IVAN AND MISHA

# IVAN

*and*

# MISHA

*Stories*

*For Mimi*

MICHAEL ALENYIKOV

*All my best*

*Michael A*

TRIQUARTERLY BOOKS

EVANSTON, ILLINOIS

Northwestern University Press
www.nupress.northwestern.edu

Printed in the United States of America

10  9  8  7  6  5  4  3  2  1

This is a work of fiction. Characters, places, and events are the product of
the author's imagination or are used fictitiously and do not represent actual
people, places, or events.

**Library of Congress Cataloging-in-Publication Data**

Alenyikov, Michael.
    Ivan and Misha : stories / Michael Alenyikov.
        p. cm.
    ISBN 978-0-8101-2718-0 (pbk. : alk. paper)
    1. Twin brothers—Fiction. 2. Immigrants—New York (State)—New
York—Fiction. 3. Russians—New York (State)—New York—Fiction.
I. Title.
PS3601.L35355I93 2010
813.6—dc22
                                                          2010024016

♾ The paper used in this publication meets the minimum requirements of
the American National Standard for Information Sciences—Permanence of
Paper for Printed Library Materials, ANSI Z39.48-1992.

For my mother,
born Bella Brovarnik (1920–1960),
who planted the seed.

So terribly many mysteries!
Too many riddles oppress man on earth.
—Fyodor Dostoevsky, *The Brothers Karamazov*


Life is weather. Life is meals.
—James Salter, *Light Years*

# Contents

—ɯ—

IVAN AND MISHA

# PROLOGUE

*Kiev, USSR, 1980s*

—⁓—

Misha's papa had disappointed before. "In the spring a new apartment," Lyov would say. "Sunlight will pour through windows. And later a dacha, where in summer my little Mishka and his brother, Ivan—my precious motherless babies—will fall asleep to the sound of crickets and wake to the smell of grass and lilies and pear trees. Just you wait. And maybe next year, no, even sooner, no more Kiev: no more gray slab buildings, sleeping three to a room; there will be an appointment with prestige to a hospital in Moscow or Leningrad. Promises have been made. And next month, next year, we will skip over the Atlantic, first stopping in Amsterdam, Paris, London, and Rome . . . My boys will see the great museums—I give my word!—until New York. And, who knows, my babies . . . along the way, perhaps . . . a new mother."

But plans were postponed, forgotten. Instead, there were card games, bribes, vodka, needles, pills. Misha and Ivan fell asleep, choking on the thick smoke of cheap tobacco and the sound of men's voices, in argument, in laughter: voices sweetly pleading, bullying.

Despite Papa's talk, jobs were lost. Reasons vague. Women stayed overnight who were not mothers. Misha remembered one: blond hair to her waist, slender, almost without hips. She sat on the edge of the bed he shared with Ivan. She wore no blouse, just a bra, and stroked his hair. Her face was small and round, a teardrop of a face. She drew him into her large, heavy breasts. How could such a slight body carry them? he wondered.

"My sweet one," she said, "How old are you?"

"I am six," he said proudly.

"And your brother?" she asked, running a finger along Ivan's sleeping face.

"Six. We are both six." He could smell Papa's sweat and tobacco on her body, and beneath, her own strong scent; it overwhelmed him as if he'd opened a newly filled pantry from his earliest memory, stocked with any number of grains and fruits to tide them through a long winter.

Ivan stirred and slung his arm roughly across Misha's chest, but remained asleep. With envy, Misha thought: You sleep through everything. Then, the sweetly rancid smell: Ivan had wet their bed again. The floodgates of shame opened before this woman. He prayed for the darkness to hide his burning crimson face.

She seemed not to notice. "Your Papa, he has eyes like a poet's, like Chekhov's. Such gentle eyes, too tender for this world. Someone must take care of him. Yes, of course," she said, nodding her head as a thought made its way through the vodka's warm mist. "Someone must take care of the doctor, too." And Misha could tell by the rocking of her body and the way she stroked his hair—her touch so light it might have been the moon's passage overhead—that a silent conversation continued deep within her. "Such eyes," she said, stroking his hair, and he fell asleep dreaming she would be there in the morning.

But in her place, Lyov once again served up new hopes with stale bread and bitter coffee for breakfast. Yesterday's promises were forgotten—or rewritten. In recompense, he read them *War and Peace* at bedtime. Also, to their delight, Papa recited plays, and more stories than they knew how to count. He did all the voices: men and women . . . children, too. There was instruction in his voice and manner: the raising of his eyebrows warned, this part is sad; the sparkle in his eyes said yes, yes, to laughter. They understood little, but they heard Papa's voice, resonant like the smooth, steady ascent of an engine's steam whistle on the edge of the city. The belief that they were headed somewhere new and wondrous settled under their skins.

One day Misha awoke to learn that Papa's promises were also stories. It was a morning like any other: outside, the air was cold, crisp, the edges of buildings and trees sharp. He had often watched Papa carefully trim his beard in the bathroom's cracked mirror, the golden scissors—a gift from their mother, he was told—dancing across the field of black. Misha waited for the door to close, for the sound of the toilet flushing, for his father to claim his few minutes alone. But this morning the door did not close. This morning, Misha watched his papa stare intently into the mirror, his breath made visible by the air's chill. "Chekhov's face," the woman had said. Misha mouthed the name silently and took pleasure in the way the syllables moved the air through his mouth and shaped his tongue and lips. Papa removed his teeth (how had Misha never seen this before?) and his father's handsome face sank into itself, as if crushed by a fist. He rested his hands on the edge of the sink, letting it support his weight. Misha feared it would collapse. Watching his father at the mirror, Misha had caught him thinking, doubting.

Ivan and Misha were rarely apart, and when they were, they shared all at night; they whispered details in soft voices so as not to wake Papa. But this, *this* Misha knew he must not tell Ivan. All that day at school he recalled the image of his father. Did Ivan know? If he did, Misha could not tell. That year, Misha had suddenly grown taller than Ivan. Was that why he could see more clearly?

Years passed, and one day people were talking about a wall. *A wall had fallen*. On street corners men argued as never before. The eternally sour faces of babushkas laden with bread and potatoes were lit with smiles. These sights and what came next made fairytale sense to Misha: a wall had fallen and in only weeks, a month later, they were on a jet plane to New York. For such an occasion,

Misha and Ivan insisted, only a jacket and tie will do. "There is no time," Lyov said, but Misha and Ivan, as one, stood firm. They were eleven now. They combed their hair with grease, as in the pictures they saw of American boys, in magazines that appeared everywhere.

And on their first night in New York, Papa said there was only one way to start this new life: in Central Park, seen before only in movies, he rented a horse and buggy. Clippety-clop, clippety-clop, the horse trotted on roads covered with yellow leaves. Wherever he looked Misha saw trees, branches barren of leaves, coated white with snow that fell from a bright gray sky, rose colored along its edges and pierced by unimaginably tall buildings. Once, the horse lost its footing in the leaves and slush and Misha felt his heart clenched as if in a handgrip—now I will wake up from this dream. But the horse regained its footing and clippety-clop, it marched on, gaining speed as if preparing to take flight. Large wet snowflakes fell on Misha's glasses and he saw buildings through a crystal lens splitting colors into fragments, adding to the magic.

Misha held tight to Ivan's hand, its scratchy feel of wet wool a warning that Kiev was still near and the dream could end in the sound of Papa's voice, waking them for school in the morning darkness. Ivan slept, his head on Papa's lap, which did not matter because later that night Misha whispered into Ivan's ear about all the wonders he'd seen.

"How, Papa?" Misha asked. "How has this happened?" Then he leaned his head so far back he felt the skin and muscles of his neck strain to keep it from falling off. His mouth stretched wide to swallow the snow and the stars; his ears were attuned to capture the muffled sounds of distant cars; his eyes were wide to take in the tall buildings, each with a shape of its own, as if they were a crowd of people who'd gathered to welcome them.

"I called the maitre'd. It was all arranged for my boys."

"A magician, papa?"

But Lyov seemed not to have heard; he waved a hand toward the sky, the trees, the brightly lit buildings. "Only the best in America, only the best," he said, wisps of snow clinging to his coal-black beard. "Only the best," he repeated slowly, sonorously. "Only the best."

# Ivan and Misha

*New York City, July 2000*

—⁓—

Ivan calls at three. "Meet me at the Odessa," he says. "Thirty minutes. You won't regret it. I've got this idea."

"But," I say. I don't know what else to say so I say "but" again. I'm standing naked, water dripping on the white carpet in a circle, me in the center. "Okay," I say. "But first, Ive, where are you?"

Geography is not a minor detail with my Ivan. He's a little bit bipolar and drives a cab. He is fearless and will go anywhere with a fare: Poughkeepsie, Newark, Hoboken, Harlem, Philadelphia, Coney Island—to him they are all the same. And his mind takes ideas and travels to places I cannot reach. He schemes for riches to share with me; he has dreams of a better world for all mankind, which is wonderful, but too often to count they have taken him to Bellevue, and once he was found shot and left for dead in front of the Brooklyn Museum. When Ivan bleeds, so do I. When we were very young, Louie, our father, would say, "The whole is greater than the sum of its parts," tapping each of us in turn on the head with his gold-plated fountain pen. So last month Ivan bought me a new cell phone to calm my fears. To this one, only he has the number. "We'll stay in touch better," he said. When he calls, it plays the opening notes to "Back in the USSR."

We're fraternal twins, me and Ivan. Fraternal, for the most

part, although once I went six months without talking to him. Not an easy thing to do. Maybe it's because he's all I've got— by way of family, that is. There's my father, Louie (Lyov back home; "Call me Louie!" six months into America), but Louie had a stroke last year and in his mind he's more often playing pinochle in a Kiev cafe arguing Gorbachev than in New York City, planet earth. He isn't quite our father anymore. He's more like a moving, talking memorial to the guy we loved: something holographic, so when you put your arms around him for a hug you're stuck hugging yourself.

Water drips from my hair and into the phone. Can a wet cell phone kill you? Like if your hair dryer falls in the bathtub and you're fried in water? Smith's sitting at the kitchen table. He shoots me a sidelong glance. Another kind of electric. Smith's family, but of a more uncertain kind. He's been studying *Details* for a new look while deconstructing a croissant. Smith was Robbie Doddsworth from Michigan's Upper Peninsula when I met him last year, a psych major at NYU by day, a short-order cook by night. Every few months he puts on a new persona. This summer it's Philip Marlow meets the Vampire Lestat. I indulge him because he's young. He's barely nineteen. At twenty-three, I feel waist deep in the muddy swamp of maturity.

He licks his fingers, then brushes the remaining crumbs onto the floor. He's passive-aggressive and plays on my fear of roaches and water bugs. I insist water bugs are not roaches. They're large enough to be pets, I argue. I give ours names: Fido, Spot, Mrs. Butterworth. Fido loves to frolic in the kitchen sink; Spot prowls the bedroom; and Mrs. B. is the czarina of the bathtub. The ploy doesn't work. They enter my dreams, like meat-eating extras from *Jurassic Park*. Smith says water bugs are just roaches, but big, linebacker roaches, as opposed to the little running backs that sprint across tables and floors. "It takes all kinds," Smith says, his favorite expression.

Now, Smith pushes his plate away, then turns the page of his magazine. He wiggles his chair and the linoleum squeaks. *Stay home* is in his every gesture, but Ivan plays on something deeper in me and I feel trapped. Smith knows this.

"Ive, where are you?" I ask again.

"I'm . . ." his voice fades, lost in static. His cab is passing under steel or concrete. *Pickup for two, Sheepshead Bay, headed Kennedy.* The radio dispatcher's voice, filtered through Ivan's cell phone. Then Ivan fades in: "Near Z . . . 'tween X and Z."

First I think: he's given up an airport job for me and his new scheme; then: did he check in on Louie? Louie lives in an apartment—assisted living for seniors, they call it—in Brighton, just past Avenue Z. But if you could map his mind, he's way past Z, past the Belt Parkway, past New York Harbor and Liberty's statue and across the Atlantic, far away in a place we left long ago. They called it a *mini-stroke*. *Mini* means he's lost no more than 10 percent of his mind, the doctor said. It means he has his good days, and days his mind opens to greet the morning like a door with rusty hinges, liable to get stuck in the oddest places.

Just last Sunday I was off to buy bagels and the *Times* and found Louie around the corner, sitting on a bench in Tompkins Square Park. He was feeding pigeons from fingertips yellowed by a lifetime of cigarettes he rolls by hand. He was as elegant as ever, his beard trim, a rich black shafted with gray. "Zdravstvui, kraisvy Amerikanets," he said. "Hello, my handsome American." His clear brown eyes gazed sweetly at me as if we'd shared a private joke. He speaks Russian now with an American accent he's picked up like lint on a fine dark coat. He could pass for an exiled scholar, in New York for a conference on particle physics or the semiotics of Turgenev.

Have I mentioned he looks ten, fifteen years younger than his age? The life he's led does not show on his face. In that he is lucky; I think petulantly of my fair skin and its early crow's feet and laugh lines. ("Pigments of your imagination," Smith has said, suppressing a giggle, peering over my shoulder in the bathroom mirror.)

But he was wearing an overcoat on a summer morning and it tore at my heart to see him feeding pigeons in the park, dressed for the wrong season. Still, it was a nicely tailored overcoat: gray charcoal, silk lapels, well cut at the wrists and knees. His yellow tie had a coffee stain the shape of Florida, but he'd had a good haircut, his nails were trimmed, and he'd arrived unharmed—a few items for which to be grateful.

"How did you get here?" I asked.

He waved his hand, dismissing my question. "Ya prishol. Eto ne dostatochno?" he said. "I came. Isn't that enough?"

I took him home for breakfast, where he joined me and Smitty. He smeared cream cheese on his bagel and picked out a small slice of lox.

"Take more," Smith said, amiably, sliding a plate of onions across the table—they're a mutual love fest, those two.

Louie added a slice of red onion and placed it with care on the lox and cream cheese. "My Mishka," he said to Smith in English. "He looks just like his mother." He says this to Smith each time he sees us, as if for the first time, or, I've begun to fear, for the last. He did not ask about Ivan.

Ask about Ivan, too, I said to myself, ask about Ivan, Papa.

"Don't let me down, Mish," Ivan says. Then the sound of static, like someone's taken a jackhammer to my ear drum, brings me back to being wet, naked, and making the decision not to tell Smith I'm meeting Ivan.

I dry off, slip on jeans and a shirt, and plant a peck on Smith's shaved head. "I'll do groceries," I say. A lie of omission. Small, harmless. He licks his fingers and growls. I forget my umbrella. Two blocks away the sky opens. I'm wetter than I was before. The heat makes the sidewalk steam.

I arrive at the Odessa early, but Ivan's already there. His cab, with its IVAN THE TERRIFIC plates, is parked out front on Avenue A. Orthodox crucifixes and the Star of David, tokens of our mostly forgotten heritage, dangle from the rearview mirror. The red meter flag is up and a soggy parking ticket is tucked under the wiper blades.

Ivan waves at me from a booth. He is arm in arm with Gino and Sylvie, models I know from shooting TV commercials. I am a production assistant, better known as a gofer. They are saying hello and good-bye at the same time. Sylvie kisses me three-cheek style. I fumble the third kiss and our noses collide. She has wild red hair and dark eyeliner. She models hands and fingers. Gino looks like those guys you see stretched out on the sides of buses. All his clothes are skin tight to show off his muscles. When he moves, he willows, like he's an undulating sine curve come to life. To compensate, he gives me a "regular guy" handshake. They leave—Ivan interests them more than I do. Ivan's looks draw men and women. Who can blame them? What he does with them, he never says. It's the one thing we don't share. Sometimes I think, nothing much. I think he's just social, that he belongs only to me. Sometimes, when I'm asleep and dreaming sex with a hot guy I've passed on the street, Ivan appears. He watches and, in the dream, when I come, our eyes, mine and Ivan's, lock onto each other's.

Ivan's wearing a long-sleeved white shirt: silk, buttoned to the neck, a red bandana tied loosely around it. Despite the heat, he looks fresh, hair slicked back and wet. He lives around the corner. We've both moved a dozen times in five years, circling around Avenues A to D, and we're never more than a half mile from each other. Sometimes I wonder if this means something. I asked Smith once—a mistake I won't make again. He rolled his eyes until they were epileptic-white. "Duh," he said.

Looking at us, me and Ivan, you'd never take us even for distant relations. He's a head shorter. He fidgets like he's a lamp plugged into an unreliable wall socket giving off sparks. I'm quiet, watchful. Smith says I move like a tree. A big Michigan oak. Ivan has olive skin, long, straight black hair, and dark brown eyes that grow wide and shine when he's selling me on an idea. "Misha," he'll say, preternaturally still, "this one will set us up—I

mean set us up—*for life.*" I'll groan and *his* eyes will tear up. He
makes me feel like I'm jilting a lover when I turn down one of
his schemes. And that's how we are to each other, it occurs to
me not for the first time, as I elbow my way through the crowd
in the Odessa. To look at him, he's just like Louie: the dark hair,
the olive skin, the long, sharply angled nose. And, like Louie, a
seducer, a gambler. Ivan was born twenty minutes before me, and
our mother died two hours after I oozed out—*died in childbirth,*
as they say—leaving just the three of us. Once, when we were
seven, maybe eight, Ivan, in a rage, never repeated, blamed me
for her death. *You came last . . . If it weren't for you . . .* I look
like her in the old pictures: blond hair, round Slavic face, high
cheekbones. In the photos that Louie's saved, she's a chameleon:
shy, coquettish, maternal, angry, sad—it's all expressed in her
mouth, while her eyes gaze at Louie behind the camera, which
captures her brushing strands of flaxen hair that an unseen wind
blows in front of her face. She is my age or a few years older. Her
name was Sonya. In my favorite picture she stands in front of
a field of wheat. It is late summer. She has a look of serenity. I
believe that one reveals her true self.

"Phone booths," Ivan says, after I sit down. He's already ordered
me coffee.

"Phone booths? What about phone booths?" I sip my coffee.
It's cold and bitter. I was expecting a condo turnaround deal or
Ukrainian bonds or an Internet IPO.

"Phone booths," Ivan says. Steam coats the restaurant's windows. A crowd huddles by the door waiting for a break in the rain;
their hushed attention to the weather soaks up the buzz of voices
rising from Saturday brunchers. A cathedral of quiet shelters me
and Ivan. He is so beautiful that I've an urge to run my fingers
through his hair (do all twins feel this way? I've often wondered),
which is in constant motion, along with the rest of him, the ends
brushing his shoulders back and forth, like a pendulum.

"Misha," he purrs, "we each put 5K down, own a string of two hundred phone booths, and lease them to the city."

I groan.

"No really, they're moneymakers. Guaranteed cash flow." Ivan leans in toward me and cups my hands in his. His skin is soft and warm. "Mishka, this can't go wrong."

"How can 10K buy that many phone booths? It's got to cost more than 10K. Ivan, please, *give me a break*." I'm thinking lithium, feeling disloyal. On lithium he's not my Ivan. When he becomes that stranger, Who am I? is what I think, feeling like I'm filled with helium, unmoored.

He's pulling me in. I hate myself. His hands are pressing down on mine so I can't move unless I go for a violent gesture. Maybe I exaggerate, but that's how it feels. What if we had been Siamese twins? Where would we be joined, I wonder: shoulders, head, heart, hips? I imagine us connected at our navels, destined to stare into each other's eyes, he lost in my pale blues, me in his dark browns. Or sharing one set of testicles, or one cock. The thought excites me.

*Not that anyone's asked,* Smith has said, in his matter-of-fact Upper Michigan nasal, *but a little less thinking about your brother would do you some good.* I wrestle my hands free. Ivan's face saddens. He pulls his knees up into his chest and leans back against the restaurant's grease-stained wall like he's going fetal on me. He looks so much like old faded pictures of Louie that I fall into a trance—which is not to last.

"It's like buying on margin, Mish," he says eagerly, reminding me of why I'm here: Ivan's idiotic phone booths. But the words *buying on margin* dredge up a bad memory of last year's Ukrainian oil deal. Ivan knows he's made a misstep: his eyes grow wide with a touch of naked pleading; they gaze at me, innocent and vulnerable. With his properly buttoned white shirt and red scarf, he's now an altar boy. I can smell the incense. It's like I'm negotiating with a twelve-year-old.

"Misha, this can't go wrong. I swear."

The waitress refills our cups. "You guys want anything more?" she barks, already three tables away before the words crash in my ear like a five-car pileup.

"Pierogies!" I shout. "Pierogies and applesauce. Two orders." I feel weak and fight an impulse to ask the waitress to sit down and argue my case. Ivan takes on an aura of hot reds and icy blues. I feel a migraine coming on and rest my forehead on my hands, rubbing my eyes hard with the soft part of my palms. The sound of nearby voices hits me like spears.

Ivan runs his hand through my hair. He whispers into my ear: "It's okay, my Mishka. I will make the pain go away." We are sharing a bed again in Kiev. Louie is playing cards in the kitchen. Strangers are shouting. The pain is so intense I whimper.

We sit like this for a long time.

When the pain is gone, I remember. "Ivan, why for chrisfuckingsake phone booths?"

He uncurls his body, leans back with a broad, self-satisfied smile, then ties his red scarf into a Boy Scout knot. "Li'l brother," he says, "there is, you see, *an angle*. A totally awesome, can't-miss angle. And you will thank me for this. That's what I predict."

I cringe when he calls me "li'l brother," reminding me of his extra twenty minutes. Tears appear in his eyes. He knows he's upset me, but our wires are so crisscrossed, the tears come from his eyes and not mine. And the idea, his idea, is so good, he thinks (and I know how he thinks faster than he does) that it bubbles up explosively like uncorked champagne.

"It's a favor I'm doing for you. A fucking gift. The phone booths, you see, they're these really authentic English kind. The English don't want them anymore, so I got a deal on these beauties. They've got so much class. People here will love them. Imagine, Mish, you're flying low over the city. On each corner, standing guard, is one of the queen's own regiment. Gives the place a little dignity, don't you think? It'll make people feel secure, proud. And a little of that gorgeous red color will lift the spirits of each and every working slug, crawling their way underground back to the Bronx, Brooklyn, and Queens. No doubt about it."

"No," I say, trying to resist the purr in his voice, and his eyes— Louie's eyes; I'm really fighting against them both.

"Take a chance. Just do it. *Trust me.*"

"No!" I shout, "No, no, no!" I pull my hands away from his. The waitress appears with the pierogies. She thinks I mean her and looks confused. "No, yes, no—yes, we want the pierogies."

"Look boys, do kissie-kissie and make up." Her chipmunk face mixes scowl with smile, a cross between Judge Judy and Dr. Ruth. The pierogies glisten in the light. I take a bite. It's dry, tasteless. I bury the rest with applesauce.

"Look, li'l bro," Ivan says, slurping coffee, ignoring the food. "You're a writer, but you don't write. And why?" he asks, snapping off a rhetorical question that engraves itself in my heart like an unwanted tattoo. "Because you work all the fucking time for that shit-assed so-called movie primacocainedonna producer of yours. Get a little vision. This is your ticket. Be an artist, like you want to be." Ivan says *artist* with a sense of awe. I feel like a fake, but Ivan thinks I'm something special, something he can never be. These schemes are his gift to me. And, since Louie lost his 10 percent, Ivan's desire to give to us both has taken on a special urgency. "Kills two birds with one stone," he has said. "I help you be a writer *and* there's money left to take Louie back home to Kiev." Forget that Louie hated Kiev, that Petersburg was his real home. But now home for Louie is a grave where his Sonya is buried, and a grave is not a home. I don't try to explain this to Ivan, because it would break his heart. And it would not make Louie bestow his gaze upon Ivan with the pride with which he looks upon me. There is nothing Ivan has to give that Louie wants. Which breaks *my* heart.

I lean forward and rest my forehead against Ivan's. He leans against me and we form an arched bridge like we did as children when we whispered secrets to each other while Louie read his newspaper. "How soon do you need the money?" I ask, grasping his head between my hands, squeezing tight. He plants a kiss on my lips. "Lov'ya, li'l bro," he says.

Last year: "He's lost 10 percent," the doctor said to me and Ivan. "Only ten." He was a short young doctor.

Maybe we could negotiate, I thought.

"Which ten?" I asked calmly. He dug his hands into the pockets of his white smock, eyes downcast. Maybe I could choose. It would be like shopping. Leave behind his bad memories; that should take up 10 percent if the doctor is a skillful surgeon. Yes, please, doctor, take away his sadness. Two months into our life in America, Louie had started asking us, "Should we have stayed? Don't forget, your mother's buried there." His eyes would moisten. He had been too old to start over as a doctor. English came slowly; in those first years in America he'd stubbornly held on to the Russian he revered. And the joke is, I got my wish; in his mind, he's more there than here. Louie's happier than anyone I know. And if you think about it, the snow and grime in Brighton isn't much different than Kiev. Who wouldn't be confused? And Brighton's Tower of Babel suits him: a little Russian here; the dem's and doe's of ancient Brooklyn; a bit of Spanish, Armenian, and the faded remains of Yiddish. "Pidgin Yiddish," I say to make Smith laugh.

The little doctor brought his hand to his mouth and coughed politely. "He's not paralyzed," he squeaked, furrowing his smooth young face to squeeze out a few wrinkles on his forehead. "His right arm is weak, but we expect that to improve quickly."

"But what about his mind?" I shouted. And, turning to Ivan, "Coney Island Hospital is a dump. I don't want him in this dump."

Ivan took my arm and pulled me aside. "Calm, li'l bro, calm," he said, firm and gentle in his voice, newly minted. "We'll deal with it later."

Ivan always says, "We should be like family," but after one day I was stuck with Louie. It was me who told him who he was every morning. Me who descended into the level of hell Dante left out because he'd never had to deal, as I did, with a social worker thirty years away from loving humanity and two years from early retirement. Me holding the bedpan, while Ivan, a few days later, calls me from the Long Island Expressway on his way to Montauk.

"A monster fare," he said. "What can I do? Dump this guy in Floral Park? His wife, she's slashed her wrists." I could hear the pain in his voice. I know when Ivan hurts. And I'm quick to forgive.

But a week later: "I'm working on a deal," he announced, calling from San Diego. "We'll put Louie in the Kiev Taj Mahal. Real estate and Baja, software and digital chips." All this he said into my silence. He'd never heard my silence before. Maybe it scared him. It scared me. And that's when I didn't talk to Ivan for those six months. For six months, he called from up and down the West Coast, leaving messages unanswered by me. Then, one day: "Mish, pick me up tomorrow at Newark, okay? Use my cab. I wouldn't trouble you, but I'm out of cash." I expected the worst, but next day, Ivan, he never looked better. We hugged and I pointed and said, "Meet Smith. You remember him?" hoping it might hurt Ivan, my having someone new—me having secrets, too.

Summer flies by. It rains every weekend. No beach days. Ivan calls every day. "Soon, soon," he says, meaning phone booths. "Trust me."

On Labor Day it rains again. Smith swats mosquitoes, me roaches. Division of labor, I call it. Smith says, "Come with me to Michigan, to see my sister? On Thanksgiving."

"Sure, why not," I say, feeling not sure at all, only now remembering we met one year ago this day. "Do you think it's time to meet your family? Maybe it's too soon."

"She's all that matters to me."

I think of the car crash that killed his parents, and feel ashamed. "Maybe," I say.

Smith picks up the yellow pages and slams it on the floor. "Yeah, right. Maybe." It isn't like him to be this direct. To my horror, the yellow pages kills Mrs. Butterworth. Out of respect (for me? for Mrs. B.?), Smith washes the dishes for the entire holiday weekend.

His sister calls when he's at work. "Don't tell Robbie I called," Joanne says. "He told you our parents are dead? In his dreams. Daft, for sure, but not dead. Robbie likes to pretend."

"Tell me about it."

"I want to meet you. But I can tell from your voice I can trust Robbie with you."

"His name is Smith, now, not Robbie," I say, trying to figure how you can trust a person who's only a voice.

"Back in the USSR!" The Ivan phone wakes me in darkness. "Mish, Mish," Ivan says. His voice is frantic. It sets my heart racing, my breath comes in staccato gasps. Phone cradled between ear and shoulder, I reach with one hand for my watch and with the other for the reassurance of Smith's warm flesh, his reedy bulk. My hand moves through empty space, landing awkwardly on a patch of flannel sheet rubbed smooth over many months by his butt, which has this routine of sliding one way, then another, while he sleeps, pivoting between the two positions that never quite provide him with peace. I reach further into the dark and find him on the far edge of the bed. His chest moves quietly up and down.

"What is it, Ive? What's wrong?" Images of blood, torn flesh, and Bellevue compete for space between my ears.

"They're late, real late. Maybe months. I'm sorry, Mish. I know how you were counting on them."

"Counting on . . . counting on what?" I slip quietly out of bed and pace around the room in the dark. My knee hits the hard edge of a chair. "Shit," I say. "Oh, shit." The pain is sharp; it feels permanent.

"Mish, what's wrong? Talk to me, Mish, talk," Ivan says to my muffled "Shit, oh shit."

I sit down and look at my glow-in-the-dark watch. Smith

bought it for me on Canal Street for my birthday. It's 4:00 A.M. "Ivan, what are you talking about? What's late? Where are you?"

"I'm home. Just got off work. It's the phone booths, Mish. They won't be here until at least after New Year's. I just thought you'd want to know."

"It's four in the fucking morning, Ivan. You woke me at four in the morning to talk phone booths."

"But, Mish . . ."

"Ive, next time use e-mail." Ivan knows e-mail. Ivan even has a Web site: www.Ivantheterrific.com. It's just he likes to talk, but he has no inner clock; when God made him, he left out the gears and mechanisms that make for a circadian rhythm, for knowing day from night.

"But Mish . . ."

"Please, Ive, middle-of-the-night is what e-mail is for." Do twins talk to each other before they've been born? Sometimes I feel as if Ivan and I had the same conversation in our mother's womb. Me a bit hesitant about this birth canal project and Ivan saying, "Mishka, Mishka, trust me on this. You're going to love what's at the other end," his voice layers of echoes as it bounces along the moist dark passageways. Blinding light, a smack in the rear, and blood and slime in my throat was what I found, but Ivan had already moved on.

"But Mish . . . ," he says again.

I implore: "Please, please, Vanushka, don't wake me in the middle of the night." I force calm into my voice, wary as I am of Smith's closed eyes, open ears, simmering opinions; and also not wanting to stir Ivan's pot, which would only—I know from experience—make him more excitable.

September cools into October. Ivan calls less often. He grows somber with winter's approach. The phone booths fade into memory, though at times, scurrying up Fifth Avenue after a quick lunch, I picture a red English phone booth standing with an unflappable dignity amid the jostling midday crowd. I don't dwell on the money I've given him. Money does not come between us. But sadness lingers, a dull ache near my heart that I feel whenever one of Ivan's schemes evaporates, and each time we part.

"Shit, man, I'm wasted." Smith is home from work. He's wearing a trench coat and dark glasses. It's late October and the days are suddenly short but the Indian summer air is five degrees hotter than hell. It's six in the morning. He pokes me hard in the kidney to double announce his arrival. My shoot's in an hour. I'm late. Smith's dressed all in black: trench coat, jeans, T-shirt. He throws the coat on a chair with a touch of the dramatic. His skin is so pale that next to the black T-shirt his arms, neck, and face pick up the ambient streetlight and glow in the dark. He peels off his clothes, then rubs his five o'clock shadow and growls, "I want sex." He bites my neck. "I vant to give you a hickey," he says.

"I vant you to take a shower," I say, pulling him under the covers. I coil myself around him and pull open his belt buckle with my teeth. He bites my neck and gives me that hickey. We wriggle around naked. Our bodies stick together from sweat and heat. His mouth tastes of garlic and his skin smells of olive oil and tomato sauce. Each pulling apart of one limb from another makes a puckering sound. We wrestle for position and the puckerings sound like kids making gross-out farts. Smith gracefully does the necessary but unspoken rubber thing, then guides me inside of him. We seem to be getting somewhere when I hear "Back in the USSR!" from the Ivan phone.

Smith rolls over. "Fuck this shit, man." He never talked like that when we first met. He was soft-spoken; he had such nice manners. But New York has that way with people: they go native in about one week and you'd never guess they were nice, polite people from Texas, Montana, or Michigan.

I crawl over Smith, who's biting the other side of my neck (double hickeys will really get attention from the straight boys at the shoot) and muttering, "Fuck, fuck, fuck." The cell phone is in the kitchen. I flick it on. Ivan's in mid sentence: ". . . so I was feeling kind of lonely and thinking about you and me and Louie, and li'l bro, I just started to . . ." Static. For a few seconds, I lose him, then "There I am, Mish, stuck in traffic on Kings Highway talking to this dude who's pouring his heart out to me. He's an Orthodox Jew in full drag. He's going to tell his wife he's a homo, that's what he says, 'I'm Schlomo the homo,' and he laughs like I figure you do before they fire up the electric chair. I'm feeling sorry for the dude, but I'm thinking of you and Louie and there's Thanksgiving coming up and I'm crying. I'm feeling so all by myself, Mishka. We're all we got, remember that," he says, like he's twenty years my senior, not twenty minutes, but he's got me thinking of Thanksgiving, how we never made plans last year and who knows how long we'll have with what's left of Louie. "Mish, so I've got this idea."

I crawl back into bed in time to see Smith's pale white butt disappear as the bathroom door closes behind him. My neck is sore where he bit me. In a panic, I untangle sheets, fearful that Fido's crawling up my leg. This is what Ivan's ideas do to me. *There's like, you know, a pattern here* Smith's taken to muttering when the Ivan phone rings.

"You see, li'l bro," Ivan says, his voice now urgent, insistent. "I've got this idea so we'll be like family." But I'm stuck on Thanksgiving and feeling like I'm falling down a deep well: there's the damp smell of loneliness that makes me ache around my solar plexus and all I can think of is to grab hold of Ivan. And now I'm sobbing into the phone. Suddenly, I think to ask: "Ive, where are you?"

"Scarsdale, li'l bro. Monster fare."

"But what about Kings Highway?"

"Oh, yeah, that was yesterday." Static. "Oops, got to go, Mish. We'll talk." *Pickup for three, Mamaroneck, headed Newark.* Silence.

I get into the shower with Smith. He's peering into an old-fashioned round shaving mirror, the kind with an extended accordion arm. He studies his face closely (he hates to miss a spot), ignoring me. I squirt a glob of green liquid soap on his body and rub him from top to bottom with the smell of pine needles. I want to make him feel good, maybe because in my head I've just promised Thanksgiving to Ivan. He studiously pays me no attention until I tweak his nipples and he falls back into my arms and lets me bring him to a sputtery, wheezy orgasm. We slide to the bathtub floor, the shower spray in my eyes. I'm thinking about being late, about the double hickey straight boy jokes on the shoot, and about how I've got to clean the bathtub someday. And even though I'm holding Smith in my arms and feeling all the muscles in his body he's let go soft to show he loves me, I'm thinking of Ivan being alone on Thanksgiving. Of Louie being alone. When Ivan and I have the same feeling at the same time, I almost forget who I am. Reminding me is Smith, whose limp postcoital body is in my arms, and who asks now in Robbie Doddsworth's sweet, slightly nasal Upper Michigan voice, "Who do you love more, him or me?"

"What's love got to do with it?" I say, relieved that he can't see my face.

The troika: Tolstoy, Chekhov, and Gogol. Endlessly read. A Mount Rushmore carved inside my head, too high and treacherous to scale for poor dyslexic Ivan. "Bipolar is no obstacle," the 100-percent Louie once said. "Could even be an advantage," he added, forgetting Ivan was in the kitchen. "But he has no feeling for *words*." A misjudgment of Ivan, if my opinion had been asked. And, I might have told Louie, had he asked, that Mother Russia has produced other great minds. Take Pavlov. Not someone I'd given much thought to until the night Ivan was shot. The phone rang that night, two years ago: a landline with the old-fashioned kind of ring, each one rippling the air so they overlap, and before one ring ends, the next begins. There were three, each louder in my memory than the one before. Ever since, when a phone rings, beeps, whatever, I gasp for air. *Pavlov.*

That night, I cabbed it to the hospital. Overcoat over underwear. Shot in the chest, they said. In front of the Brooklyn Museum. Three doctors, two nurses, and an orderly. Too many for just one Ivan. A bad sign. They spoke in one voice, a chorus: "He needs blood. His blood type is rare. We have sources, but time is running short. It may not arrive in time. You're his brother. We can test you in minutes."

"I'm his twin," I said. "So much the better," sang the chorus. People were being wheeled all around me attached to rolling IVs. "You don't understand. My blood is no good. My blood is no damn good," I said to puzzled looks. Tears dripped down my face. I wiped them away with my wool mittens. "I am healthy but my blood is infected. *I cannot give my brother my blood.*" They looked confused, exchanged glances. There was blood on the floor. It was wet and looked fresh. Feeling desperate, I thought: Maybe that blood will do. One doctor kept his eyes on me, his lips shaping an "oh," and then an "ah," the international signs of comprehension, or so I needed to believe. He had dark curly hair and walnut-brown eyes. Tufts of chest hair stuck out from the V of his blue doctor shirt. He stood a step or two away from the others. He touched my arm. "Sit down. Rest," he said. "Everything will be all right." There was relief that I didn't have to say the words. Until then, only Smith and Ivan had known. Ivan had screamed at me, "*You stupid fuck, you stupid fuck.* How could you let that happen?" It was like the time he blamed me for killing our mother: a flash of anger, water boiling over the sides of a pot, the fire sizzles, and then there's calm. Our foreheads had touched. "Vanushka, Kevin lied to me. He said he was negative. But he loved me. He really did. He loved me and he lied to me."

The blood came in time. Coptered in from Philly. "Monster fare," Ivan called it a few days later when he heard the story. I forced a laugh. Ivan flirted with a pretty blonde nurse and the walnut-eyed doctor. They hovered about him like butterflies.

Yesterday, the leaves began to fall. Funny how that happens in New York. They go green to yellow to brown; for a week they dangle precariously, then a bruiser of a storm blows through, and the air smells of wet sidewalk. Windows, stiff in their casements, slide shut throughout the city to an almost audible grind and thump. The memory of fireplaces, real or imagined, fills seven million hearts with longing, and in the morning, the ground is thick with sticky wet leaves.

Ivan and I are in his cab, driving south on the FDR Drive. It's the day after the leaves have fallen and there's an icy chill in the air, a preview of winter. Leo, Louie's next-door neighbor, had called. "Yah betta get down here real rappido, you kids," he said. His voice was hoarse and raspy. Leo'd had his voice box removed two months ago. Cancer. It was hard on the ears but I had to applaud the guy; he was a yapper before and a yapper still. Nothing tragic can happen to a guy like Leo because he just won't admit to it. His wife died year before last. Fifty years together. Next, he's made Louie his soul mate. An odd couple to be sure: the man who'd owned a chain of carpet stores and the dapper former doctor from Kiev who'd read *War and Peace* and *Anna Karenina* more times than a life had hours for, if he was to be believed. "Caviar for the soul, Mishka, my how-do-you-say 'wannabe' writer son," he'd say, proud of the American lingo he'd learned from Leo. Once, when I was in high school, I'd worked up my courage to ask Louie about the great Dostoevsky. "Such crap," he'd said. "So many words wasted on God."

"Your father, he fell. He's okay, but a little, you know, more confused than usual." Leo lowered his rasp to an imitation whisper. I pressed my ear tightly to the phone. "He's been crying. I never seen Louie cry, so's that's why I'm putting you guys to this trouble, otherwise we, you know, take care of each other here."

Ivan's changing lanes like a stock car driver, as if he feels the need to fill in any and all empty spaces. He's babbling about the stock market. "Trade by day, drive by night," he says. To change the subject and because I am more than a little irritated, I ask about the phone booths. "Back burner, li'l bro, back burner. I'm into wireless now." The Verrazano Narrows Bridge looms up ahead. Dense, low clouds obscure the view of Staten Island across the harbor. Ivan never lets go of any of his ideas, so I know the phone booths still exist in some gaseous cloud nebula spinning wildly between his ears.

He exits at Ocean Parkway. Snowflakes float about in the wind—or is it the white soot from incinerators? I am easily fooled. On the street people walk swiftly, staring at their feet. Overcoats have made their first appearance of the season. I'm tuning out Ivan and thinking of the day when Louie brought us to New York. How he unhooked my glasses from around my ears and tried to dry them with a handkerchief. Melting snow dripped from his hair. Then he carefully replaced the glasses, placing first one arm around one ear than the other. My glasses cleared only for a moment, but, nonetheless, he was my Houdini. This one master trick—me, him, and Ivan in Central Park—wiped away all the failed promises. I was filled with a kind of love and joy as pure as I'd ever known. But what had Louie wanted out of life? I assumed he had lived for me and Ivan. Pretty damned selfish of me, I think, as Ivan weaves in and out of traffic. I want to feel my heart explode with that joy again, but it does its everyday thump-a-thump-thump.

As if reading my mind, Ivan says, "So here's my idea: we take Louie to the country for turkey day. I mean the real country. I've got this house from a friend who owes me a favor. We'll be like family, li'l bro." Ivan circles the block, then parks in front of a fire hydrant. Is the house for real? I want so much for it to be true. I can see Louie's face light up with joy and the light turning on Ivan. I want it more for them than for me. I can take care of myself.

"Ive, is this house for real?"

"For real, Mish," he replies, his brown eyes, dark caffeinated pools of espresso, wide with possibility. "I swear."

We ride up in a graffiti-covered elevator. Leo's door is open a crack. Music trickles out into the blue-tiled hallway. I knock, then push open the door. Louie and Leo are slow dancing. Ella

Fitzgerald is singing "Bewitched, Bothered and Bewildered." When they see us, they stop. Leo says, "Everything's okay. Don't you kids worry. Like I always say, we take care of each other here." Louie gives me a sheepish look. "I'm learning American music," he explains. There's a half-empty bottle of Stolichnaya, two shot glasses, and a deck of cards on a rickety TV tray table. "And my comrade Leo is learning how to drink vodka the proper way. Right, Leo? Can you believe, he sips it like brandy." He gives me a big hug. Ivan gets a cuff to the side of his head.

Tomorrow is Thanksgiving. We're on Route 17, heading north after having had lunch in the town of Liberty. A tuna salad sandwich sits uneasily in my stomach, a stab at independence on my part. The others—Ivan, Louie, Smith, and Joanne—had corned beef, at Louie's insistence. Joanne ate her sandwich in cautious little bites, as if sampling camel meat in Uzbekistan. Ivan's passing yet another sixteen-wheel truck. Sleet slices its way down from a grim sky. The truck churns a steady barrage of slush under its wheels, like a cement mixer determined to bury us alive. The windshield wiper blades labor valiantly, but in truth, Ivan's driving blind.

If Ivan has taken his lithium, there will be a house in the country where we will celebrate Thanksgiving tomorrow. If not, we are headed somewhere that exists only in his mind. I imagine a campfire in the woods over which we will warm the white containers of takeout Chinese food—Szechwan beef, mu shu pork, lemon chicken, and steamed dumplings—that Ivan's brought for tonight's preholiday dinner. An IHOP in Binghamton beckons to me like the Four Seasons.

Almost until the end, Smith held his ground. "I'm going to Michigan to see Joanne. It's time you met *my* family." He crossed his arms, stretching himself lengthwise to look taller and unmovable. His shoulders lost their gentle stoop; they became wide and sturdy. He stared me down, his gray eyes radiating no warmth. I chose not to mention the small secret about his alive-and-well parents. I think: he will tell me in his own time.

Later, while putting away the laundry, I found a note "hidden" in his sock drawer: "Misha: I'm I'm I'm I'm leaving leaving leaving because because because love is like arts and crafts, which was the only part of high school worse than gym." It looked like he'd written several versions, cut them up, and pasted parts back together. But why leave a good-bye note that stutters? And, besides, he'd told me he'd been on the swim team in high school! But most perplexing: was the note left there for me to find? I could only assume. Between him and Ivan I felt like a hockey puck whacked on both sides.

The cab hits an icy spot. The back wheels spin out, but Ivan regains control. Louie sits up front, next to Ivan. In the back seat, Smith had deftly steered Joanne between us, so that he sits behind Louie and I'm behind Ivan. All that past week, Smith and I slept together like a couple married ten years staying together for the sake of the children. Finally, I decided to call Ivan and say no to his Thanksgiving, sparked by the discovery of a feeling I hadn't noticed before, like something misplaced, hidden by a pile of dirty clothes: *Smith is the best thing ever to happen to me.*

But at the last minute, it was Smith who cracked. "Okay," he said, sighing dramatically. "I'll go if Joanne can come too. But don't think I'm doing this for you," he added. "It's for Louie." Maybe *I'm* the best thing that's ever happened to him, I thought, which made me feel good until I remembered nervously that I was the *first* thing that ever happened to him in the love department.

For a long time we are all quiet, hypnotized by the hum of tires on the slick, icy road. Joanne breaks the silence: "Your father tells me you're a writer." She has Robbie's little nose and nasal voice. She also has a dark tan from a trip to Bermuda. She's a travel agent. "No," I say, "I'm a gofer." The sudden roar of a passing truck makes it hard to hear. "Did you say you were a groundhog?" She gives me a half smile, mouth open, revealing a thin line of unreasonably white teeth, the expression Smith has when I can't tell if he's joking or serious. Is this how everyone looks in Michigan's Upper Peninsula, or is it a brother-sister thing they share?

"No, a gofer. I make coffee and do errands for people who snort cocaine and make TV commercials."

Joanne sniffs the air. A cold? A sense of humor? Louie twists his head back. The bones in his neck crack. "Don't you believe him. My Mishka will be famous someday." I cringe. Being a writer is all talk, no action. Louie wants it more than I do. My application to film school is secreted in *my* sock drawer, past its due date.

I lean forward and rest my chin on Ivan's shoulder. Louie may be sitting next to Ivan, but talking about me is more important than Ivan's Thanksgiving gift to him.

Last night, Smith and I packed without talking. You can say a lot, pointing and grunting. After a while, I thought maybe I should study signing for the deaf—make a contribution to the world. But now Smith, whose arm has been resting around Joanne's shoulders, extends his hand and tweaks the back of my neck. I'd like to think it means he won't leave me when the weekend is over. On the radio, a lament from a country western song, "You're gonna miss me when I'm gone," hangs in the air. I sit back in my seat. We sneak quick looks at each other over Joanne's head.

An hour later, Ivan exits at a sign that reads FISHS EDDY. "Shouldn't there be an apostrophe, you know, like in the possessive?" Joanne asks.

Smith, waking from a nap, says, "Joanne, who really cares?"

"I heard there was a guy named Fishs who lived here," Ivan says gamely, giving the word an Arabic pronunciation.

"But what if it's a mistake?" she asks, in a big sister voice.

Smith retorts, "Leave it alone, Jo," in a kid brother's voice. So Joanne and I discuss the ins and outs of punctuation in a part of New York where maybe one in ten can even read.

We cross over a narrow wooden bridge, then drive past a cluster of trailer homes and shacks. A sign cautions: SLOW DOWN

FOR CHILDREN. "Fishs Eddy!" says Joanne triumphantly. Low clusters of green surrounded by wire fences suggest vegetable gardens. There are dashes of red, the last surviving geraniums of summer. Several houses still have soggy Halloween pumpkins with toothless, maniacal grins; a few sit atop rusty mailboxes on the road's edge, others in curtainless windows. Children's bicycles are strewn across barren lawns. Some houses have pickup trucks; others have cars without wheels sitting on concrete blocks.

"Our father who art in heaven," I say, with mock solemnity. "Say it ain't so."

"Be nice," Joanne says, sotto voce, into my ear, her breath smelling of spearmint gum.

"Not to worry, li'l bro," says Ivan. "The best is yet to come."

And there is a house. A few miles down the road, Ivan turns into a long dirt driveway. The car stops in front of a plain white clapboard house. I breathe a sigh of relief. Yes, there is a house. But there is also a sign. The sign hangs from a post. The sign reads: ASSEMBLY OF GOD. The sign flaps about in the wind. The house is a church. It sits in the middle of what appears, in the dark clouds that hug the earth, to be a pasture. Jesus, are we in trouble; Louie and God *do not* have a good relationship.

We sit quietly in the car. I roll down my window. The air is fragrant; the damp smell of snow-laden grass and moldy leaves is heavy and sweet. The only sounds are Louie's wheezy breath, the wind, and the sign creaking on rusty hinges.

"This is it," Ivan says.

"But it's a church, not a house." I try to keep hysteria out of my voice.

"We are going to church?" Louie says. "Why is this? Why is this?" There is a spasm of coughs.

Ivan puts his arm around Louie's shoulder. "It's in transition, Papa. One of my regular customers bought it. It's being renovated."

"What is this word *renovated?*" Louie asks. He stares fiercely at Ivan. "Skazhy mne, syn," he says. "Tell me, son." Then, he opens the car door, but Ivan holds on to him and Louie is not strong

31

enough to break his grip. He turns to me, Smith, and Joanne in the backseat; fear and rage share his face, which is drained of all color. His voice trembles. "What is this word that makes a church not a church?" he asks. Smith and Joanne exchange worried glances. I order my voice to speak, my muscles to move, but they ignore me. I tell myself in the language of calm: this is not happening; surely, this is a mistake.

Ivan releases his grip on Louie's arm. We all get out of the car and stand in the cold wind. Small pellets of sleet and ice sting my face.

Suddenly, Louie lunges at Smith, grabbing hold of his scarf and pulling hand-over-hand as if climbing out of a deep hole. "Kakoi koshmar!" he cries out. "What a nightmare!"

"Let's get our asses inside before we freeze to fucking death," says Smith, doing his Philip Marlowe, drawing a sisterly stare from Joanne, who apparently does not recognize Upper Michigan practicality spoken in the language of New York. His words ignite me and Ivan to action. First, I disentangle Louie from Smith's scarf; then I take him by one arm. Ivan copies me and takes his other. Together we support him in the blustery wind.

"Pochemu tserkov? Pochemu, pochemu? Ya eto ne ponimaiu!" he shouts. "Why a church? Why? Why? I do not understand this!" Louie is shivering from cold and agitation. I fear he has lost another 10 percent, which may be good news; once inside, away from the sign that creaks in the wind, maybe he will forget it's a church.

The front steps are soft and rotting. We enter a square room with a low ceiling. There's a rank, pungent smell, as if some animal died inside the walls. On the left are church pews, twelve rows deep. On the right is empty space and floor covered with sawdust and ripped-out planks. Underneath where the pews had been, the floor's shade of brown is light in color. In between, the brown is mottled with water stains and the scuffing of shoes. New windows, floor to ceiling, line one wall, flooding the room with gray winter light. The other wall has two hexagonal windows.

They are oddly close together, as if they were old-fashioned spectacles created for the former parishioners to gaze through, perhaps to bring a hostile world into sharper focus.

"Oh my God!" Joanne screams at the tat-tat-tat sound of scurrying feet. A raccoon runs past us in pursuit of a cat. At the sound of her voice, the raccoon stops, turns, and gives us a territorial stare, then saunters out. Ivan runs to the cat, picks it up, and cradles it in his arms.

"Come, look," Ivan says, leading us through a door in the back. There's a large room, half kitchen, half living room, all flea market: overstuffed chairs and a sofa covered with cheap floral slipcovers in a dandelion motif. The kitchen has a long, free-standing modern butcher block work surface, covered with beer, soda, wine, vodka, and stacks of thick, heavy plates and mugs, which look like they were bought at a fire sale from a roadside diner. There are also two large commercial-looking refrigerators and a massive old stove with twelve burners; three square Formica tables have been pushed together to form a makeshift dining room. Filling out the space are a monster TV, a VCR, and a stereo.

Joanne sits Louie down on the couch. Smith pours him a glass of vodka. "A drink, Pops." This is new language for Smith. Louie's dark eyes, which had taken on a dull, vacant look, come alive again as if his soul had left his body but returned after briefly considering the alternatives. He chugs down the vodka and puts the glass on the floor. Color comes back to his face. No one has ever called him Pops before. I smile. The church is forgotten. Joanne and Smith sit on either side of him. He takes each by the hand and gives them a hearty shake.

I sneak a look inside each fridge: one holds two large turkeys, the other is crammed with bowls of cranberry sauce, sweet potatoes, salad, and stuffing, along with four pies. I have a light bulb moment: Ivan's been up here all week, shopping!

"But where are we going to sleep?" Joanne says, which begins Ivan's tour. "I get the couch," he says. "And here," he adds, guiding Joanne through a door between armchairs, "is your room." It has a simple bed, a chair, a dresser, and a window. Offsetting its plainness is a glass vase on the dresser with fresh white roses.

Smith and I have the same room on the kitchen side, but with two windows and no flowers. One window is open a crack. I feel an icy breeze. It brings with it the rushing sound of a mountain stream.

"But look, guys, you've got to see the upstairs. It's for Louie." He tugs on my shirt. I take Louie's arm. We climb a narrow winding staircase. He's a little shaky on the stairs. He stops halfway, takes out his handkerchief, and coughs large globs of mucus, then returns the handkerchief to his pocket. He does the ungraceful with grace. But Louie is an old man—my father is old and frail. Under the wool of his sweater vest, his arm has more bone than flesh.

Upstairs is one huge bedroom. Totally renovated. There's a bigger-than-king-sized bed. The floor is brown and smells freshly lacquered. Louie slips on its smoothness. I catch him before he falls. The ceiling slants and comes to a point. One side of the slanting roof has a large new skylight; the other side is mirrored and reflects the light. Even under the dim November sky, the room is bright. Louie smiles. Happiness unfolds on his face like a sixty-second Polaroid snapshot. He coughs again. His body quivers and stiffens.

"There's a hill behind the house," Ivan says. "And a mountain stream. You'll see tomorrow if the weather clears." He fidgets with his hands, touching Louie gingerly, as if afraid his hand will be swatted away.

The storm eases and the slush on the skylight slides off to reveal clouds beginning to rise and the lower slope of the promised hill. I lower my eyes and, transfixed, watch the faces of Louie and Ivan, so alike.

At the sound of a sharp thud against the skylight, I look up, alert to any signs of disaster. There is a clump of red, brown, and gray against the glass. "It's a bird," Ivan says. "They don't see the glass." I look closely at Louie to see if this will steal his joy, but he's bouncing on the bed like he's in a hotel, checking to see if he's gotten his money's worth. Ivan's stopped his fidgeting. He looks at me and I see something new in his steady gaze: pride.

Then Louie stops his bouncing; he rises, awkwardly. I go to help him and he embraces me, planting a sloppy kiss on my cheek. Which confuses me, until I realize he thinks it's all my doing. Like Ivan was just the chauffeur. Ivan's busy scurrying around, unpacking Louie's clothes—too distracted to notice is what I hope.

Music floats up from downstairs. Mozart. We are quiet together—me, Ivan, and Louie. A stillness that's rare. Then Louie says, "Nice music, but don't they have Ella or that Frank Sinatra, maybe?" He looks at Ivan like the choice of music was his fault. "Papa," Ivan says, "we've got *everything*." Louie gives him a hug. He gives me a hug. Louie's eyes are alert. He looks at Ivan with a sharp, appraising stare. For a precious moment the 10 percent is back. It's an unexpected look of appreciation and love, which Ivan does not see because he has raced downstairs to find Ella and Frank.

Smith's in charge of music. Mozart is off, Ella is on. Later, Ivan heats the Chinese food and Joanne sets the table. Yesterday, Ivan's every move made her left cheek twitch, but now it's like she'd rather have him for a brother than Smith. She still calls Smith *Robbie*, which makes *his* left cheek twitch. He's brought a stack of videos. *Casablanca, Velvet Goldmine, Maltese Falcon, Rocky Horror*. Noir meets glam is the theme. Smith's choices meet mine. In the video store on St. Mark's, he'd said, "We'll drive a post through the heart of the postmodern." Now, still wearing his trench coat, which is dark and blotchy from the rain and sleet, he says, "I'm falling in love with you, sweetheart," like he's Humphrey Bogart, and leans me backwards across his arm, tango-style. Before dinner, under the influence of *Velvet Goldmine*, he's rouged up a bit and added glitter and eye shadow. It becomes him. Over dinner, Joanne says, "Robbie, would you please wash your face?" He ignores her until the third or fourth time she says it. He flips a dumpling at her. "The name's Smith," he says. She giggles. I can see them as kids. Maybe she's decided it's okay not to be in Michigan. Louie laughs so hard he shakes the table, then stands and circles around filling shot glasses with vodka. "A toast," he says. "A toast to family." His voice is deep and strong. "Drink in one swallow," he instructs.

I wake to early morning sunlight. It fills every corner of the room. Smith sleeps, an arm resting on my chest. He snores sweetly, a musical rumbling. I lift his arm gently so as not to wake him and go to the window. My feet are bare and the wood floor is cold. Outside, I see two deer, a mother and her fawn. They tiptoe cautiously in the front yard. With each step, I can hear through the open window the cracking of the thin sheet of ice that covers the ground. Each crack startles the mother, who looks back protectively toward the fawn. And, in the distance, the sound of the fabled mountain stream, reminding me of Smith's way of modestly gargling water after brushing his teeth so as not to wake me.

Then I hear the Ivan phone's "Back in the USSR!" "Shit," I say under my breath and flip it on before it wakes Smith. "Where are you, Ive?" I ask. But before I remember that we're in the same house, in the country, and he's in the next room, Ivan says, "I'm upstairs with Louie." His voice is dry and tight. "Come quick," he says. "Please, Mish, come quick."

I put on a robe and go upstairs, two steps at a time. Ivan is on his knees beside Louie's bed. He is mumbling prayers in Russian. His brown robe has slipped off his shoulders. He looks like a monk in prayer, but a monk whose bare skin arouses feelings that confuse me.

"Ive, what's going on?" But when I reach the bed, what's going on is clear. Louie's eyes are open. He does not blink. His chest does not go up and down. His skin is a kind of gray in the middle of turning blue, or maybe the reverse. For a moment I get stuck on figuring out this puzzle. On his face is a smile. It could be a happy smile or an ironic one. I cannot tell. All I can tell is that it is a fixed smile and that he is dead. His fingers are stiff and crooked as if in his last moment of life he grasped at something that had been hidden: an angel, the meaning of life, Sonya's face. Who's to know? Maybe something simple, like a plane ticket back home or a glass of the best damn vodka ever made.

Ivan cries quietly. "Papa, Papa, ya tebia liubliu," he says. "Papa, Papa, I love you." I am more watching Ivan and Louie than paying attention to myself. Did Louie get to see the sun rise from behind the hill? Did he live to hear the mountain stream? These are my thoughts, until I notice that Ivan has crawled into the bed and lies clinging to Louie, as if trying to use his own body's warmth to bring Louie back to life. With a finger I close one of Papa's eyes, then the other. His eyelids are cool and stiff. They close like parts to a machine, not a person. Immediately, I regret not looking into his eyes one last time. To remember. But the thought of prying them open again makes me shudder.

I gently pull Ivan away from Louie's body. He responds easily to my touch. We hold each other. Ivan says, plaintively, "He'll miss Thanksgiving. He'll miss the turkey." I feel the warmth of Ivan's skin against mine.

"But he saw the sun and the hill and heard the mountain stream," I say. "He heard Ella and Frank, and drank good wine and vodka with me and you and Smith and Joanne last night. We were family, is what he last saw and felt." At first, I don't believe my own words—I say them to comfort Ivan—but as they tumble out, I remember last night and see a truth in them that comforts me.

"No, no, no. I fucked up. I royally fucked up. It was too much for him."

I know with a certainty I've never felt before that Ivan is wrong. I am full of gratitude to him for giving all this to Louie. I stroke his hair and cover his face with kisses. We sink to our knees, forehead to forehead. My robe opens. We lie yin to yang on the smooth hard floor, skin touching skin, curled into each other. Ivan kisses me on the mouth. It is not a brother's kiss. He touches me. I grow hard. I think of Papa's dead eyes, of Smith, but these thoughts do not save me. I wait for the feeling of sin to fill me, but in its place feel the heat of Ivan's firm body, his sweat-slicked skin. I explore his mouth with my tongue and feel him grow hard against my stomach. He twists in my arms and turns his back to me. I know what he wants, without his saying, but resist until he begs: "Please, Mishka, please do it."

"No, Vanushka. You know I can't."

"Sdelay!" he says. "Do it!" His voice is harsh, demanding. "Sdelay" he repeats. "You owe me." And I remember the blood-stained hospital floor and my own tainted blood, of no use to my brother when he lay near death. I lick the sweat from the back of Ivan's neck. I have the taste of my brother in my mouth, indecently smooth and rich, like pecans. We rub against each other in a rhythm that surely must date back to Sonya's womb.

"Don't move," he says. Then my body spasms.

"Idi k chortu," I say, gasping. "Damn you." I fill his body with all my love and rage and the mistake I never speak of until, spent, I roll over on my back. I breathe deeply and stare up through the skylight at the cloudless blue sky.

In December, Smith leaves to spend Christmas with Joanne in Michigan. Ivan calls daily, in his voice an unfamiliar reticence. Smith calls every few days, *his* voice noncommittal. Limbo is where I wait; the choice is his. I have made mine. Smith doesn't care if I am a writer, a gofer, or a banker. With him, I can breathe easy.

December dissolves into January. Smith returns. No phone call. The doorbell rings. "Hi," I say. He wears a tie. Striped. And a sports coat. "Welcome home." There is light brown hair on his head.

"My name is Leon, now," he says.

"Like in Trotsky?" I ask, but he looks at me blankly.

"Whatever." Maybe they don't study Russian history in Michigan. "Okay, Smith, Leon it is."

To my surprise, we settle in. I am happy. We feel like family. In a matter of days, he is Smith again. To me, Smith, Leon, who cares. He is home.

One Sunday morning I go out for bagels and the *Times* and see a handsome old man with a dark beard sitting on a bench. I think: Oh, there's Louie, then quickly remember. When I go home, Smith and I crawl into bed. For the first time I cry in his arms, and for the first time I say "I love you."

A March snowstorm leaves sidewalks icy, and bitter winds make most everyone irritable, but Ivan takes his lithium and stays out of trouble, and for that I am content.

One morning, the first of April, I'm snuggled into Smith, a tangle of arms and legs and sheets, when I wake to a sound like someone tapping at the window, or maybe it's hailstones, I think. Half in dreams, I go to the window to see. In the middle of the street is Ivan. "Open the window!" he shouts between flurries of pebbles. So I do, thinking: Why no cell phone? Then I remember: it's our birthday. We were Papa's April Fools. Ivan's voice echoes off the buildings; there's no competition on the quiet early-morning street. The air is warm, the sky faintly blue and pink—a dawn sky. Ivan stands by a pickup truck. In the back, tied by heavy rope, standing tall, are two glorious and unlikely objects: telephone booths, one as red as a fire truck and the other Irish green. Uncertain, I fumble with the snap on my eyeglass case and put on my glasses, and, yes, what I see is an English phone booth and its Irish mate.

"There's more to come, li'l bro! We're on easy street. Trust me!" And there he is, my Ivan, face smudged with grime, hair sticking out this way and that, a runaway garden, waving his arms and hands wildly, eyes wide and the sky growing brighter and bluer. I hoist my butt onto the window ledge. And there I am, half-awake, feet dangling, two stories up, waving back with one hand and holding on with the other.

# Barrel of Laughs

—⟋⟍—

I discovered time today, its essence. Hormonal fancies of some teenage kid, you say. Think you've got me pegged. Wrong. I'm at the other end of it all. Decades past that epiphany. If you're thinking philosophical nonsense from an old man, you're onto me. But go ahead, humor me along. What harm is there?

I was gazing out the window, sitting at my dining room table, a small one that seats two, squeezed into what you Americans call an "eat-in" kitchen.

My view from the fifteenth floor is meager: a mix of red and gray brick buildings, dotted with windows and sad little terraces—used as closets or gardens—and down below the small figures of people moving about, so many specks under a microscope. I'd think myself a god if it were my only view of humankind. And cars, row upon row of them in what you call parking lots—though why it is called a "lot" I don't know. Maybe it was a word used by farmers. I've asked Leo about this—Leo, my neighbor and explainer of all things American, now that my sons, Misha and Ivan, have decided they are fully grown and busy, always so busy. But Leo could not puzzle out this parking-lot business. "You fuss over words too much," he says, to cover his ignorance, so typical of Americans, who have no feel for history, revealed by the way they recklessly mint new words from old.

"Life," Leo says when he feels picked on by me, "is so much

41

more than words and meanings." And then he'll grow misty in the eyes and I know he's thinking of his Rebecca who'd shared fifty years with him, and I touch his hand in comradeship, recalling my brief five with Sonya, the mother of my children, so long ago.

But I've digressed. I was staring out the window, from which I can see a sliver of ocean—the Atlantic—along the Brooklyn coast. There is a beach, Brighton, but I must conjure the sand and the boisterous people promenading along the boardwalk. From here, caught in the space between two buildings, I see only the finger-sized sliver of blue—not quite the width of a thumb, more like an index finger—the sight of which evokes a smile, whatever my mood.

I was sitting there for heaven knows how long when Leo tapped me on the shoulder. "Earth to Louie," he said, to accompany this gesture.

"Who are you?" I asked, angrily. The teakettle was whistling, the room was filled with smoke; something was burning: it was porridge. Why am I cooking porridge? Sonya will have one of her fits. I hate it when she twists her face into a red knot and screams—it's the anger and despair of an insatiable child. "Why can't we eat meat?" she'll demand. "You starve us, me and my sons. You bastard!"

"It's me, Leo," Leo said, giving my shoulders a good shake. "Are you all right?"

Suddenly all was clear: Sonya was the memory, Leo the present, whose creased face was worried and sprouting the early layers of a beard. Recognizing him, I felt foolish, knowing that for some unknown number of minutes I was "clueless," an expression taught to me by my two boys when they were first absorbing English like thirsty sponges after we'd arrived in New York from Kiev ten years ago. Embarrassed, I watched Leo open the window. As the smoke cleared, I was aware of another smell, uncertain if I'd wet my pants or if it's the odor I fear I've taken on in old age.

"Louie, you can smell the smoke all the way down the corridor!"

"Oh," I said, with insufficient urgency to appease him.

Leo stood on a chair and reached up to the smoke alarm above the front door. He pressed a button and waited.

"The battery's dead. How many times have I got to tell you to replace the effing battery?"

"But I did, just last week."

"So how come this battery is dead? I swear, Louie, sometimes you and the truth are allergic to each other."

Looking up at him wagging his finger, I was struck again how in the photos that chronicle Leo's adult life, he was once a barrel-chested man whose upper torso slid down over the years to his stomach, creating a large bulge above his belt. But his anger did not upset me; it's all in his voice, not his face, which, the beard barely begun, still had the kindly jowls of a Saint Bernard and not a Moses or Abraham on some hilltop, waving a staff.

"How long have you been sitting like this?" he asked, like a worried parent.

Yes, how long? I wondered, and that's when I discovered time. It filled me with a sense of joy I'd thought lost forever: greater for sure than the meager pleasure offered up by my finger-sized view of the ocean. I had no idea how long I had been sitting here "like this," as Leo said. It was in the losing of time, you see, that I'd discovered it.

*The losing of it.*

Thanks to a small stroke, I am losing more and more of my time on earth. But where earlier it had caused fear and dismay, I now saw only its blessings as Leo, humming a jolly tune, made us breakfast while warm summer air—a humid, medicinal healing—filled my kitchen. How amazing, in my seventy-fifth year!

Not that I hadn't ruminated on the nature of time before. How slowly it passed when I was a child, school out, staring at the sky under a warm sun, chewing on a daisy or playing a nonsensical game with my friends. During the war against the Germans, time moved like a traffic jam, a jagged flow of stops and starts when there was no food, no medicine for the sick and wounded. Soldiers, workers, peasants, intellectuals, party members—there was little difference in the war years; we had a truly classless society! And the unexpected ways time comes to a complete halt: falling in love with Sonya was my first genuine taste, and I'd thought, yes, this, the stopping of time, is a wonder sweeter than any pomegranate. Such a philosopher I was. And again it stopped when she bore me two sons. She gave me what my other two wives could not—and in my fiftieth year! She had missed the war, the famines, the purges, all of which, perhaps, are not good for the ovaries. Then, for a while, time ambled like lovers strolling aimlessly in the woods. There was little money and we were forced to live in a village many hours from Kiev. But who needed Kiev or the pleasures of far-off Moscow and Leningrad? I was a doctor with a fine wife and two sons. And, as the boys began to crawl, took their first steps, spoke their first words, Sonya, for a time, was happy.

"Do you trust me to make coffee?" Leo asked, knowing how fussy I am.

"Yes, please, I trust you today, but just for today," I teased.

He scavenged around my cabinets and in the refrigerator. "Where are you hiding it now?" he asked, with good humor. "Under the bed?"

"The vodka?" I asked, playing the innocent. "I no longer indulge. Didn't I promise?"

"Louie, you're trying my patience."

"Oh, the tobacco. Not in three weeks, as was my word."

"The coffee, Louie. The goddamn coffee."

"Oh."

I pointed above the microwave with a little wave of my hand.

When my boys were just months short of their second birthday, time stopped again. Stopped horribly. I do not to this day understand why Sonya took the razor blades to her arms. Such delicate arms. I loved to trace the pale blue veins that ran under her skin. Why, you might ask? Was I not a doctor? Did I not know the proper label for her despair, her tears, her grandiosities, which emerged in speech and visions that rushed ahead like a train out of control? To say I've forgotten would be a lie. But to give it a name, a diagnosis! Ask me first to defile her grave.

I never told my boys. I said she died in childbirth, that she was joyful and happy, a guardian angel looking down on them. Could I have invented a better story? A disease: TB, diphtheria, meningitis, perhaps? You be the judge. But I never spoke of the dark circles under her eyes after she'd lock herself in the bedroom for weeks; the sound of her weeping; the nights she disappeared. How her face would be distorted by rage, unrecognizable, then wide-eyed with grand and impossible schemes. Their memory of her—if it existed—had no more substance than a dream. Of that I am certain.

Yes, losing time.

It can be quite fascinating.

Not long ago, I remembered that Anna threw herself in front of the train. For days I could not recall how that novel ended. I've read Tolstoy's book four or five times, at least. With a few vodkas I can talk about it for hours. I was certain a few months ago she'd married her lover, then with equal self-assurance that she'd returned to her husband; one night, drifting off to sleep, it came to me she'd accidentally drowned her child. Pride kept me from going back to the book.

The train! I awoke only just the other day at dawn, startled. How could I forget? I'd never believed it anyway. I'd ranted on about how she'd never kill herself. Count Tolstoy made her do this. *He* threw her in front of that train—Anna would never have chosen that fate. Never. She was too proud. Too strong. It was the count's guilt: he was ridding himself of his mistresses, or killing himself, or in anger, destroying his long-forbearing wife. Why on earth would an intelligent, beautiful woman do such a deed?

I've digressed again, I fear. The kitchen table, the smoke alarm, the whistling teakettle and, yes, Leo, making toast (which he burned), scrambling eggs, pouring coffee. My index finger of ocean was gone, faded into the gray clouds above. And down below, trees. Sickly city trees surrounded by pavement and patches of grass. Have I told you about these trees? Have I?

Leo cut away the burnt edges from the toast. "But that's my favorite part," I said in mock anger. When he worries about me he is fun to tease. He ladled the eggs onto my plate. "Dig in," he said, with gusto, pulling out a chair for himself.

"But you forgot to butter the toast."

"Coming from you, that's a barrel of laughs."

"I like that, 'barrel of laughs.' You teach me so much, my friend." I sipped some coffee. "So, what does this mean, your 'barrel of laughs'?"

A few months ago, I reluctantly moved into "assisted living for seniors" housing. Such a graceless collection of words, don't you agree? My sons, having turned twenty-two, united in one voice to say that I could no longer live completely on my own. A small stroke, the doctors said, but one which left me forgetting to turn off the stove and wandering about, finding myself in strange surroundings, no memory of how I got from one place to another. There was some small paralysis on my right side, which cleared up quickly but left my arm weak. I did not tell them about the coffee cups I dropped, the plates, too. Meals I scraped off the floor. But one day on a visit, they witnessed. "You must move, Papa," said Misha, his jaw set, brushing away the hair from his eyes. "Yes," echoed Ivan, a little less certain, perhaps nostalgic for this apartment off Avenue U. To me, it was quite ordinary, lacking any detail worthy of nostalgia. Yet it was larger than any I'd had in my life; perhaps it was my employment as a doorman that clouded my vision. Compared to West 77th Street, where I worked before my stroke, with its grand canopy, its elegant mirrored lobby, Avenue U disappointed. I'd expected more from America. Of course, now that I've been here ten years, I realize that everyone expects more from America, not the least her native-born.

46

But I was not happy to move. I was cranky toward them, testing their will, thinking, perhaps, they were children and would give me my way. My boys—have I told you?—are twins, but in looks and temperament they could not be more unlike. Mishka's hair is yellow like corn, skin so pale as to be translucent; "more sun," I tell him to the point of nagging. He is tall and slender— he seems to sway in the wind—with a mild manner that masks great ambition: to be a filmmaker. "My Sergei Eisenstein," I tease, fearful, knowing that time is not as abundant as he believes. And Ivan, my Vanushka, short, hair dark as coal, whose moods, mercurial, swing wildly like the pendulum of a mad scientist. "A real motormouth, that one," is how Leo puts it. It is said that parents cannot love their children equally; I do not believe this to be true. Certainly not for me. But on any given morning since my Sonya died, when I awake, my worries dwell more on one or the other. I have no control.

Yet, for all my complaints, my sons dote on me. They have cell phones and call every day. Ivan, who drives a cab (that he left college, I confess, is a heartache), will say, "Papa, I'll be there in a nanosecond." My love for him is strong and steady, but surges unexpectedly when I hear the very American way he says *nanosecond*.

I find English to be unfussy, lacking in frills; utility is its greatest value and for this I give it much credit. But rarely, to my ears, does it rise to poetry. Yet *nanosecond*, as spoken by my Vanushka—there's a beauty to its sound that touches my soul.

"I'll give *your* bacon ten extra minutes," Leo says. "It carries diseases, you know." It's been a week since the smoke-alarm incident and I've given Leo keys to my apartment, "Just in case," he'd insisted.

I notice that he calls the bacon mine. "I don't myself partake," he says. He does that business with his nose to show he's squeamish, and then holds his palms out, looking to heaven as if for moral support.

"Louie," he says, "it's none of my business, but I don't understand how a fellow Jew, from the old country no less, can partake in eating bacon."

That I'd almost burned down the building last week was, apparently, not the only shock to Leo.

But Kiev, "the old country"? And me, "a fellow Jew"?

He is so earnest that despite my best efforts I laugh.

"What's the goddamn joke?" a somber Leo asks.

When I catch my breath I see the wounded look on his face. Yes, even after six months, we are, to some degree, strangers. It is fascinating to learn more about a friend each day, an unexpected detail revealed: what makes him laugh, hurt, what he can talk about, what he can't. During the months I've known Leo, he still talks little about his Rebecca of fifty years.

"What's so damn funny, Louie?"

"Leo, where did you live most of your life?"

"Sheepshead Bay. I've told you that already."

"So, is that the old country?"

"No, it was home."

"And to me Russia was home."

"Oh," he says and returns to the stove. "Whatever you say."

Leo once managed a chain of carpet stores. He believes I am smarter than him. Often this pleases him and he is deferential. This, I confess, pleases me. Sometimes, though, he turns grumpy and I believe he thinks I'm making a fool of him. In several of the pictures that cover a wall in his living room, he is taller, an athlete in high school, later a strong, healthy man in his army uniform. Now, he is a little stooped over. It hurts him to be an old man who's lost some height. "Height is not stature," I tell him. "Many things can take away a man's stature, but not his age." This is a subject me and Leo *can* talk about.

So far we've avoided the subject of religion. It's best that way and it's deliberate. Leo, like most Americans, does not understand the luxury of choosing among gods and rituals from which to find solace and hope. In "the old country," an unguarded conversation about religion could lead easily to the loss of work, if not to a gulag or a firing squad.

But, I must admit, their innocence has a certain sweetness.

"Five more minutes," he says, turning to face me, spatula in hand.

Five minutes? I recall him saying "ten minutes," but it feels like no time has passed. Where did those five minutes go? This is upsetting as I'm not sure if I was "lost in thought"—Leo's expression for when I lose my memory of recent events—or just lost in my thoughts like any man with time on his hands, a window to look out of, waiting for his breakfast.

We are back on the subject of time. Did you notice? Did you perhaps notice before I did? That would be a delicious irony, would it not? Was I lost in thought like any ordinary man, or did I lose five more minutes of my life on earth?

Leo sets up the TV tables in my living room. He likes to eat and watch TV. I call this an abomination. We compromise. Today, he gets his way. I carry the plates into the other room. I've been working with a physical therapist and my right arm is stronger. Leo pours the coffee. While he stares at the TV—I think he has a crush on the young woman who hosts the *Today* show—my eyes settle on the old mirror across from us, its edges gilded, as if it once hung in a castle or grand dacha, the mirror's coating chipped away in places. It was a gift from Ivan, one of his "finds" as he calls them. Ivan gives gifts exuberantly. (Leo has said, "The boy has a good heart, but, Louie, maybe he should get married. A good woman would settle him down.") And there's another plainer mirror behind me. While Leo watches TV, I become lost in the images within images, a carnival funhouse effect; layers of Louie and Leo, extending out endlessly, growing smaller and smaller. Perhaps that is where time is leading us: not to extinction, but to endless diminution. Perhaps those dark flecks I see in my vision, floaters they are called, are diminished people: old friends, former tenants who haunt this apartment, perhaps even Sonya or Rebecca. This thought pleases me.

I've gone, it seems, from being a physician to a metaphysician, thanks to my stroke. Before, I idled away my time on nostalgia and regrets. But I've no such luxury now. A doctor of metaphysics: a strange fate for a man who valued money and the ladies and, most of all, survival—yes, survival was my metaphysics. It was everyone's back in "the old country," especially during the war when I ate horsemeat for dinner or amputated a boy soldier's leg without anesthesia; and I was a boy myself, with one hurried year of medical school (but no shortage of cadavers)! So, please, Leo, don't bother me with this "Jew from the old country" business, or someday in a foul mood, I will introduce you to horrors.

"That pisses me off," says Leo, startling me. "What people get away with."

"What?" I ask, and then realize he's talking about a news story on TV. "Oh, yes. Quite shocking."

"More coffee?"

"Yes, my friend."

Leo struggles to get up. His back is weak. He stands still for a moment too long, like a tree quietly searching for its roots, and then strides ahead, his left heel grazing the floor ever so slightly. When he returns we drink our coffee in silence for a few minutes, watching the news.

"Leo, my friend, change the channel. The news is too grim." I let him be lord of the remote control. I've observed that it is of great importance to men in America. I care little for the honor and, besides, it is an easy kindness; he is, after all, lord of little else.

We agree on what he calls a "sitcom," which to me means a piece of theater where an invisible audience laughs at equally invisible jokes.

"Louie, no way those kids look anything like their parents." He points at the actors on TV.

"Quite true."

"Now that kid of yours, the motormouth: he's the spitting image of you."

"Yes, so I've been told," I say, finding this subject disagreeable.
"The other one, no way. You say he looks like . . ."
"Leo, can we please just watch the show."
"Okay, didn't mean to ruffle your feathers."
"My feathers are not ruffled. They are fine."
He sighs heavily. "Don't be such a . . ."
"Sourpuss?" I say, finishing his sentence. "Yes, perhaps today I am a little."

There are things they don't tell you about children. They say, "He looks like his father." Or his mother, or a dear old aunt in Moscow. They say this as if it is sweet, a wonderful phenomenon; but when I'd look at their young faces, I'd see Sonya, always Sonya, in Misha's fair hair and skin and sad blue eyes and in Ivan's sweetness and his grandiose schemes, always so urgent and demanding. Do you know what a horror it is to see your dead wife in your children? In their everyday look and gesture? Can you even imagine? A blessing some call it. They are fools and if you think like this you are a fool! I had to keep it hidden from them. And I swear to you, I did. They never knew.

I see her in them still, and then I lose time, which is a blessing to this Jew from the old country.

I'm standing on the boardwalk with Leo, wearing a heavy wool military overcoat. I've told Leo it's from my service in the Soviet Army, but to be honest Ivan found it in a secondhand clothing store in his neighborhood, which he calls the East Village. It is all New York, America to me. Dividing cities and countries into easts and wests, norths and souths, brings to mind memories of war, whereas to Ivan neighborhoods are fashionable playthings, as they are to Misha, too. One side is "cool," the other is not, Ivan says. But bickering, splitting hairs is an old story between us and I grew quarrelsome with him when I'd meant to be grateful. And I am grateful, as the coat keeps me warm even on such a cold and blustery day. About their East Village, I can't make up my mind. It is both dingy and playful but my boys are proud of it. It is "up and coming," they say. That certainly cannot be said of me. There is less of me each day. You could say I'm "down and going," if that makes any sense in English.

I try this "down and going" on Leo. "Leo," I say, "we are down and going," and give him a hearty slap on the back.

"Speak for yourself," he snaps, looking as if he's bit into a sour candy.

"Only a joke, my friend."

"We've lots of good years in front of us." He is encased in an oversized green parka which would do well for him in Siberia. He looks all puffed up, with small head and skinny legs. A strong wind and I imagine him knocked off his feet, rolling along the boardwalk like a barrel or a beach ball.

"Sure we do," I say, to reassure.

We've walked a mile, perhaps. The boardwalk is mostly deserted. The frozen wood groans under our feet. The few people we pass are all old. Leo nods and waves to people I barely recognize as if he were a small-town mayor. Do only the old enjoy a bracing walk in winter? Odd, if that's true. Since our arrival here in America, I've never been able to get my boys out with me in this weather. In Russia the cold was their element, they were like fish in water. Here, they say, "Papa, it's too cold for you to be walking." I think they've become very lazy, very American. I tell them about the healthy effects of negative ions in the ocean air, a tidbit learned from Leo. Ivan groans but keeps his smile; Misha rolls his eyes and frowns. From an early age, Misha's expression could be read as a frown or a pout, as if he'd been given a shot of Novocain. I never knew if he was happy or sad, sulking or daydreaming. In his eyes, I read judgment of me until I said just the right words when, like a spark to dry wood, his face would explode into fiery joy. One day—a day I wish I could forget—we exchanged angry words and it was my father's face I saw in him: the judgment, the stiffened jaw, the loathing in his eyes, which in my father's case, only vodka released.

"Louie, you must have had too much of that foreign coffee of yours. I can't keep up with you," Leo says.

"Sorry, my friend." We lean against the railing. His breathing is noisy and labored. Leo has a touch of asthma, only a "touch," he insists. He puffs on his inhaler. The sand is dark brown from a cold overnight rain. If I squint, the ocean, flat and gray on this cloudy day, could pass for the Black Sea. It was on such a day in Odessa, on the Black Sea in fall, where I fell in love with Sonya.

Although I'd been courting her for several months, it was not love at first sight. She was a nurse in the hospital where I worked. She was lovely and charming but I was not yet in love. Forgive my hubris in saying this, but I was near fifty and had seen too much death, and been in love far too often. I knew little of her past, nor she of mine. Secrets, discretion, were second nature in our world back then, as natural as breathing.

For a time we gazed silently at the waves from the window of our hotel. I'd borrowed the money for the trip—she'd wanted it so much. We had the hotel to ourselves, as who would vacation in November, even in Odessa? We sipped strong black tea, both of us quiet after making love. At one point our fingertips touched across the lace-covered table and she began to cry. It was a funny sound she made. I took it for hiccups at first; her chest rose up and down, ever so slightly. "Are you all right?" I asked. Then I noticed her tears. She had been so gay, almost buoyant since we'd met, not a moment of sadness or anger, not even irritations.

I rushed to comfort her, rattling the table, the cups and saucers, the heavy silverware. Even the samovar threatened to tip over.

"The sea makes me sad," she said.

"But you wanted this trip so badly, dear."

"I know. But my father died on vacation here. It reminds me."

"You should have told me," I said, not to reprimand but in honest confusion.

"I thought with you it would be different."

She baffled me. This held no logic. I did not take offense,

but rather felt the warmth of her need for me, which evoked a tenderness, a piercing love in me, such that I'd never known.

"You will never leave me?" she pleaded, tightening her grip on my hand. "Promise me that."

"Never." I'd said this to women before, but for the first time I could feel in my heart—or whatever organ holds such emotions—that for once I'd spoken the truth. Stroking her fragile hand, I thought I could count every bone.

"You are the kindest, most honest man I've ever known," she said, resting her head on my shoulder.

"Time heals all wounds, my darling," I said, a nostrum that I did not believe, but hoped might soothe her nerves.

She lifted her head and pursed her lips, and a wry, mocking smile appeared that I'd not seen before. "Is that a prescription, my handsome doctor?"

Yes, my Sonya had a sense of humor, the memory of which always surprises.

That she left me—and in a manner more cruel than if she'd run off with another man—what can I say? That it was a long time ago? That I've forgiven her? That I blame myself? You be the judge. Yes you, if you must.

And now I am looking out on the Atlantic in winter, which looks nothing like the Black Sea, and Brighton Beach, despite what some say, is not Odessa and never will be.

"Leo, time to head back?" I suggest.

As is our custom, he replies, "A knish and a hot dog on the way?"

"But of course, old friend. Of course."

We find a small deli with a few chairs and tables. Inside it's as warm as a Turkish bath. Traces of mustard cling to Leo's beard, which is long, gray, and unkempt. He is transforming himself into a biblical prophet, after all, though a sleepy one. Warm and a bit sleepy myself, I await prophetic words. There still lingers in me a need to have the mystery of it all explained. Instead, I hear the wind's howl, the windows' rattle, and Leo's sloppy chewing. I'd hoped for a prophet and instead sit across from a hungry old man. My mood sours. The mustard clinging to his beard annoys me.

"Leo," I say, pretending to wipe something from my beard. I do this several times, attempting to mime.

"Louie, you got a napkin compulsion?"

His eyes twinkle and his lips form into a cryptic smile. I am furious with him. I want to say, "Wipe that smile off your face and the crap from your mouth," but I hold my tongue. I imagine holding my tongue literally, buying time to replace anger with amusement.

"Leo, you've got mustard on your beard, that's all."

"If that's the worst of my sins, then heaven's a slam dunk." He finishes off the last of his hot dog in one messy swallow. Then, with a dramatic flourish he wipes his face. The mustard, though, still clings to his beard. "Are you ready to go?" he asks.

"Not yet. It's warm in here. Let me finish my coffee." I'm in no hurry now for the cold wind outside. Leo is a messy man— messy with his clothes, his body, his emotions. There was a time I could not countenance a friendship with such a man and, to be honest, I've always favored the company of women; but life is full of surprises and I find Leo's messiness endearing. Besides, the women in our building are not very appealing. For a time, I courted a widow of sixty-eight, a certain Sylvia, who had the kind of bone structure that holds up with age. Leo said she had great "knockers." He congratulated me on "scoring," which was crude, but he was right. Sylvia, though, had surprising delicacy for an American woman. We were taking our time, but alas, she did not live to see the age of sixty-nine. And, while I scored maybe twice, depending on how one defines that word, I grew fond enough of her to learn that love is just as perilous at my age. When my boys and I first moved to America, I was stronger and unafraid to swim far out into the ocean. Once, I was caught in a powerful current. I was helpless in its grip. I fought it until a whisper in my ear—a tap on the shoulder, perhaps, from the God in whom I do not believe?—or the weariness of the fight itself led me to ease up and swim parallel to the coast. Later, I added the word *riptide* to my growing vocabulary of English expressions.

Riptide. Love is like that.

"Louie, can I ask something personal?"

"And when has that stopped you before?"

"Your kid, the blond one. It doesn't bother you he's a *feygela?*" Leo makes that mincing gesture with his wrist and purses his lips. "He's a great kid, don't get me wrong, but don't it bug you any?"

I raise a hand to the waiter. "More coffee, please." When it arrives I make a great show of thanking him, ignoring Leo, who shifts about uneasily. Although I dislike sugar, I tear open a packet, pouring it into the cup, stirring it slowly. What I crave is vodka and tobacco, but I've made Leo that silly oath to forswear.

A man enters, leaving the door open to the cold.

"People like that guy really piss me off," Leo says.

"Why not just close the damn door?"

"That's not the point."

"Yes, it is the point."

"Okay, okay," he says, rising.

I gulp the coffee; it's hot and gives me a coughing fit, allowing me more time to gather my emotions.

Leo sits back down.

"No, Leo, my friend. It does not *bug* me any."

"But . . . ," Leo says. I raise my hand to silence him.

Quite unexpectedly, when Misha was eighteen, one year into college, he announced he was moving out. He'd already found an apartment. "Nonnegotiable," he said, with his downturned mouth and jaw stubborn as granite, impervious to argument. He had taken a job as a waiter to pay for it. Besides, he'd moved nearby. And not a day passed when I didn't hear from him. I missed my son, but held that back. Let him test his wings. I knew that Ivan would leave next, and prepared myself for the loneliness.

I had a habit, from the old country, as Leo would say, of "dropping by." One brisk fall afternoon, when the sidewalk swirled with dry leaves that crackled under my step, I went to Misha's apartment and asked for tea. He had none. "Coffee will be fine," I said, but he said "No, Papa, if it's tea you want I will go all the way to China," and he hurried out to the nearest store, several blocks away. Children grow so fast; an open book, transparent for so many years, they become, if we are fortunate, affable, affectionate strangers. Perhaps, if he'd been born to me when I was younger, I could look forward to knowing him when he'd reached middle age and we'd be less a mystery to each other.

While he was gone, I snooped. I opened drawers, looking for clues to his life. He had an old hardwood dresser with hand-painted details, one of Ivan's finds. One drawer was enough to open. I found condoms and marijuana and magazines with pictures of naked men. Maybe it was his way of telling me: to leave me alone. All I know is that when he returned, I screamed at him. I was profane toward my boy. "Idi k chortu!" I cried. "Damn you!" I had never behaved like this with Misha or his brother. Never. I beg you to believe this.

He stood there and took all my words. His face grew red. His arms crossed his chest. The set of his jaw hadn't changed since he was two. When I ran out of words I threw those magazines in his face. Then we stood in silence. I was emptied of feeling. Numb. So bewildered I forgot the cause of my rage. Do you have any idea how terrifying that silence was to me then? It was the silence between a father and son that if not breached can last forever. I know. I did not speak to my father for his last twenty years.

"Papa," he said, calmly, steel in his voice. "If you do not accept me for what I am, I will see you next at your funeral."

We stared at each other. Neither of us gave ground. Time passed. I don't recall if I'd ever stared so long into another man's eyes—and, yes, I could see what I'd been missing for too long: that he was no longer a boy.

Then, I looked away.

And of course I had no choice: accept him or lose him, really quite an easy decision.

A few years later, two or three, perhaps—he had moved into the East Village by then—I saw the bottles in his medicine chest. Snooping again. Though I have not practiced medicine for many years, I knew what they were. Did he forget to hide them, or was this his way, again, of telling without words? This time I kept silent. Although I am not a believer, I pray that I die before he does. I think the odds are good now that I will. I follow the news, after all. But they are not great odds. When I gambled I would not have taken these odds.

"Earth to Louie," Leo says, waking me from my reverie. "I wasn't knocking the boy. He's a great kid. Both of them are. But can we go now?"

"Yes, my friend. Let us go. But please do not use that word to describe my son. It lacks respect." I think that this business of losing time may be a gift, so that if anything happens to my boys, I will not remember long enough for grief. For my grief will crush me more heavily than the weight of all the stars in the universe.

"You're not mad at me for asking?" he says, forgetting that he's asked before. I think he truly wants to understand what to him is unfathomable, so I forgive him, because, to be completely honest with you, I do not fully understand what my son does with men, or what he feels.

"No, I am not angry, my friend, just cold and tired."

It's a long wait for the elevator. Someone is holding it for a neighbor. It's rude, though we all do it. I'm patient today, while Leo taps his foot in irritation, mumbling, "Some people, they have a nerve," to no one in particular. We take turns with impatience. Today it's his turn, tomorrow will be mine.

The elevator arrives with a noisy bounce of metal on metal, betraying its age; like the tenants, it too has its ailments. The doors open with a velvety swoosh and the lovely Estelle emerges. She is a new arrival. (Just yesterday, Leo pointed her out to me— with all the grace of an excited schoolboy—as we walked along

Neptune Avenue. How he discovered her name so quickly, he did not say.) We each nod to her and she bestows a nod and a cool smile to us both. She clutches to her bosom a bouquet of tulips wrapped in paper. The petals peek out. Their tips are yellow. Elevators, like women, are a mystery to me. You push one button and they go up, another and they go down. Doors open, they close. But, with some effort, elevators—mechanical creatures—can be understood. A doctor can understand and perhaps fix a defective heart, but he is helpless before a broken one. The hearts and bodies of women open, enveloping you in their warmth; but while their love also rises and falls, there are no reliable buttons. Should there be a heaven, and should I meet him there, I will suggest to Chekhov that he write a story about women and elevators.

I have yet to hear the sound of Estelle's voice, but her scent—of peaches and talcum—makes my blood quicken, my heart beat faster, which may or may not be good for me at my age. But does a man have a choice at any age? Ask me when I'm ninety, if I'm so lucky.

Inside, Leo and I are quiet. When we reach our floor, he says, not looking me in the eye, "She likes you."

"It is you she likes, my friend."

"No, Louie, you've got me beat in the looks department. I say you should go for it."

"You speak nonsense," I reply, feeling flattered and uncomfortable. How quickly a woman can make rivals out of two men. "Besides," I say, "I have not yet recovered from Sylvia's passing." I mean this as the truth, though it is Sonya's life—and her death—that has never released its grip on my heart. There were women before and after but for me only one woman has ever taken breath on this world. How I long to break this grip, yet I fear my love for her is what keeps me alive. Yes, I must confess, even more than the living, breathing presence of my sons, my treasures.

Typically, Leo and I play cards or watch TV after our walk, but today we go our separate ways. Has Estelle done this to us? Who's to say? Perhaps it's the rhythm of friendship.

Alone, I gaze at my view of the ocean. The large book of Van Gogh's paintings sits in front of me where I'd left it last night. A gift from Ivan on a visit we'd taken to the wondrous Metropolitan Museum of Art. At the time I was puzzled by his insistence that we go together. "Just us, Papa," he'd said. Quite unlike him to drag me to a museum. Misha, yes, but Ivan is easily bored. This trip was not to include Misha, he made clear, also so unlike him. Now, each turn of the page deepens my understanding. Each painting is a cri de coeur from Van Gogh, sometimes hushed, other times raging, as if the colors, the brushstrokes, speak: simple objects that adorn a cozy room, but a blanket of piercing red and two pictures on a wall, which may or may not be of brothers; wild irises with hearts of yellow reach for the sun; a hospital behind twisting, inconsolable trees; the lone figure of a man staggering through a field on a hot summer day; a radiant starry night, painted as if clawed at with uncut fingernails. It is a guide to Ivan's life, behind the facade of "happy-go-lucky," as Leo describes him—the emotions that too often drive my precious son to Bellevue.

And so like my Sonya, these rhythms. I would like to write a letter: Dear Mr. Van Gogh, please explain to me this joy and this despair, these wild visions that remake the world. Do not the commonplace pleasures of life make it all worthwhile? Is there no sensible middle ground to stand on? Maybe I'm too simple a man to understand, but was taking your life so necessary? I ask because I am still trying to understand my Sonya. So tell me, why couldn't she take strength from my love and the innocent smiles of her adoring sons? Tell me, I'll demand. I fight back tears, helpless with the fear that my Vanushka will do as Sonya did. Tell me, Mr. Van Gogh, why is it that my love for him and his brother's, too, may not be enough?

I pour myself an inch of vodka from the bottle I'd hidden in a closet, then roll a cigarette, lighting it, inhaling deeply, exhaling, and waving the smoke out the window.

Mr. Van Gogh has left me only his pictures, which, after all, is more than most, certainly more than I will leave. So, Mr. Van Gogh, you're off the hook, as Leo might say, for today.

Every Sunday morning Leo and I go out and splurge on breakfast. He calls it brunch, to which I reply, "Whatever you say, Mr. Au Courant. But brunch, I believe, is for yuppies."

To which, Leo says, "Okay, Mr. Have the Last Word," and I nod as if to give *him* the last word, though a nod is akin to a word, don't you agree?

We go to Belinsky's coffee shop. Lately, Belinsky's has introduced espresso, maybe the last place in all the five boroughs. I am teaching Leo to develop a taste for the thick dark drink with its many layers of complex flavors. The American version is not as good as the Turkish drink one could, on occasion, find in Kiev, but more often on trips to Odessa. Coffee from home (I will forgo mention of the Soviet version) was a more complicated affair, as was life; its bite echoed the bite of life—I was not one to sweeten it with sugar—its bitterness, the bitterness of life.

Life today is much simpler for me and Leo sitting in Belinsky's. He gulps his espresso. "Sip," I say. "Savor it. If you rush, you are rushing through life, my friend. And where at your age are you rushing to?"

Leo smiles indulgently. Belinsky himself serves us. This time I join Leo in his haste, rushing through pancakes awash with butter and maple syrup. We sit in a booth upholstered with red vinyl. My seat is patched, and creaks each time I move. Leo picks out a slice of my bacon without looking me in the eye. "Don't you think the pancakes are exceptional today?" I ask to save him embarrassment. The air smells damp from the wet overcoats piled on seats, hanging from hooks. The excess heat of Belinsky's has fogged the windows. It reminds me of a railway car somewhere between Leningrad and Moscow. They did have dining cars once, though the food was not as rich as Belinsky's. The rain has been a steady pitter-patter, but now it strikes harder against the window. Hail, perhaps. Against my will, I recall the sounds of fingers clicking, then rifles discharging bullets in bursts of three, always three. Neither thought is very pleasant and I try to wipe them both from my mind. I'll stay in the dining car, if you please, Mr. Conductor, wondering if there really was a dining car. It seems so unlikely. Yet the memory is vivid and I can't shake it, try as I might.

Click-click-click. A steady tempo. Now I'm working in a prison hospital outside Moscow. The war is over and the purges have begun again, though they lack the demonic energy they had in the thirties. The Old Man is no longer young. War and age does that to the small and the powerful alike. Whenever a prisoner is due to be executed, the others click their fingers in the hours before dawn. They are all prisoners before they are patients. The irony is that no one knows who will be executed, only that it is someone. Click-click go the prisoners, in imitation of bullets.

"Louie," Leo says, "I've been thinking."

"Yes, my friend." I am eager for distraction.

"You have the wrong name."

"And how is it I have the wrong name?"

"I was talking to Ira on the fourth floor and he knows some Russian."

"Yes. So what does Ira say?"

"He says there's no name in Russian that translates to Louie. He says your name was probably Lyov or Lev, and in English you should be a Leon maybe or a Leo, but you can't be a Louie."

"Is that so?"

"Yeah, that's what he said."

"So maybe I should be Leo and you should be Louie?"

"No, you should maybe be Leon so I can stay Leo."

"No. I want to be Leo if I can't be Louie."

Leo waves to Belinsky. "A cup of real American coffee, please," he says, then stares at me with that look he gets when I'm teasing. "Louie," he says, "I just want to know the truth. It's no skin off my teeth. I just want to know what's real."

"Skin off your teeth? This expression is new to me."

"Louie, cut the crap."

I'm startled and amused he takes this so seriously.

"Be careful about this truth business. Please, my friend, just let me be Louie. It's done no one any harm. We can pretend it's *Louis* pronounced the French way."

"But that's still pretending, Louie. It isn't the truth."

The pounding rain has diminished. I remember the day Sonya first called me by my name and not Doctor: a dreary fall day, that wry smile, the challenge in her sparkling blue eyes; there's more to me than you know, they said. And my name, spoken in a way I'd never heard before. I felt like a newborn child birthed from her lips—*my Lyov, darling Leova.*

"Louie, are you paying me any attention?" Leo's voice, not a sweet sound, brings me back to who I am now.

"Okay," I say. "Let's compromise. I promise not to use this Louie name for too many more years."

Dessert arrives: Danish for me, cheesecake for Leo. Waistlines are for the young. Besides, our spats are rare and dessert is a guaranteed change of subject.

But Leo is still red in the face. I don't know why this is so important to him. I sense it is one of his mysteries; which makes for satisfaction in a friend, not at all unlike the layers of flavor in Belinsky's unexpectedly fine espresso.

The first day of spring, sunny and brisk. Not a cloud in sight. Leo and I are wading up to our knees in the ocean, pants rolled, shoes and socks left on the sand. Both shivering. And why, you might ask, at our age? It seems my tales of the old country have come back to haunt me. The tradition, for example, of diving into the sea in winter. Yesterday, quite out of the blue, Leo said,

"Prove it." His eyes gleamed with the need for adventure. Yes, especially at our age there is the need for adventures other than ambulance rides to the hospital. Did I ever make like a polar bear when young and strong? It's doubtful. The stories I tell Leo and the facts of my life are producing offspring that are neither here nor there. "Half-baked" is what my Mishka calls them when he is irritated with me.

Small waves now lap against my calves. The cold rises from my feet and spreads throughout my body.

"Louie, I think this is enough."

"Yes, okay, enough is enough. Let's go back to the beach." I say this sadly, as if it is his fault I must turn back. I might have stripped bare and dove into the waves is in my voice. Although I have won a small victory in this game of chicken, I feel no pleasure. He, after all, has conceded the lovely Estelle to me. This is not bluffing and counterbluffing over cards and vodka; a friendship is not to be toyed with too roughly, I think, feeling a warmth for Leo that's quite the opposite of the still wintry Atlantic.

We sit on a large beach towel and cover ourselves with blankets. I can feel the sun's heat on my face for the first time since fall.

Leo looks chagrined. He's shaved his unruly gray beard; only a pencil-thin mustache remains. Beardless, he looks younger and, as I have bested him in this silly adventure, he looks vulnerable.

This mood of Leo's will not do. He'll grow maudlin with words about the children who rarely visit. "You're a lucky man, Louie, you are," he says, when my boys visit or escort me back into the city.

"Can I share with you a secret?" I ask, thinking a confidence will do him good.

"Of course."

"You must promise to tell no one, especially my boys."

"Scout's honor. Hope to die," he says, a smile on his face.

"Scout's honor is good enough. Hope to die is an excess."

"Louie, get to the point."

64

"I have never told you how I managed to bring my family from Russia to America."

"Sure you did. You flew." I can't tell if Leo is, as he often says, pulling my leg.

"Yes, but how did I pay for the plane? And where did I have money for rent and food when we arrived?"

"Are you trying to tell me something?" he asks, frowning. I imagine he fears I had some connection to the Russian Mafia, which is the whispery talk of the neighborhood. As if saluting me, he brings a hand to his eyes, shading them from the sun.

"I sold my Sonya's wedding ring and all her jewels. Her family hoarded them through the October revolution, the civil war, and the war against Hitler. When she died I swore an oath to keep them. The jewels and a few pictures were my sons' only link to her. It broke my heart, but it was the only way."

"Gee, Louie, that's tough, but surely they'd understand. Considering."

"I substituted shiny fakes that cost a pittance. They were young and easily fooled, but I feel a shame, at times, that I cannot erase."

"Louie, you do what you got to do in life is all I can say." He gives me a clumsy hug. "You've nothing to be ashamed of in my book." He takes out a thermos filled with coffee and a touch of brandy.

"A toast," he says. "*L'chaim.*"

"*L'chaim*," I echo.

The sun is lower, a winter sun again, a pale yellow adornment in the sky.

"Time to go," I say, stretching my arms. It is, after all, only the first day of spring. There will be time enough to feel the sun.

Walking back, I wonder, briefly, why I made up the story of Sonya's jewelry. There seemed the need of it at the time, but now I feel real shame. And this is when I lose some time and find myself in bed—no memory of walking home—in my pajamas, huddled under my blanket, fearful, remembering the tale of

65

Sonya's jewels, not sure, in the dark, if it was a dream or the truth; and, getting up to pee, I decide to call it a myth, which, in its way, satisfies me deeply, as does the emptying of my bladder.

Coffee this evening at Leo's. "We're always at your place," he's grumbled lately. Which is true. I blame his American coffee, little better than tepid brown water. But the truth is that his apartment faces away from the ocean toward the highway and city streets with the never ending hum of cars, the roar and clatter of the elevated train, and car alarms that remind me of war.

I am worried. I see more than Leo realizes. In recent weeks the shuffling of his left foot has grown worse. And now, pouring coffee, some in the cup, some in the saucer, a few drops on my pants, it's clear the tremor in his left hand is worse. These are details a physician notices automatically. I have not told Leo my profession before coming to America. To my way of thinking, if I do not do the work of one, it is no longer of importance. He knows only that I was a doorman on West 77th Street. And Leo has not told me that he suffers from Parkinson's disease. He respects my past by not asking questions and I respect his present and likely future.

"Did I ever tell you that my Sonya had a beautiful voice?" I say, to get us past the spilled coffee and Leo's shame.

"No." He cleans up the mess, avoiding my eyes. Although in personal grooming, Leo is lacking, his apartment is tidy. A curious contradiction: dishes in place, no musty piles of newspapers, magazines, and books. My place he'd described as a kind of forgivable squalor. "You're a real intellectual," he'd said.

To which I'd replied, "I keep up. Nothing more," feeling a quiet pleasure. "Why 'forgivable'?" I'd asked.

"Because you're my friend is why forgivable."

Now he lowers himself onto his large leather recliner and we drink our coffee in silence. His living room is filled with odds and ends of furniture salvaged from his home in nearby Sheepshead Bay. One can barely move without bumping into a table or chair.

Leo has managed to rest the saucer on his chest, while his elbow is braced on the chair's arm to steady his hand.

"Yes, Sonya had an incandescent voice. It was a gift and she treated it as a trifle. Her parents, when she was young, imagined her in the Leningrad opera. But Sonya sang simply for the pleasure it gave her."

"That's sweet," Leo says, putting the cup and saucer down. "I can't carry a tune. I'm a great dancer, but can't carry a gosh-darned tune to save my life." I imagine the younger Leo guiding his slender Rebecca on the dance floor.

"Sweet, yes, but also selfish. A career on the stage would have brought a larger apartment and more income to help her parents. By the time she met me she was too old—still young but too old to begin proper training for a soprano."

"Rebecca was a great dancer, too. How we loved to dance."

"Sonya, when she was pregnant with my boys, sang the most beautiful lullabies. In bed I'd lay my head on her belly while she sang to them. I think, now, those were the happiest moments for us both."

Leo sighs. I don't know if it is for me and Sonya or for his Rebecca. I am not so content but try my best to reflect Leo's smile. Sonya was Beauty and the Beast rolled into one. And I cannot recall the lullabies without the madness. Can I confess to you that the other women I saw, that I was driven to them by Sonya? I will not even try, and it's best not to ask. Enough of lullabies, madness, and war. "Water under the bridge," as my Misha said, when I smothered him with apologies for my anger that day I discovered his magazines.

To my relief, Leo asks, "A game of cards?"

I add, "Before the news?" finishing his question, as is our custom.

He walks to his desk for the cards. The shuffle is gone. And the tremor is much reduced, so much so that he cheats with ease, which is also our custom.

We are finishing dessert, Estelle and I, at an Italian restaurant far beyond my means. Who am I trying to impress? Estelle, apparently, but in that mission I believe I've failed. Seduced by her scent of peaches and talcum and her still shapely figure, and curious to hear this woman of mystery speak, I asked her out during a rare elevator ride without Leo. She said, "Yes, I would be delighted," in a cultured voice. I feared that Leo would be jealous, but I was lonely for the pleasures only a woman can bring.

She puts on thick glasses to scan the menu, bringing it close to her eyes. Too close. Now I know why she has moved in among us: she is very likely going blind—a disorder that will be slow but pernicious. Maybe I'm wrong, out of date. I can only hope. I would like to reach out and touch her hand and say, "I understand." But, alas, our conversation over dinner has dwindled to an awkward silence. When I was younger, I could flirt effortlessly with a woman, talking of dreams for the future, treating her to a well-phrased compliment—even anger at the Soviet state could add sauce to an overnight tryst. But now we talk of loss or how it will end and that is too sad, so we retreat into silence. Flattering her good looks fails when we're both past seventy. I ask about her family—a widow for five years, four children in California and Oregon. "Too far away," she says. Of her husband, "He was not a bad man." Of her children, "They send postcards, they call." She seems far away, lost in her past, and perhaps in shock that it's all gone. "I was a secretary at City College for thirty years," she says, as if they betrayed her.

I ask, she answers.

A violin fills the gaps. The waiter, young, with admirable posture and a stiff white jacket adorned with silver lapels and gold buttons as if he were in the navy or, perhaps, a cruise ship, asks, "More wine?" I look to Estelle, who places her palm over her glass and shakes her head.

"Yes," I say. "Just a little."

I have a mouth full of tiramisu when she says, "Louis"—she

calls me Louis with a sibilant *s*, which is of mild annoyance. "Louis," she says, "are we not both exiles, you and me?"

"What do you mean?" I say, trying with great difficulty to swallow.

"We live here among strangers, separated from our real lives, which occurred in another time and place."

I am not sure if she is talking to me or to herself, she seems so inward and despondent. I touch her hand but she pulls it away.

"I am not an exile," I say, which is only a small part of what I feel.

"You live far from the country of your birth. I live far from the life I lived as a mother, a wife, my career, such as it was."

I think of an image from far back in time—I may have been three or four years old. My father, who was a burly man, is hoisting me high in the air. I am dizzy with fear and laughter. I look down on him from that great height and up at the spinning sky. I am the repository of that moment. When I die, it will die with me.

"Estelle, I have learned to live wherever I find myself. If I could, I'd strike the word *exile* from every language." I wipe the traces of tiramisu from my mouth, then wave a hand to the waiter for the check. "Yes, for me, I do regret leaving Russia or Ukraine or whatever they call it now. I do not belong here. I look at my sons' faces for signs that they miss their homeland, but see nothing, only America. And I must make my home near them. It is such a romantic fashion to be an exile. Careers and lives are built on it. But to me it is a pose to earn sympathy, to appear as a person of depth and mystery." There are tears in her eyes. I've been too harsh, I fear, but keep on:

"True exile is a place in the heart. It is a sunken ship, rusted and metallic, where one's vision is obscured by silt and seaweed, one's taste overwhelmed by bitter salt. It is too private, too painful to parade about."

I hear in my voice the maudlin poet that emerges with alcohol.

"No, Louis, exile comes in many forms. I had a husband,

children, a home, good health, a job and I thought, foolishly, I had a life that would last as long as one of those castles in Europe Herb and I saw on TV and visited when we could. I walk about now as if I were already dead and returned as a ghost." Now she surprises me with the touch of her hand on mine. "Shall we go?" she asks.

We walk in silence the half dozen blocks to our building, our place of exile, one might say. The evening had started warm, but now there's a chill breeze. Spring is tentative. Estelle is wearing a gray sequined blouse. In her hand, she carries a blue sweater. "Brrr," she says, laughing, and hands me the sweater.

I hold it out so she can slip one arm in, then the other. "That's better," she says.

The sequins glitter in the moonlight. I am content. Though I may not remember this evening, I know the feeling of it will stay. Still, it may all be lost in time. I make an effort to forestall this. I note the buds on trees, the hum of cars, the voices of people who pass us in the street; English, Russian, Armenian, and Spanish are the languages I recognize, but there are others. I breathe deeply the smell of ocean air and note how it mixes with the fragrance of an early-blooming plant and Estelle's peaches and talcum.

I regret failing to notice the color of her eyes.

"Lilacs," she says, as if reading my mind. "They bloom this time of year, especially after a cold, rainy night."

She leads me down a side street. "Look," she points. "Down there." She kneels at a cluster of plants neatly lining the front of a house. She buries her face in them. She motions for me to do the same. I kneel, as instructed. The cold grass dampens my knees. "Bring your face into them," she says. I feel foolish but do so and the smell is both wonderful and sad. It reminds me of a happier time, at my parents' dacha.

We go on our way. The streetlights glow and I am determined to remember each of them as well as the one up ahead that flickers and is partly hidden behind a tree. She takes my arm and I hold to the gesture; a timeless one that women know so well. I give her a smile and etch in memory her delicate shoulder blades that look like the furled wings of a swan. On the corner of Ocean Parkway we wait for the light to change and I'm determined that the moment when red changes to green will not be forgotten, that if I can note every detail, one will remain and I can follow it back to the whole. The moon is full and only Venus is visible. I pull her closer. Will the gods of moons and suns, burning bushes, and bloody crosses give a damn about my holding tight to this evening?

"I had a lovely time," she says. Sonya had said that to me often in the old country when we'd courted.

"As did I."

In the elevator, Estelle still carries the scent of peaches and talcum, and I have, perhaps, the aura of the true exile. We wait. Once in, she presses 5 for her floor. I hesitate, then reach to press 15 for mine, but she stops me, takes hold of my hand, folding it firmly into hers.

Leo is alone in his kitchen. The silence and the impulse toward tears are one, as is often the case these days. His stomach rumbles. The sound is a relief and prods him into action. He opens a can of tuna, drains the water, turns the can upside down over a bowl, and taps it four times until all the tuna is in the bowl—a trick he learned from his mother—then adds the chopped celery and a dollop of low-fat mayonnaise, spreading the mix on whole-wheat bread with a layer of lettuce and tomato. He's made an effort to add healthy food to his habits. Rebecca often said, "Leo, you are such a creature of habit." It keeps her alive in him, such thoughts. Rebecca would shake her head in disapproval, but the laughter in her eyes took the edge off her scolding.

He likes to cut his sandwich into fourths, another habit. He'd known the statistics: women live on average longer than men, so in some corner of his mind lay a decades-old assumption that he'd never be faced with losing her. He sits on the sofa that had fit in their home but was too large for this apartment. He'd held on.

Not to everything, but he couldn't make a clean sweep. Rebecca had been his wife and his best friend. He'd not felt the need to make others. The men and women who worked for him at the carpet stores brought a kind of camaraderie that reminded him of army days, but when he sold out he lost touch. His children called regularly. He could travel; there was enough money in the bank. But Rebecca was right. He was a creature of habit. And now, of course, the Parkinson's.

Friendship with Louie was something new and it was a kind of traveling, with Louie's touch of the foreign, his thick accent, and tales of life in the old country. Hard to know with Louie what was bull and what was true. And now Estelle. An attractive woman tests the best of friendships. It was true in high school and it was true now. He considers going to Louie's for that card game but pride holds him back.

Leo turns on the TV to pass the time, but a local news story about a murder is followed by one about a fatal car accident. Changing channels brings him a plane crash, then a famine in Africa. Another channel has a game show where people shriek about something he can't figure out. He presses the mute on the remote. Flickering images are enough.

# It Takes All Kinds

—⁓—

They never got naked, so Smith figured it didn't count as cheating. It was a hands-into-unzipped-pants, shirts unbuttoned kind of business and the other guy—a Danny or a Tony, Smith wasn't all ears when he'd said his name—called him *dude* in a husky voice, which was a turn-on the first time, but by the fourth or fifth time after he'd guided Smith onto the leather couch in his apartment, it was a major *turnoff* and thus something of a relief.

Okay, they had kissed, which was a turn-on. His touch was rough, quick, searching, and yes, it was new, *unpredictable*, but just as Smith began to lose himself he thought of Misha: Misha's unhurried ways, his whispering "I love you" before they came. How Misha played Smith's body like a sax or an oboe, his instinct for shifting intensity and tempo with tender talk in English and Russian before they came together. How did he pull off that trick? No American-born man could make love like this. Smith, whose experience had been limited to boys from Michigan, had concluded it was a gift, ancestral magic passed on from one generation to the next, known only to men from frigid, faraway Russia.

Misha had a soul—*dusha* in Russian—and Smith wished he could steal it and make it his own.

Staring into Danny's or Tony's vacant eyes (he'd given up on Smith and was trying single-mindedly to get himself off), Smith thought of Misha's sad blue eyes waiting for him just three blocks away. The pain in them, were he to find out. They had rarely fought in their two years together. Skirmishes, of course, but quickly repaired. Misha's too-present brother, Ivan, was often the cause, until Smith learned that if he wanted—and he'd come to crave—Misha's near-mystical way with love, an unbounded affection for family was the price.

Smith's sense of family was American, prickly, unsettled. "Mish, I have very ambivalent feelings toward my family," he'd explained. "There's no word in Russian for ambivalence," Misha had said. Smith doubted this. And the truth is that he missed his family, especially his sister, Joanne. When Jo had visited last year, Misha said, "She is wonderful. Explain your silly ambivalence to me." Then Misha, poking a finger into Smith's chest, had declared, "Smitty, it is time to give up childish nonsense."

Now, Smith buttoned his shirt, zipped his pants. He scooped up his bag of groceries—the tomatoes and red peppers, the pale green lettuce wilting in the summer heat, the ice cream melting— and cast a backward glance at the dude-guy, whose muscles were tensed, his face contorted and sweaty. He looked like a laborer at day's end lifting one last pile of bricks, not at all like a man reaching for ecstasy.

"You can't go now," he said.

"Sure can," said Smith, halfway to the front door.

"It's rude, man, really rude."

"It takes all kinds," said Smith, closing the door quietly behind him.

Smith hated to fight. And he hated to cheat. But he had worries and this Tony or Danny with his lean body and muscle T-shirt seemed a solution of sorts. Spotting him at the Korean's on Avenue A, Smith, who'd been tapping cantaloupes for ripeness, had followed him into the Odessa, taking the open seat next to him at the counter. Before Smith could order an iced coffee, the stranger said smoothly, "Come see my paintings," stroking Smith's arm, after barely a nod and a hello. "I live upstairs."

Smith now raced down those stairs and stopped. He had three blocks to collect his thoughts. He'd been faithful to Misha for two long years—eight seasons in all! How could he be so stupid? *Come see my paintings.* Such a pathetic cliché; Smith blushed at the memory. And what if Misha found out? He could blame Ivan for taking up too much of Misha's time. But that was old news. I've never sown my wild oats, he thought, trying out that old line. But it too was another cliché. He was turning twenty-one next month. That had more potential. It was substantial, a birthday of consequence. A time for reflection, decision. I won't be young anymore, he thought, reaching for the right note of vindication. But the sound he heard was the errant clank of a child at the piano. More to the point, their anniversary was Labor Day, just one week away, and Smith was learning to say, to pronounce properly, I love you—*Ya tebia liubliu*—in Russian, as his gift. It had proved harder than he'd expected. Ivan was an impatient tutor, no substitute for Louie, Mish and Ivan's father. (How Smith's heart ached at the memory of the old man!) And often, of late, he didn't know if it was true, this sentiment: this I, Smith, loving you, Misha. And sometimes it was so true it frightened him.

Smith took the long way around Tompkins Square Park. The sun was hot, but cooled with each passing cloud, fall's chill fingering its way through the late August heat. He looked up, squinting at the sun. Was love so important in the greater scheme? Was it not more than a little self-indulgent? There was the thinning of the ozone layer, after all, and the melting of the polar ice caps, about which Misha had said, "Who cares, Smitty?" One year into the new millennium complacency reigned. At times, Smith believed he could see the earth's atmosphere escaping into the emptiness of space, the vacuum of the cosmos sucking him up with all those he loved. He'd bought a ticket to Antarctica, an excursion with Greenpeace. He'd not told Mish, not sure why until this very moment, clutching the bag of groceries tight to his chest: he might not come back—to school, to New York, to Misha.

And now Jo was about to visit. A whirlwind trip, she said, to see my only brother. She avoided discussing her engagement: his Jo planned to marry a dentist! Only he could save her from this foolishness but he had so much on his mind and though he loved her dearly he'd not found the courage to say, "Not a good time for a visit, Sis."

All reasons enough for a slipup on Smith's part.

He had a way of analyzing problems that was half his own and half his mother's influence. It hadn't been easy having a psychologist for a mom in Ann Arbor. She analyzed everything. She'd probably know exactly why he'd told Mish he was from Michigan's Upper Peninsula, why he'd lied about something so small.

The language stuck in his head: low self-esteem, projection, transference, the strengths and weaknesses of the ego, the power of the unconscious. Plus it had humiliated him when she took up with a graduate student half her age: Henry, a student in his father's department. Henry was skinny, still had zits, and sprouted pathetic patches of fuzz on his boyish cheeks. He called her Mrs. Doddsworth when he first came to the house for a meeting with his father. Soon she became Helen (a name she'd later spurn for Helena), then sweetheart. Henry breezed into the Doddsworth split-level like it was his, lengthening his spine so his head—in his dreams!—was positioned for a crown. Who did he think he was, master of the house? It made Smith sick.

She was the cheat! And when he learned that his father, Charles Doddsworth, professor of mathematics, had his own half-his-age mistress—at the same time!—who called him Chuck, he was crushed. Jo, older, trying on blasé for size, said, "Everyone's parents do it, why not ours?"

That's when Smith, born Robert (Robbie) Doddsworth, first changed his name.

If they could change, so could he. He waved hello to Z-man, a runaway street kid, a twig of a boy, who sold weed and kept Smith abreast of the latest happenings; to Sue-Ellen, pushing a stroller, hugely pregnant since he'd last seen her, who'd sighed about giving up her law job and treated Smith as if he were her only confidant; and to the quartet of old men playing chess in the shade, who still insisted they were from Yugoslavia. He felt he belonged in this teeming postage-stamp-sized neighborhood, this East Village, as he'd never felt he belonged in Ann Arbor.

He'd called himself Lawrence for a while. He'd seen *Lawrence of Arabia* at the campus theater and been mesmerized: sand, flowing white robes, desert dust storms, camel caravans, Peter O'Toole's bare chest.

Death too young on a motorcycle was very cool. No one got the reference, of course. Jo did with some explaining, but wasn't impressed. His mom said, "You're my Robbie. Whatever you do, I love you." She suggested he play his music louder as therapy when he lamented losing his dad. "Robbie, he's not exactly lost," she said. "He's five miles away."

Then the diagnosis. His mom was dying. The end came quickly. At the funeral he called himself Zero. His dad, distraught, confused, asked tersely, "Zorro? Are you calling yourself Zorro now? Robbie, it's Mom's funeral. It's time to grow up, son."

He'd never called him *son* before.

"No, Dad," he'd said, as a gentle drizzle fell over the large gathering. "My name is Zero."

Smith's father was tall, wide in the shoulders, and leaned over so often to hear people talk that there was a permanent curve to his spine. As the rain grew heavy, he opened an umbrella and tilted it to cover his son. Smith often replayed the scene in his head, like a movie whose meaning shifted on repeated viewings; it made him dizzy how quickly memory created a father at his mother's grave who spun from strong, to lost, to bitter.

He stopped. Something was wrong with his memory. He struggled to recall what was missing. Jo! Why wasn't Jo at the funeral? He did remember that everyone took his new name, Zero, to be a worrisome sign: "low self-esteem, unresolved grief . . ." The obvious was missed in Ann Arbor's culture of self-analysis: the mathematics of zero, the jargon of Dad.

He was paying homage.

"Yo, Smitty," the super's son, Julio, greeted him, wakening Smith to the heat, the groceries, and . . . Damn! He'd forgotten to buy the liter bottles of Diet Sprite Misha loved.

"Hey, what's happening?"

"You know, everything, nothing." Julio, pants below his waist, backward baseball cap and down jacket in the summer, looked the part of a drug dealer. But he was his father's eyes and ears, keeping the street safe—a dying breed in this gentrified neighborhood. Smith had seen a touring company perform *Rent* in Ann Arbor a dozen times and ached for the bad, good old days he'd missed when the neighborhood had an edge, a soul—when, legend had it, art and danger combined to transform life into an elixir to be drunk with abandon, or so he imagined.

He jiggled the key to the lobby. His was the second set of Misha's original. Ivan had the first, but Smith still thought a second copy gave him distinction. He knew little of Misha's old boyfriends, although he'd once overheard Misha and Ivan in a heated argument, whispering *Kevin, Kevin* as if the name were a tennis ball smacked from one brother to the other, Ivan's tone bitter, Misha's chagrined.

Afterwards, he'd asked. "An old boyfriend," Mish said, yawning, rubbing his eyes, as if he'd been questioned about the weather. "Do not concern yourself, Smitty."

This was another worry: was he good for Misha? How could he know if he didn't know Misha before they'd met?

"Do I make you sad?" he'd once asked when Misha's expression turned inward, and Misha smiled. "I am from Russia. We are born to be sad."

If Smith understood human nature at all, it ended at Misha. Mish was the unknown. Smith wanted a time machine. He wanted a snapshot from the past, home movies. Louie had known, but it was a parent's knowing, and Louie was almost one year dead.

Do a thousand *I love you*'s from Misha keep their meaning forever?

The hallway smelled of cat piss—the old Puerto Rican lady on the first floor or as easily the old Polish man, her neighbor. They hated each other. You'd think at their age they'd have something in common, reasons to be friends, but *people don't act sensibly* was one of the few rules in life Smith had learned that stood the test of time. Misha's loving him, for example, was not sensible. And labeling his own feelings low self-esteem did not help with this puzzle.

When Smith left for New York, Charles, or rather Chuck, drove him to the airport in his yellow sporty Mazda. Breaking long silences, he'd said, "Keep in touch, Robbie," and "I'm up to be departmental chair soon," and "Call collect." Smith didn't remember in which order. The word *love* floated unspoken in the tight confines of the car. Politely, Smith said, "Sure," "Great," and, "Call collect? Dad, that's so last century." He felt unforgiving. Chuck never knew how to say what was in his heart. Smith had promised himself that he'd not make this mistake. At the airport, his father wrapped his arms around him; it had the awkward sense of discovery, as if this were the first hug ever between two people, a grand revelation akin to solving a mathematical puzzle, Fermat's equation, perhaps, that had resisted the best minds over the centuries.

Smith now raced up the stairs, two at a time, ravenous for Misha.

"Mish," he croaked, his voice strangled by panic and guilt. What if he carried the dude-guy's smell on his body? He wanted to dive into bed with Mish, vaporize the recent past—the little cheating business (he'd reduced it to that) and a long string of pasts back to snowy Michigan Sundays, when he was Robbie Doddsworth and Robbie would burst into his parents' room and snuggle the morning away in bed with them.

"Hold it a minute, Smitty," Misha said. "I'm on with Ivan. Some kind of trouble." Smith dropped the groceries just loud enough to suggest annoyance. "Oh, and Jo called. Your Mom's coming, too."

Smith sighed. The funeral scene had been so comforting. The fantasy of his mother's dying was not new, but never so real. It had taken away the shame of what he'd just done. But the good-bye from Chuck was painfully true. He put the groceries away, half listening to Misha chatter in English and Russian.

At work the next day, Smith was relieved to be chopping onions. He'd spent the evening preparing potatoes for the latkes—the restaurant's claim to fame—although he preferred the pierogis and blintzes. Shredding those stubborn potatoes was an uncreative chore. But onions! He'd mastered dicing them to the edge between being and nothingness his father might appreciate. Besides, they made him cry. He needed a good cry, even if dicing onions was an artificial means to that end.

Smith had been worrying about the rain forests when Uli, his boss, switched him to onions. Uli was German, a barrel-chested brick wall of a man. Smith had been hired thanks to a brief conversation—in German—between Ivan and Uli. Ivan drove a cab. He was smart enough to do better, but didn't seem to care. "I like meeting people. What's the crime in that?" he'd say to Misha when the brothers quarreled—more often since their father's death. Smith wanted to learn Russian. He wanted to speak to the brothers on their own terms. He still knew so little and was especially confounded by their way with consonants: the unnatural acts with his tongue that Ivan insisted were required and which made Smith sound like he was lisping.

But the poor rain forests. They were disappearing. He'd read about it in *Time*, *Mother Jones*, and *Scientific American*. There were urgent warnings in *National Geographic* and *Nature*. *Nova* reported the consequences in somber terms; literature from *Greenpeace* was his bedside reading. A documentary etched forever in his mind the huge swathes of forest and jungle cleared for profit. But culpability was confused. The indigenous peoples were both victims and perpetrators. Smith preferred good and evil more clearly defined. He did not like this unfamiliar territory where right and wrong were muddled.

He'd been deeply troubled, outraged! . . . by a map illustrating how New Orleans, Bangladesh, Amsterdam, the many islands of Japan, Indonesia, the Philippines—and Manila, poor Manila!—would vanish beneath rising seas.

When his cell phone chirped, his hand slipped and he cut his index finger.

"Fuck it," he muttered. He grabbed a clean towel and wrapped his finger, listening to Joanne, irritated by her Michigan accent, so apparent to him now after two years in New York.

"No, not you Sis," he said.

"Robbie, what's wrong? Is everything okay?"

"Yes. No. Hey, bad time."

"Robbie, getting married isn't the end of the world."

"To a dweeb it is. Have you lost your mind?"

"Then let's talk about where Mom and I will stay. Like, you know, you little twit, to make *p-l-a-n-s*." Smith pretended to hate it when Joanne spelled out words, but the truth was it made him feel protected, that she was still watching out for him. "Stop avoiding me," she said.

"I repeat. Can't talk and *p-l-e-a-s-e* get the *n-a-m-e* right. It's not Robbie and you're a twit for bringing Helena. So, so, so . . ." Smith was stutteringly mad: "bye-bye, ciao-ciao, do-do svidanya." *Good-bye* was the one expression he could say in Russian!

He'd adored Jo for as long as he could remember. "You are in my thrall," she'd say when they were young, in the voice of a stage hypnotist, subtly mocking Helena's therapy voice, wiggling her fingers in front of his eyes. They were each other's confidants. He was Robbie then. Helena was Helen, Chuck was Charles, and they were a family. Jo and Robbie were raised to amount to something. They were assumed to have prodigious talents in keeping with their parents'. Helen Doddsworth (born Smyth, she was one-quarter Welsh) had regretted taking her husband's name. She'd had brains, looks, and ambition but had given in to an archaic romantic fantasy. When Jo was born, she put off graduate school to be a stay-at-home mother. None of her girlfriends had proven so weak. To what syndrome had she succumbed? One day—with Joanne a toddler and Smith just learning to crawl— sick to death of diapers and baby talk, she'd bought seventy loaves of bread. (Seventy had a biblical ring to it, she thought.) They littered the kitchen floor, spilling over into the dining room. When Charles came home he'd raised a questioning eyebrow. "Asshole!" she screamed, throwing loaves at him. "I won them. I can be a breadwinner too, damn you."

"Bread pudding for dessert, sweetheart?" Charles had said, retreating to his study.

She returned to school, earned a Ph.D. in record time, and became a psychotherapist; she wanted to help others strip away their romantic fantasies and see the world as it was.

Helen had been an English major and named Jo for the Jo in *Little Women* and Robbie for *Robinson Crusoe*, markers to remind them to be independent, inventive. Their names sat in the unconscious of Jo and Robbie like pacemakers, reminding their weak-willed hearts to beat with ambition.

When Jo showed an affinity for math, Charles took a fatherly interest in her for the first time; he smiled with delight whenever she spoke. Charles Doddsworth was establishing a major minor career in the world of mathematics. An article, "Parsing Infinity: The Cosmos and Its Kin," had caused quite a stir and not a little celebrity. He became a popularizer, settling for book tours in place of discoveries in the realm of higher mathematics.

Robbie was a good listener, with a gift for empathy, Helen noted. Helen acted pleased that he and Jo were not conforming to gender stereotypes, although secretly she was uneasy. But she believed in working with what was at hand and not with what-if's. She taught Robbie that problems in life have causes that can to some extent be understood, and from understanding will come insight and action. He began to nod thoughtfully when listening to others. He took to saying "to some extent" precociously.

Jo, older by two years, grew disenchanted first. In high school, her quest to understand the mathematics of infinity was postponed when her body matured. In quick succession, she slept with a boy in the senior class, her high school math teacher, a student of her father's, and then one of Charles's colleagues. She saw a succession of sexual partners stretching as far as the eye could see. This, not guilt or shame, horrified her, this infinity of human connections, none of which would satisfy. At first she told Robbie everything. But in the winter of her junior year she grew silent, withdrawn, sulky. Robbie was too young, too vulnerable. She wanted to spare him her knowledge. But he pestered her. He wanted his sister back. And in the spring, as the ground thawed, so did Jo. She confided again.

"Robbie," she said, "it's time for a new approach. *I have decided we will squander our talents. Toss them to the wind.*"

"But Jo," he said.

"We will amount to nothing in the eyes of our parents. We will swear a blood oath."

"But Jo . . ." He didn't think he had any talents to squander, he wanted to say.

She took out a pocket knife, cut her thumb, then took his compliant hand and made a small cut in his.

"Ouch," he said, as she rubbed their thumbs together. Despite his reservations, he loved being close to Jo again; he reconsidered his mother's wisdom that problems can to some extent be understood. He thought about this until his brain ached. To make the pain go away, he finally accepted that he understood nothing.

"Of course they will stay here," Misha said the next afternoon, folding the laundered shirts with precision. "There's always room."

Twice a month the stars aligned to give Smith and Misha the same twenty-four hours free from work. Usually savored, today the day had taken on a vinegary taste.

"They'll stay at a hotel," said Smith, rolling socks into balls, army-style, side-arming them against the wall like baseballs.

"No, that's impossible. And rude. They are family and will sleep in our bed. We can sleep on the floor or," he paused, tilting his head as if to let one side communicate better with the other, "they can stay at Ivan's." Whenever Misha tilted his head in this fashion, his smile turned sly and Smith imagined a dialogue going on between the little Misha who'd lived his first eleven years in Kiev and the hip American Misha who had been constructed on top. It was like talking with two people.

"With Ivan! Mish, are you crazy too?" Two months after they'd met, after a night spent in the Bellevue Emergency Room, Misha had explained that Ivan was "a little bit bipolar." Two years later, Ivan's emotional life, its carnival ups and downs, was routine. To Smith, he was handle-with-care Ivan, but no longer a diagnosis.

"No, well, maybe not with Ivan."

"What's impossible is that they stay here. Have mercy on me, Mish. Please." Smith was tempted to spell out the letters to *mercy* and *please*. "They're my mother and sister, not just any family."

"Family is family. I don't understand your distinctions. Besides, there are obligations. No, I'm sorry. It's a no-brainer. They stay with us."

Misha's English was impeccable, but when he used idioms— "no-brainer," for example—there was an over-learned quality to it, a rumbling Slavic undercurrent. It was seductive and typically Smith succumbed. But Helena staying in his home would be unbearable. Eagle-eyed Helena was sure to spot the cracks in his hard-earned new life, her insights scalpel-sharp.

"They'll stay in a hotel." Smith upended the folded laundry and stomped into the bedroom, slamming the door behind him. He was embarrassed; Misha, a film school student at Columbia, would think the door slamming was out of a Bette Davis movie.

But Russians were not above their own melodrama, he thought, in consolation.

The door opened a crack and Misha's head appeared. "I don't understand why we can't talk."

"There's nothing to talk about. You either get it or you don't."

"Get it? Get it? That you wish to treat your family as if they were strangers, or worse, like vermin."

Misha's cell phone chimed the opening chords to "Back in the USSR."

"Yes, Ivan. No. Yes. Yes. No. No. *Nyet*. Maybe, later." Smith's thoughts drifted to the rain forests again, the melting ice caps, the spread of diseases that had existed for eons in isolated jungles. These concerns frightened him but were easier to understand than family. This, Misha would never get. Feelings about family were like religion Smith had learned since being with Mish. The differences were as profound as the approach to God defined by Catholics and Protestants, Jews and Muslims, Hindus and Buddhists. And just as irreconcilable. In Misha's world one was loyal to the death for family, even if they drove you crazy, even if they were crazy.

"Ivan says hello and that they can stay with him." He crawled into bed next to Smith and they lay side-by-side, facing each other, but not touching. Smith felt them breathe in tandem. Why was it so hard for Mish to understand? "Yes, your mother is a psychotherapist, and yes, she may be, as you insist, larger than life and so very demanding. But why," Misha had asked, "is this such a problem it cannot be solved? They are people. All people are too much of this, too little of that. What is the big deal, Smitty, if they love you?" Unspoken was Misha's loss, his mother's death in childbirth.

"In a hotel," Smith said.

"Okay, have it your way. In a hotel." He lifted Smith's chin up. "Smitty, look me in the eye?"

"I am."

"Yes, now, but lately only if I ask."

"Not true," Smith said, kissing him softly on each eye, feeling Misha stiffen, then tremble, brushing Misha's lips with his.

That night, Smith lay awake, eyes closed, while Misha slept, clinging to him lightly. Polar icebergs shone radiantly white under a full moon. They stirred, as if from a long sleep. His breath came in stops and starts, in synchronicity with the crack and groan of glaciers, shattering the Antarctic silence. The wind howled like a pack of wolves, like lunatics in an asylum.

The year before their divorce Charles and Helen had taken him to Los Angeles. A convergence of conventions for the parents. Jo had stayed behind. He'd been fascinated by the La Brea Tar Pits. He tried to grasp how the dinosaurs and countless other creatures could disappear from the earth. There was so much about life he did not understand. The black tar pit—its ability to trap and kill—was the unknown. It was infinite and lurking. That night he'd dreamed he was sinking in tar. He awoke before dawn: death, divorce, the end of what appeared solid, filled his mind. If the dinosaurs could be snuffed out, what chance did people have? He'd already sensed that Charles might leave Helen, that marriages, love, had endings. (Riding his bike around campus one day, he'd seen his dad holding hands with a young woman.) At the tar pits, it came to him that each ending was a rehearsal for death. He pushed back hard against this new thought. Still, it took possession of him.

Preoccupied, he kept to himself at school. But he was maturing, too. He'd become a strong swimmer and joined the swim team. He noticed the sleek bodies of other boys; they were children in September, whose muscles by April were sculpted as if each boy were a quick sketch by Michelangelo. One noticed his and suggested they fool around. The sex was quick and frequent. Robbie didn't care for Toby, but craved his touch. It puzzled him, this obsession with a boy he didn't like. He felt himself come alive only when he and Toby explored each other's bodies. Life in between was a matter of waiting, planning, dreaming of sex.

He'd thought love should be a part of the equation, but it was not. There was no joy, just the pursuit of it.

He could not talk to Jo about it; it was his first real secret from her. During those thrilling, hurried minutes with Toby, he was ecstatic; he, Robbie Doddsworth, had a soul. A soul! In his boyish way he came to believe that the passion he felt with Toby was a sign that death was not the end, that there might be a God and a life after death, and that sex was the path to igniting his own pallid soul into being. Perhaps, he thought, wistfully, the dinosaurs hadn't known about sex.

Smith ambled home from work, savoring the late-night smells of East Seventh Street: of restaurant kitchens and garbage; the park, its dewy leaves and grass; the pungent aroma of weed; the air dense, sticky, oozing of sex and the instinctual. The streets were never empty, but after four o'clock there was a hush, a moment of stillness that could stretch to an hour, if you were alert to it. In this hush, Smith was wrapped in a cocoon, his thoughts clearer, less scrambled and edgy. He spit on his shirt to rub at borscht stains and lost himself in a fantasy: he'd come upon a man—strikingly ugly, but in a sexy, magnetic sort of way—lying in the street, dying from a stab wound. Smith would take him in his arms, cradle the stranger's head on his lap, raise the man's lips to his, breathing life into him as the cops swooped down and, confusing the borscht stains for blood, mistake the Pieta-like moment for an act of murder . . .

Damn! They would arrive tomorrow. Labor Day weekend ruined. No sleeping the day away. No beach. And why was Helena coming? He longed to see Jo. And then, again, he didn't. It had been almost a year. Jo had looked tired then; she'd settled into a routine at the travel agency and he'd heard of several men in her life, though she made them sound like such dweebs, so beneath her. Postcards from Paris, Venice, London—perks of her job—sounded like the self-possessed Jo of old. The last one breezily announced she was engaged to a dentist. A dentist! And a creeping *I know what's best for you* insinuated itself into her phone calls. Misha be damned. He was ambivalent. He had a new life, such as it was; Robbie Doddsworth was totally, thoroughly the past.

But Helena. She was so responsible with her patients. She never took vacations, not even in August. "Such a cliché," she'd say, year after year. In addition, there was her agoraphobia. A psychotherapist mom afraid of open spaces. By the time he'd left home for New York, she had improved from those grim days after the divorce; she could make her way around town—but two square miles was her limit. At two miles there was a cliff and a bottomless abyss, she explained. "Maybe you need new glasses," he'd said, not recognizing cruel until it was out of his mouth. And flying became unthinkable. Her agoraphobia, which had been so totally uncool when he still lived in Ann Arbor, had, up until now, proved a blessing since he'd moved to New York.

He found his favorite bench in the park, near the fenced-in dog walk. He was sweaty and tired, but still buzzed. The sky was a cloudy crystal ball, glowing gray from sleepy, half-lit buildings, street lights, and a moon near full.

He wasn't ready to see Helena yet. And maybe not even Jo. He was not finished, it occurred to him. He thought of hanging a sign around his neck: CAUTION. PERSON UNDER CONSTRUCTION. He laughed. Who else would find this funny? Misha might laugh, but he wouldn't really understand. Ivan would ask about it earnestly. Only Jo would get it. Smith believed that most people were complete, finished by his age, done deals as persons. He was the only one playing catch-up in life.

He needed more time.

And now the tears did flow.

Smith was on the cusp of leaving Misha. He'd been on this cusp for a long time. How long he could not pin down. He thought of it now—this cusp—as the line of stakes that make a picket fence: on one side comfort, routine; fenced-in, for better or worse, in sickness and in health, by Misha's at times exalting, at times unbearably deep commitment. On the other side: all he need do was run.

Misha's unqualified love had for a time been a wonder. He thought back to their first meeting. That he'd met Ivan first was a fact he often forgot. Walking in the park, he'd seen Ivan sitting on a bench. Smith was attracted to his dark good looks and regal posture, hard to place—exiled royalty, Smith imagined, from Spain or, perhaps, Persia?—and his incandescent smile, which shone on lonely, new-to-town Robbie Doddsworth. He thought it might be this very bench, which was why it was his favorite spot in New York. It had been Labor Day. He was anxious about starting at NYU; he didn't know anyone in New York. The sun peeked in and out from passing clouds. The stranger's smile came and went with the sun. Smith made the first move, so unlike his Michigan self, but it was the stranger who did the chatting, rat-a-tat-tat. When Smith suggested going somewhere for coffee, his voice going all soprano from nerves—a battle within between lust and shyness—Ivan patted him on the knee and said, "I'm waiting for my brother." Smith rose to leave but the stranger said with pride, "No. You'll like him. He's my twin."

So they waited. As the clouds grew thicker and the sun retreated, the stranger became quiet, which made Smith edgy. He'd not been in New York long enough. He didn't know the rules. He searched the sidewalk for another short, equally beautiful man with dark hair. Would he be just as chatty? Or indefinably different?

They waited and he glanced nervously this way and that. Up above, a flock of birds flew south; below, he studied pigeons and sparrows pecking at food and pebbles, candy wrappers and broken glass. Suddenly, the stranger stood. "Hi, bro," he said to a tall, fair-haired man with sad blue eyes and a big smile. The dark-haired man's face, which had grown still and remote, became animated, as if he'd been jolted alive by an electric current. The brothers gave each other a kiss to each cheek, which Smith recognized from foreign movies. They were older, he realized, easily twenty-three or four, and he was tongue-tied shy. Should he slip away? He'd imagined ending up in bed with the brother of the radiant smile, but his taller twin—fraternal twins, it was now clear— had his own appeal. He had small ears like baby bats that stuck out at wide angles. The brothers switched between English and a wonderfully incomprehensible language. Smith felt his dull, Michigan self pale by comparison. The fair-haired brother gazed at him with those sad blue eyes. Then he smiled, a smile that seemed to strain his cheek muscles; it was a defiant smile, as if to say he was happy, could be happy, but happiness took work.

Smith had experienced lust, unrequited love, and a few inconsequential events that fell in between, but such longing as he felt now was new.

He wasn't sure if he was to end up with one of the brothers, both, or neither, but it was the man with the funny ears to whom he lost his heart, when, with a formal half-bow, he said, "My apologies. We have been rude, speaking Russian in front of such a handsome stranger." He offered a hand in greeting. It was large and warm, with long delicate fingers. "My name is Misha and presumably," he continued, extending his other hand out, palm up, as if presenting someone of great renown, "you've met my brother, Ivan?"

"Yeah," Ivan said, "I'm Ivan."

"Ivan the *Terrible* we sometimes call him."

"Ivan the *Terrific*, Mish," Ivan said, and both brothers laughed.

"My name is Sm-Sm-Smith," Smith stuttered, minting this new name on the spot.

"Hello, Mr. Smith," Misha said, earnestly.

"No, just Smith," he said, still holding tight to the stranger's hand. And with the new name, his New York self was born.

It was Labor Day, and they later declared it their anniversary, although it was a month before the stranger called. After they'd met, Smith had been all nerves, eventually giving up hope as the days passed, then near forgetting, with classes to take, books to buy; and Misha, finally, mumbling on the phone, all apologies—my father took ill, my brother's in California, please be my guest for dinner? I'd be so honored. The pasta was undercooked, the sauce too thin, too sweet, but, by then, who cared?

The agitated chatter of unseen birds announcing daybreak brought Smith back to the park and the present moment. He looked up toward East Eighth Street, toward home, where pink had softened the night sky's murky gray. Was leaving Misha the same as Chuck leaving Helena? A family dynamic? A repetition compulsion? He cringed at the language in his head. He had been trained by Helena to think this way. Helena would burrow in on the cause, the psychological trigger, while Chuck would shrug amiably, a disinterested nod to the infinity of cause and effect.

"Cusp," he knew from his dad, was a mathematical term, a curve crossing itself; and Smith saw his two possible lives—the one with Mish and the one without—reduced to mathematical curves snaking toward infinity.

I'm ill-equipped for this, he thought, facing up to the dread. I'm only twenty, after all. It was Louie's death that changed it all. But death and its aftermath could not be reduced to variables in an equation or the language of therapy. And it was a burden he carried alone: Mish and Ivan never talked about Louie in his presence. His name had become taboo. He'd tried, but Misha's face turned cold, his rosy cheeks paled.

The sound of garbage trucks laboring slowly up Avenue A silenced the noisy birds: these clumsy, monstrous trucks were the city's true announcers of dawn; birds were no longer necessary, he thought sadly, although he was relieved that there were still birds!

Smith bolted up. It was maddening. Damn Jo! She was supposed to protect him from Helena, not add to his burden. He kicked a can and returned to considering the rain forests. Smith kicked the can again, deciding that the indigenous peoples were, on balance, the victims in this drama, although the wormy bother of their selling out so cheap still gnawed at him.

Smith was not ready to face up to loss, not of the rain forests and the people who lived in them, not the death of people in general or particular. He sensed that he'd reached the beginning of an unexplored continent—honesty with himself—and in doing so, glimpsed, for the first time, Helena's courage. But he'd run aground on this: death's outline beneath Misha's pale skin.

The virus in his blood.

It was this he was poised to run from, not love.

Mother and sister stepped out of Ivan's cab in complementary pastel outfits: pale pinks, Helena; pale blues, Joanne. Each wore a straw hat: Helena's was large, oversized, suitable for the tropics; Jo's was smaller, more stylish. Each had a pastel ribbon that fluttered in the breeze.

The clothes irked Smith—their matching. Had Jo morphed into a clone of Helena? Perhaps planning a wedding did this to women.

Helena looked, in turn, at Smith, Misha, and Ivan. She blinked rapidly as if her eyes were taking snapshots. He had not seen her in two years. She was smaller than he'd remembered, prettier, younger looking, and more vulnerable. Her hair was cut short, almost boyish. But her dress, in the humid air, had lost any shape it might once have had. She was pale—odd for his mother, who worshipped the sun as much as she did the psyche. She looked bewildered. Helena had clung to her children after the divorce; she needed them like a vacuum cleaner needs dust, he'd once explained to Misha, who'd snapped, "She's your mother, Smitty." No need to say "Be grateful you have one."

"So?" she said. It was a gentle interrogatory *so*, spoken in Helena's velvety therapist voice. It was followed by a medium-strength hug that suggested meanings, and an earthy "Hi ya, sweetheart."

Smith sighed. She'd found her bearings. He was relieved, but also wary. "Hi, Helena," he said. "The hotel?"

"I thought we'd stop here first, sweetie, then freshen up later."

Jo lingered near the cab, standing by Ivan. Eyes downcast, she looked defeated, her dark, dramatic lipstick the only sign of her feisty self. Ivan gave her a small push toward Smith. She looked up at him, her eyes widening as if waking from a trance. Brother and sister embraced—too politely, he thought.

"Are you okay?" he whispered. She pulled away.

Misha, who had been standing to the side, abruptly stepped in and engulfed mother and sister in a long hug.

"Welcome," he said. "Please be very welcome." Misha was so courteous when he was nervous. Smith, usually touched, now found it irritating.

Helena took the hug as if it were an expected gift to a visiting potentate. Her look was now alert. He knew it well. Misha smiled too broadly. His eyes were unblinking.

"This is Mi-Mi . . . Misha," Smith said, unnerved.

"We have so much to talk about," Helena said to Smith in a stage whisper.

To Ivan, she asked, "Would you mind . . . ?" pointing at the cab. Hadn't Jo explained who Ivan was?

"No problemo," said Ivan, his dark hair slicked-back and gleaming, his smile several notches too loud.

Ivan opened the trunk and emerged, balancing packages.

His mother and sister had come bearing gifts wrapped in paper of pale blues and pinks to match their outfits. Later, when unwrapped, the gifts were a large ceramic bowl; two books for Smith: from Jo, *Don Quixote*, and from Helena, *To the Lighthouse*; matching wool scarves, ski caps, and gloves for Smith and Misha; and a U of M T-shirt, sweatshirt, and tank top for Ivan. Also later, Smith would find an envelope in *Don Quixote* with a half-ounce of weed.

"So?" Helena asked again.

"What is it?"

"Are you all right? You don't look good." She touched his forehead. "Too thin," she muttered, as if attempting to recall lines from a play.

From Jo, impatiently: "Leave Robbie alone. You promised." But Helena, after glancing over at Misha, now turned her attention to Ivan, whose presence seemed to puzzle her.

"My brother," Misha said, still unblinking, pointing toward Ivan.

"Oh, yes. Of course."

Had she slipped from agoraphobia into Alzheimer's? Smith wondered.

"At your service, Mrs. Doddsworth," Ivan said, hand outstretched.

She took his hand limply. "I'm sorry, Igor. I'm, well, . . . a little dehydrated."

Misha cringed, as if it were his mistake.

"Helena, it's Ivan, not Igor," Smith said, testily.

And Ivan: "It's okay, Smitty. Cut her some slack. Your mom's dehydrated."

Helena pulled out a pair of large sunglasses. She briefly examined Misha and Smith again, then craned her neck to take in the tenement building her son called home. A coat of industrial gray paint had been slapped over the original red brick, and the cornice and window ledges were purple. It stood as the one failure on East Eighth Street to attain the moneyed look of recent years.

She turned back to Smith, bringing a thumb to her lips, a gesture he recognized; a sign that she'd come to some sort of conclusion.

"We have so much to talk about," she said.

There'd been a time when he'd trusted her concern for him; that he'd loved her so much and still did, despite all this sidewalk awkwardness, took him by surprise.

"I'd kill for a Diet Coke," she said.

Misha's smile vanished.

"Diet Sprite, Pellegrino, wine, beer . . ." he said, now blinking furiously.

"That's fine," Helena said.

"Unacceptable!" Misha said. "I'll be back in a flash."

"A nanosecond, Mrs. D.," echoed Ivan.

Smith glanced at Joanne. She was the one who looked tired, thin. Her eyes dull. At least she'd not cut her long, luminous brown hair. "We will squander our talents," she'd said. They'd sworn to it. She'd stayed in Ann Arbor to work as a travel agent. The summer after high school he broke the news. He was going to college in New York. "New York," he said to Jo, "is a fine place to squander my talents." "Go for it," she'd said. And later, his discovery, as the plane gained speed, its nose lifting: what a rush it is to leave people behind!

With Misha off to buy Diet Cokes and Ivan, ignored, leaning against his cab, Smith stood alone with Jo and Helena.

"We can wait upstairs?" he said. It came out as a question, when he'd meant to sound strong, decisive.

"Okay," said Joanne. There was a vagueness in her voice that matched the way she looked: a shimmering mirage, a spring flower wilting in midsummer heat.

Helena looked again at the building and scrunched her nose. "I think it best we wait for your friend."

"Mom," said Joanne, stretching out the vowel.

The two women stared at each other. There seemed a standoff as to who would decide. Jo was sputtering into life. There was anger between them; it was old, familiar to Smith, but something about it was new. People change so quickly. It was so damn unfair!

He'd been away for a long time, he realized.

Then they both swiveled toward Smith. It came to him with a feeling of pride, like a balloon expanding in his chest, that he was their host—pride, which quickly dissipated into alarm.

"Let's . . . let's . . . let's . . ." he repeated, pausing between each word, waiting for a decision to emerge from his mouth, while the two women stared at him expectantly.

And then from Ivan: "He's coming! He's coming!" Jumping up and down, pointing, as excited as if a parade were arriving.

They all turned. Yes, there was Misha, who was walking toward them so fast that Smith feared he was going to stumble and fall face forward onto the pavement, but who reached them safely with his arms wrapped around two six-packs of Diet Cokes, just as a few drops of rain began to fall and the wind stirred, which had Helena and Jo reaching up to steady their hats.

Suddenly, Ivan shouted "Wait!" and dived into the cab. He emerged with two Fairway shopping bags. Offered up proudly. Another gift. Not from mother or sister, but Ivan's very own. Two bags. They all joined together in a shared curiosity, formed a circle and looked down into one bag, then the other.

"Apples, how lovely," said Helena.

"Apples, how nice," said Jo.

"Apples," said Smith, an uneasy observation.

From Misha, "Apples? So many?" with an angry stare at his brother.

And Ivan, eyes locked on Misha's, "Apples. What's your problem? The first of the season. From upstate. You know, fall, autumn, sweet and juicy."

As it was a gift—although unclear to whom—those assembled stood awkwardly, no one sure who should take the bags Ivan held out.

"Thanks, Ivan," said Smith, to break the tension. "We can always use apples."

And with those words they each stepped back, and the circle of curiosity that joined them was broken.

"Let us bring the gifts upstairs, right, Smitty?" Misha said. "We must show them our home."

"Yes, of course," said Helen. "That would be lovely."

They followed Misha up the stairs. At the first landing, Jo paused, took off her hat, and turned to Smith with an impatient tossing of her hair and several deep breaths of exasperation.

Wordlessly she was confessing: "Why the hell did I ever agree to bring Mom?" and it meant the world to him.

The Circle Line Cruise around Manhattan. Ivan's idea. Smith thought it dopey, uncool, but once the boat left its dock Helena was mesmerized. "Robbie, can you believe I haven't been to New York since I was ten? Why did I wait so long?" she asked, tightening her grip on his hand. At last they were not in a confined space. What a relief! These past days had given Smith the chance to see Misha's need to be wrapped in an extended clan; Ivan, Louie, and Smith were the mold, but Misha had a larger vision in mind. Did Mish know this about himself? Smith had observed the way Misha clung to Helena as if she were his mother returned from the grave. Smith was equal parts touched, irritated, and spooked.

He pulled Joanne aside. "Let's take a stroll, Sis."

"Yes, please. You can be quite brilliant, little brother."

"So, a dentist?" he asked, smirking. They leaned against the boat's railing, far enough away from the others for privacy.

"Yeah, a dentist. You've a problem with that?"

"Yeah, I've a problem with that. It's called signing on for a boring life. A life sentence."

"It's called settling down, Robbie. It happens. It's called wanting kids. And besides, he's a cute dentist." She ran a hand through his hair, his enviable curls. "I'm glad you're growing your hair back. That skin-head look last year gave me the creeps."

"Don't change the subject."

"You picked that so-called subject, not me."

Caw-cawing seagulls swooped down from a clear blue sky. Brother and sister watched as two gulls fought over a fish that sparkled for a moment in the sunlight before both let go and it fell back into the river, kicking up a brief explosion of white foam.

"Whatever turns you on, Jo," he said. Not: you look so sad. And not: I'm losing you and I'm not ready. He put an arm around her shoulder and gave a clumsy squeeze. It was his job to save her; he owed her that.

"Robbie, you look like someone's died. Knock it off. I'm getting married like most people do."

"Most people aren't you," he said. The wind picked up and the pennants strung along the boat's many lines and cables snapped, sounding like a succession of slapped faces.

"He plays the piano, Robbie, jazz and classical. He reads poetry to me. He's great in bed. Does that satisfy you? It satisfies me."

"Oh, really? But he's still a dentist."

"He was born with cerebral palsy. He spent years in and out of hospitals. He walks with leg braces. He . . ."

"I'm sorry, Sis," Smith said.

"I don't want your apologies, Robbie, I want . . ." she paused and looked up at the empty blue sky.

"You have my blessings."

She caressed his cheek. "Yeah, you little idiot." Her eyes moistened. Were they tears?

"Don't cry, Sis." Finding the right words—and saying them—was new and strange to him. He felt powerful in a way that made him queasy; or was it the swaying of the boat?

"It's just the wind in my eyes."

"Yeah, right."

"I made up the part about cerebral palsy," Jo said, sheepishly.

"Fuck, why?"

"I don't know. Maybe to break through your thick skull." She gently tapped her knuckles on his forehead.

"Reading poetry's cool enough. So is playing the piano."

"But he can't do numbers to save his life."

"Even better."

They gave each other the Doddsworth family smile—a thin line of white teeth—a look that was ironic, amused, and maddeningly cryptic to outsiders.

"Here," she said, pulling a joint from behind her ear as if it were a magic trick.

"Cool, Sis." Two puffs and out tumbled: "Why's Mom here? Why the trip?"

"You tell me. She's turning sixty in December. I think it's the whiff of mortality people get at her age. And you are her only son."

"Give me a break."

"Well, you are. She needs me, but she misses you."

The boat's engine grumbled loudly as it labored against the gusting wind. Salt spray coated their faces. Waves smacked the boat's side harshly.

Smith leaned over the rail, a finger down his throat. "Ugh."

"Don't say you're any less dramatic than Mom, you dork," Jo said, adding a quick, hit-and-run kiss to his cheek. She stepped back and took a deep breath. "Are you okay, little brother?"

"I'm just fine, big sister. Okeydokey."

"Really?"

"Yes, really." Smith had been waiting for her to ask about him and Misha. He wanted her to but he was ambivalent. He needed a booster shot, not meddling.

The wind calmed itself back into a breeze; the boat's engines resumed their soft, steady growl.

He gave her a goofy smile, his clown smile. She was supposed to tweak his nose, then he'd look at her in horror, hide his face in his hands and she'd pepper him with kisses until he'd laugh hysterically. It had been years since they'd played this game. But instead she stared at him, her eyes cool and gray.

"Can I ask one more itsy-bitsy question?"

"How itsy-bitsy?"

Her face was to the breeze, and fine strands of her long brown hair blew into her mouth. She pulled them away with a graceful, unconscious movement of her hand. He was fascinated. It was a gesture she must have mastered years ago, but he'd never noticed.

"Very, very itsy-bitsy."

Brother and sister huddled close. Smith glanced over his shoulder at Misha and Helena in an intense conversation, Ivan standing to the side, hands in pockets, smiling his smile, trying to find his rightful place when for now he had none. What were they going on about? He didn't trust Helena, her capacity for instant intimacy. He wanted to send a signal to Misha. Smith had once planned to study sign language. How wonderful it would be if he could send a silent warning Misha's way, encoded in a movement of hands and fingers, quick, delicate, precise.

"Kiddo, are you there? Don't go space cadet on me," Jo said, and squeezed his hand.

"I'm all ears."

Jo took several more deep breaths, as if courage were an inflated tire. "Are you careful?" she asked.

"Careful? Careful about what?"

"I don't know—looking both ways before you cross the street. Flossing after meals. You know, are you watching out for yourself?"

"Spit it out, Sis."

"You and Misha. Do you guys . . . take precautions?"

It was not like her to be evasive. She was nervous and now he understood why.

"You know?"

"Yeah."

"How?" he asked. Instead of anger he felt lighter, as if a long-lasting fever had abated.

"Does it matter?"

"No, not really, I guess. Okay, yes, it does matter."

"Ivan. Last year. Don't be angry with him. He meant well."

"He always means well," Smith said, relieved it had not been Misha. But what to say now? He and Misha were very safe, too safe; so safe that when he felt his greatest need for him Smith could, of late, barely tolerate his touch. That one time when they'd first met and Misha had told him he was HIV positive, they'd talked of it for hours, but never again. Back then he'd placed his bet on love over fear.

"You still haven't answered me. Are you guys playing safe?" He recoiled, stiffened. She let go of the railing, took his other hand in hers and grasped them both.

"Playing," he said. "*P-l-a-y-i-n-g*! It's not a freaking game, Sis." He'd talked to no one about his feelings because there were no words, or rather, to put them into words twisted them out of shape. And now, perhaps a little too stoned, he felt himself waist-deep in the black tar that had done in the dinosaurs: sinking, sinking, the tar rising to his throat, his mouth, pausing just below his eyes.

"Robbie . . ."

"Weren't we talking about Helena?" He pulled his hands free of hers and looked away. They—Jo and Helena—had come to mess with the new life he'd so carefully built. That was now clear. He felt closer to Misha, protective.

"That's the George Washington Bridge," he said, sternly, pointing up. "And that's Grant's Tomb," waving a hand vaguely at the Manhattan shoreline. "And there's New fucking Jersey."

"Calm down, Robbie. I trust you. Really."

"And that building there," he pointed wildly, "is, fuck, I forget what it is, Sis," and he took her into his arms as he'd never done before.

"Love you, too," she said.

Brother and sister held each other and rocked with the motion of the boat. When he opened his eyes he saw Ivan wave while walking toward them, rolling side to side, struggling to keep his balance. "What are you two talking about?" he shouted.

Smith whispered in Jo's ear, "We don't let Ivan do drugs. He's like, you know, fragile."

"I know," she said, softly, sadly. "What say we join the others?" She took his hand and they walked away as once they'd walked home from school, Ivan bouncing by their side.

"What say," he replied.

"Your mother's really cool," Ivan said. They were driving on the Brooklyn-Queens Expressway, returning from a visit to Louie's grave in Staten Island. That Louie wasn't in his grave no longer seemed to matter. He'd been cremated but his old pal, Leo, had bought a grave site and a tombstone. "I need a place to sit and talk to him," he'd said.

The brothers went each month, but never together. For months Ivan had asked, but Misha begged off; then he'd go on his own the following week. A routine was established: Ivan the third Sunday of the month, Misha the fourth. Once, Smith asked if he could come along. "No," Misha had said. It was a slow, firm "no." It had the sound of a decision a lifetime in the making.

But Ivan liked company.

"Really?" Smith said. Helena and Jo were "doing" Bloomingdale's and Macy's, and Misha was at home, working. Smith wore a tank top and shorts; he was cold in the cab's air-conditioned chill.

"Yeah. But why do you call her Helena and not mother, or *ma mère?*" Ivan asked, the French a bit odd—it was not one of his languages—although odd and Ivan were sometimes hard to tell apart. One made allowances for Ivan. But tossing in a bit of French was new. Ivan had not been hospitalized in almost a year, not since Louie's death, although there were several near misses, and Smith and Misha were alert for the signs.

"No, why should I call her *ma mère?*" Smith asked, exaggerating the accent to needle him. Then he added gently, "Besides, her real name is Helen. Helen Smyth Doddsworth, Ph.D. Licensed to shrink heads and"—he paused to study Ivan's profile—"fearless at it."

"Don't get me wrong, Smitty, Helena's a beautiful name for a mother. Flowing, like silk, or a river."

"That's what she thought. 'Who could have imagined,' she said, 'how adding a letter, a simple, little, mind-its-own-business vowel, could transform a life?'" It had marked her rebirth after Chuck left. Smith had been dazzled by her then, her dark brown eyes enormous, dominating her face because of the weight she'd lost. Reborn, she'd seemed a cross between a princess and a wizard.

"That's very intriguing," Ivan said. "A real inventive lady."

Ivan cooed a string of *ah's*, reminding Smith of whale song. He sighed. Whales and Ivan, both endangered species.

Smith envied Ivan, so pleased with this sound, this discovery. "You have the power to transform your life—it's within you," Helena would say to him and Joanne. It became the mantra for her workshops and TV appearances.

Ivan turned toward him, singing, smiling. "Eyes on the road," Smith said, when the cab wavered too close to an SUV. Envy turned into worry: was a fresh mania taking hold? It often began with infectious high spirits, but it always ended ugly. Smith recalled the sorrow in Misha's eyes the day he'd told him of Ivan's illness: "I'm telling you just so you should know." He'd cradled Misha's head in his lap, this man who was still a stranger.

"Don't worry, bro," Ivan said. He'd begun to call him bro of late, something which Smith both liked and was wary of. "Eyes are on the road, *but watch the hands*," and Ivan lifted both hands and looked at Smith in a way that was—well, Smith didn't know what it was. It was canny, almost cunning, but it could be the beginning of crazy. It put Smith on edge, which he tried to hide.

"Ivan, um . . . please . . ."

Ivan's hands returned to the wheel. "Had you going there. Admit it, Smitty."

Ivan patted him on the thigh and squeezed. Ivan don't, he thought, please don't. It was a turn-on and it was scary. Very scary. Ivan was foreign, after all, affectionate, and very handsome, but also Misha's brother. Smith's mouth grew too dry for speech.

They rode in silence, broken occasionally by Ivan cooing those *ah's*. Smith stared out the window at passing cars and the blur of low-rise buildings in Brooklyn; across the East River, Lower Manhattan pushing its way into view like the bow of some kind of ship, a naval destroyer perhaps, willful and decisive; and up ahead, the Brooklyn Bridge.

*How a simple letter can change your life.* Helena had struck again. It was like sitting next to a demented but good-natured parrot.

Smith ground his teeth. He began to sweat and bit at a fingernail, as Ivan's hand still rested on his thigh. If Ivan was going nuts, he'd timed it maliciously. Smith unrolled the window, gasping for air.

"You all right?" Ivan asked.

"Sure. Why?"

"No reason."

"Ivan, do you ever think about the rain forests? Do you worry about the ice caps melting?" Smith felt his voice rise and crack.

"Huh?"

"Ivan, do you know what's going to happen to Manila soon? To Bangladesh? Do you know what the glaciers are doing at this very moment? They're melting, breaking apart. Do you know that Ivan? Do you worry about these things?"

The cab pulled up on East Eighth Street. A light rain began to fall.

"Why are you yelling at me?"

Smith gave him a quick hug and hurried out of the cab, then stuck his head back into the open window. "No reason," he said. "I was just wondering."

"Smitty?"

"Yeah, what?"

"Well . . . I wish I had a mother like yours."

"Really?"

"Yeah. You're a lucky guy." Then Ivan took off, tires squealing, leaving behind the sickly, sweet smell of burnt rubber.

The rain became steady. From far off he heard the faint rumble of thunder. But Smith was still as a statue. He willed himself to move, to take out his keys, unlock the door and walk up the stairs, but he was stuck. This wasn't how *lucky* should feel. In his wallet, creased from countless folding and unfolding was the ticket to Antarctica, the date tomorrow; *how something so simple can change your life*, he thought. No one knew. What a rush it would be to leave all this behind. He'd be able to think clearly again. Endings, he understood; he could choose the kind. Leaving is what I do best, he thought, unsure if this was his own insight or Helena's voice in his head.

And was he leaving Misha or that virus? He was ashamed. He felt pathetic. Would it make any difference to Misha? Who could he talk to? Once, when Louie was alive, he'd teased Smith during a walk around the park. "A *constitution*," Louie called it however often Smith said "It's a *constitutional*, Louie." Smith now laughed and wiped away a tear. "Ask me for advice," Louie had said. "You never do. I'm an old man. That's what we're good for."

"Okay, how about your best shot of wisdom."

"Wisdom isn't vodka, Smitty. Give me a situation. Set the scene, as my Mishka would say."

"I don't know. Can't think of one."

"Smitty, there was a war in my country like I hope you never see. There's not much to learn from war except it stinks. But there was this time once, I wasn't much older than you, when artillery shells were falling all around. I couldn't think, let alone move. I shit in my pants, if that makes it any clearer. And this officer, a major, who'd been around, you could see from the scars on his face . . . he grabs me and says, 'Boychik, we can't stay here, so I'm going to say this once: if you find yourself in hell, keep walking.'"

"That it?" Smith said, confused, but wondering if Louie had known he was terrified and was giving permission, maybe sizing Smith as too puny for the job of taking care of his son.

"Yes. Now let's play a game of chess in which, as you Americans say, 'I will wax the floor with you.'"

"It's *mop*, Louie, not *wax*." He'd almost called him Dad.

"Same difference."

Smith was now soaked. He stood no more than twenty feet from the park where he and Louie had talked. A loud clap of thunder startled him. No, it was not the time for leaving, not today, not tomorrow, not yet.

Smith was early. Four coffees at home. Nerves ragged. He ordered a pot of tea and waited. He'd been surprised when Helena named a Chinese restaurant on Third Avenue. "We need to talk alone, us two," she'd whispered, slipping him a note last night; it had the name and address of a place he'd never heard of. The note, the whispers—it felt clandestine, as if they were spies. He didn't like that she knew of places in New York.

"We need time together without your little Misha," she'd said.

He poured tea into a small ceramic cup. It was decided: he'd not put up with her games! But she had a way of making him feel important, the lead actor in her psychodramas. It was such a cliché. He was such a cliché: the gay boy with a special relationship with his mother. He groaned inwardly and pulled his baseball cap down. *If she can't see my eyes, I'll have an edge.*

He gazed out the restaurant's large window at a handsome black man leaning against a car, holding a skateboard by his side. The silver wheels glittered in the sun. A slow grin spread on the man's face . . . an *I dare you* grin. The man with the mocking, lazy smile winked at him. It was a turn-on, for sure. Still, it would be another cliché: the black man and the skinny white boy from Michigan.

He felt blood rush to his groin, and the sensation of tiny pinpricks on his palms, his cheeks. He struggled to breathe; it was desire and he was tempted.

"Hi, hon," Helena said, floating into the seat across from him. She dropped a Bloomie's bag on an empty chair and leaned over to plant a kiss just to the side of his mouth. She was dressed in khaki shorts and a white U of M T-shirt; around her neck was a long blue silk scarf.

"Hi," he said.

"So," she replied, "alone at last," rubbing her hands playfully. She looked at the dark circles under her son's eyes, his unshaven cheeks, the napkin he was nervously picking apart.

The black man gave him an exaggerated shrug and took off.

"Yeah, obviously," he said.

"You're looking pale, sweetie." She fingered her scarf.

"The ozone layer, you know. Can't be too careful these days."

"Very funny."

A waiter took her arrival as his cue to appear.

"Order something, Mom." Calling her *Mom;* he'd give her that today.

"I'll have one of those," she said, "and that one, over there," pointing at various men on the street.

He laughed. "Where's Jo?"

"She's out with your little Misha and his very handsome brother."

"Misha's not little. Please stop calling him that."

"Let's not fight, sweetie. Okay?"

She tugged on his fingers as she had done when he had been very young and upset. He clenched his teeth to hold back a smile.

"Please, sweetie. Let's have a nice afternoon. It's been two years."

"Okay, okay." He held her hand in his and gave that smile. She'd come a long way, he had to concede. After the divorce, she'd retreated to her room, eaten almost nothing, and grown unnaturally quiet. She lost twenty pounds. It came to him and Jo that she was starving herself to death. They'd taken turns spoon-feeding her baby food. Over many weeks, they'd coaxed her out of the house. He was shaken again by the memory of his mother trembling during the short walk to the car, son holding one arm, daughter the other. Agoraphobia on top of anorexia. He'd loved her then more than ever before.

The waiter hovered over them. "I think you should order, Mom."

"Hmmm . . . I'll have . . . whatever it is they're eating," and she pointed to the next table.

"I'll have the same," he said, not hungry, not caring.

Smith poured them each some tea.

"Thanks, Robbie."

"Smith," he said, tersely.

"Okay, sweetie . . . I mean, thank you, Smith." They both laughed.

She looked to him like just another person in New York and he wondered if they could have a normal relationship, might even be friends. A new idea. This was going forward, not backwards.

The waiter returned, deftly arranging steaming plates and bowls on their small table.

Helena surveyed the food, picked up her chopsticks, hesitated, and then asked, chopsticks pointing at Smith, "So, how are things going with Misha?" Her voice was smooth, noncommittal, a therapist in full-interview mode. "Are you two happy together?"

"Happy enough. Plenty happy." He tensed, certain he knew where this was leading. But instead, a winsome smile and an "I'm glad for you both" led to an easy silence between them as they sipped their hot and sour soup and ate their Szechwan beef and eggplant, listening to the rattle of the air conditioner and the murmuring of lunchtime voices. Yes, perhaps they could be friends.

"Hon," she said, tentatively. He noticed a piece of food, something green, stuck to her front teeth and fought not to giggle. It looked deliberate, as if she were a clown and the tooth, makeup. "Honey, there's this spot."

He thought she meant the food stuck to her teeth and was about to say in their newfound friendship, I know.

"The doctor's found a spot. On a breast."

Smith flinched. "Oh," he said. He almost added, "Whose breast?" but stopped himself: he was emptied of feeling; then a wordless terror filled the void.

"Robbie . . ." she began. She looked at his face, which had gone pale, almost gray. She reached out and touched his unshaven cheek.

Smith looked past her at a man across the room. His hair was a white mane, his face creased, rough, pitted, as if he'd once been scalded with boiling water. When he caught Smith looking at him, he mouthed some words that Smith couldn't make out but that seemed to be a taunt of some kind. Then he threw back his head and laughed; Smith quickly looked away, back into his mother's expectant eyes.

"Oh," he said, again. "How serious?" His voice level, calm. There was that familiar pull again, to sit by her bedside, to hold her hand. But what about Misha? Didn't Misha need him too? Misha had Ivan. Was Ivan enough? Would Misha's life crumble if Smith left him? Smith had never considered this possibility that Misha depended on him. Being a man, Smith concluded, meant taking a stand . . . one family or the other! . . . or was it every man for himself?

"They don't know yet," Helena said. "I'll take more tests when I get home." She reknotted her scarf. Smith looked around, expecting stares, but there were none. The waiters navigated soundlessly between tables. He looked for the man with the long white hair and horrid face, but he was gone. This was what he loved about New York: a mother close to tears, her terrified son—*a scene*—and no one notices, or if they do they'll be damned if they let it show.

"I'm sorry, Mom." He tried to make the words sound as if they were from one friend to another; but a friend would be stunned, compassionate. If he had a soul, a *dusha*, he'd know what to say. He imagined that he could disappear, that he could stand aside and watch this scene between mother and son, study it, learn from it, anything but be a part of it.

"Robbie, you won't have me around forever. You do know that."

"I know," he said, pulling the baseball cap down over his eyes.

That night, Smith was startled awake. He was trembling. Sweat-soaked. He'd been frightened by a dream he couldn't recall. He slipped out of bed and walked to Misha's side. Misha slept facing the window, his breath even and steady. Moonlight left him half in darkness, half luminous. He snorted, then turned away, kicking at the sheet that had covered him, all of him now in shadow. Smith studied his spine, his neck, the muscles of his back, and his hair, unruly in sleep.

He tiptoed naked into the living room. He could see the moon through the barred window. It was a yellow summer moon, a slice nicked off short of full. He felt as if he had entered a stranger's house.

On the kitchen table was the ceramic bowl, Jo and Helena's gift, filled with Ivan's apples. It had a glazed pattern of thorny fantastical flowers. He wondered if it was from an elegant boutique or a Target, bought at the last minute.

He sat down. The trembling grew worse. What had the person who'd painted the bowl intended? Were the flowers a vision or was there no intent at all?

Smith was scared and he was angry. He took one apple, bit into it, spat it out, and threw the apple across the room. Then another and another. Soon the floor was covered with apples, each marked by a single bite.

He crawled under the table, brought his knees to his chest and held them tight. He lost track of time. Then, mysteriously, Misha was touching him on the knee and the room was filled with daylight.

"Smitty," he said. "Are you all right?" Again and again, "Smitty, Smitty, Smitty . . ." Misha kneeled down and their faces were inches apart. "Robbie?" he asked and Smith looked up. On Misha's face, that defiant smile. He wore his enormous white bathrobe. Smith had laughed when he'd first seen Misha swallowed by it. Misha nervously brushed away hair that fell over worried eyes that had never looked so intensely blue.

"I don't know why, but I can't anymore," Smith said, and began to rock.

"What do you mean?" Misha sounded like there was a damp cloth covering his mouth, as if the room was filled with smoke and breathing was dangerous. "Please come out from there. Please."

Smith asked himself: What do I mean? But there was no reply.

He remembered a therapist with a pipe asking him, "What's your first memory? Your very first?"

"Cold water," he'd said. Some kids had pushed him into a pond. Jo had walked him home, holding his hand.

"Please come out," Misha said and pulled harder on his arm. Smith gave in. They stood, and then Misha opened his robe and wrapped the two of them inside. It was warm and Smith stopped trembling.

It was a mistake to have let Helena and Joanne come. And it was a mistake, this new family; it was a mistake to have stayed.

"I don't know what I want," he mumbled.

"Does anyone?" Misha said and held him close.

"*Kakoi koshmar!*" he whispered into Misha's ear.

"Yes, indeed, what a nightmare! Who taught you to say that?"

"Louie."

"Papa?" Misha held Smith's face in his hands, a challenging look, as if Smith were a medium invoking Louie's spirit.

What he'd meant to say was "I love you" in Russian.

It was Labor Day, their anniversary, but that other phrase, spoken by Louie last year on Thanksgiving, had wedged itself in memory.

"I'll make some coffee," Misha said. He gave Smith his robe and sat him down in a chair.

Smith watched Misha put a filter into the coffeemaker, measuring the grounds, adding water precisely. He was so very familiar. He opened a cabinet, took out two mugs, placing them on the table. Only then did Misha bend to pick up the apples, not asking about them at all, as if, yes, he did this every morning and would all the mornings of his life.

# Whirling Dervish

—⟋⟍—

The day Ivan met Taz, the mercy of sleep was stolen from him. Slender, lanky, bubble gum–chewing Taz—self-named after a post-collegiate trip to Tasmania had turned his world upside down, freeing him to ride the jet stream to anywhere but home, the anywhere being, at the moment, New York. He was, with his wispy blond beard and pale skin turned pink from the summer sun, a fresh-scrubbed newbie from Los Angeles, or La-La Land, as he called it. "What's La-La Land?" Ivan had asked the day Taz materialized in the half-light of the garage, leaning all nonchalant against a sooty yellow cab. Ivan knew full well he risked appearing dim, or worse, foreign-born—very, very not American.

"L.A., Los Angeles," Taz had said, drawing out each syllable with contempt. But to Ivan the words were sweet. Thereafter, each time he saw him at the garage or when they'd meet to take a break during the night, he begged Taz to repeat them. Taz's voice made Ivan's skin tingle, reminding him of one of those long ago crooners his papa so loved gracing their audience with a ballad.

"Where you from?" Ivan asked for days after like a pesky kid brother, just to hear him say it.

"La-La Land, dude," Taz would say kindly, along with a gentle swat to the side of Ivan's head.

Ivan did not sleep that first morning when he returned home from work, nor the day after. He lies in bed now, cuddling Nicolai, his rabbit. It has been a week without sleep, his chest branded by the sound of Taz's voice, or each time Taz's name is uttered by another, be it Tony, the shift supervisor, or any of the other drivers. It is painful, but as necessary a pain as he has ever known. Ivan himself cannot say the name. It dies in his throat as if it were too beautiful to survive the passage into sound, or too holy. It has been a week, and he's yet to learn Taz's given name, nor does he care to.

Ivan lives simply: a small kitchen with a table for one and a hard wooden chair, and a futon lying square in the middle of his studio on East 12th between B and C, obtained thanks to the old Ukrainians, fast dying off, who hold faith in helping their own kind. There's no closet, so his clothes are folded and neatly piled on the floor. Two windows, shades drawn, look down onto the street. It's his first home since leaving his papa's apartment in Brooklyn—since dropping out of college and, he believes, breaking Papa's heart. Though who's to say, as Papa waves off any such suggestion with the sly smile one expects from a man who once gambled at cards.

Beside his bed is Nicolai's cage. Nicky stares at him, eyes concentric circles of pink—delicate eyes, sensitive to light, requiring the shades to be drawn, especially in summer. His ears stick back crookedly, antenna-like. He is not just any old rabbit; Nicolai is an albino rabbit.

It is late August. Ivan lies under a ceiling fan. The air feels good against his skin, which is coated in sweat from the summer heat and the warmth of Nicky's fur. Ivan feels the rapid ticking of Nicky's beating heart. Nicky smells of the grass he feeds on and Ivan is transported to a meadow, a memory of being a boy on a picnic outside of Kiev. He is lying on the grass, eyes closed, alive only to the smell of spring flowers, a nearby apple orchard, and the murmuring voices of his papa, his mother, and his brother. He knows this is impossible. His mother died eighteen years ago, laboring to give birth to Ivan and, twenty minutes later, to his brother Misha.

"Ivan, Ivan, Ivan," he says to himself. It is 6:00 P.M. and he is surrounded by clocks, large and small. Each day without sleep he has bought a new clock: digital clocks; clocks with hands; clocks that wind; clocks that tick; clocks as silent as a winter dawn on the steppes of Russia or the Spanish Steps in Rome. He has been to one and dreamt of the other.

Five days ago he began to add watches. He now wears three on his left wrist and two on his right.

He is tired down to the neurons that fire his brain.

It's become a cross to bear, not sleeping, nothing to brag about (although he is quietly proud); and it's become a mission of sorts to keep track of the time. The clocks and watches are all off by minutes. But Ivan is not fussy. He knows that this matters only to him.

"I am a prophet without a people," he says to Nicky and laughs, then stretches his foot. He sprained an ankle last night. The sprain is in his left foot and he's found a way to move it that releases a jolt of pain; the pain keeps him alert to traffic lights, pedestrians, passengers, directions, and the business of counting change—the nuts and bolts of his job.

Tony sent him home after two twenty-four-hour shifts. "Kid," he said, "get some sleep."

So Ivan goes home, lies in bed for hours, and returns with a smile for Tony—bouncing, he says, "Rested!" and gives Tony a neck rub, which makes him sigh and, Ivan well knows, makes Tony hard.

"I'm my own man," Ivan says to Nicky, not that he needs reassurance. Not Ivan.

To pass the time, perhaps to lull himself to sleep, Ivan recites the names of Kiev subway stations: Slavutich, Osokorki, Bortnichi. Each name unlocks a door to memories that are rapidly clouding with time. (Did he live near one? He no longer remembers.) In Kiev, he often wandered the streets alone, leaving small footprints in the snow, convinced each time that he could retrace his steps, forgetting how quickly they were covered by fresh snow or erased by the larger boots of older children and grownups. But it never frightened him, being lost. He was seven years old and without fear. Sooner or later, Papa or Misha, often accompanied by a neighbor, would find him, or he'd magically find himself in front of his tall, shabby building, cold, tired, and hungry, chattering of his adventures to a distracted Papa and to Misha, who'd listen, ravenously curious, disbelieving, envious.

This habit of wandering Papa scolded when he noticed, which was less and less often, as for him drinking was becoming more and more *his* habit. Misha, dutiful Mishka, searched for him or sat at home and looked pale and worried when Ivan returned. In time, Ivan learned the names of subway stations and each morning, Papa, resigned to his wandering, made sure to leave him coins.

Ivan has painted three walls of his room a gold-infused yellow, the color of the sun and the sky in a painting by Van Gogh (he'd bought the poster at the Met) of a man walking (in desperation? ecstasy?) toward that yellow sky—or was he running away? The poster is gone now. On another wall there'd been a Matisse from the Hermitage in St. Petersburg, once Leningrad, where Papa was born and where he'd promised to take his sons, but money, alas, had been lacking. That poster was special. He'd seen it in a book and sent money to Russia: it is a picture of a young woman. She has his brother's yellow hair, Misha's ears that stick out like saucers, and his long neck and pale skin with its faint suggestions of pink, hinting at powerful emotions just under the surface. The woman in the painting was Russian, Lydia Delektorskaya according to the book, but he thinks—in secret—she is his mother. He understands there's no logic to this belief, but he felt her watching over him nonetheless, felt her compassion, her love.

That poster is gone, too. In their place Ivan's hung his clocks and calendars; he's counting down the days, months, and years to the millennium. It is 1994, time enough to dream up something spectacular—perhaps simple, yet perfect—for Papa and Misha.

One wall, painted white, is his shrine. On it he's written the word *love* in many different languages. The letters intersect as if he were filling a crossword puzzle. He works on this when sleep eludes him. On his third day without sleep, he realizes the interlocking words were forming a shape: sending a message or perhaps it is a map? He isn't sure which but knows an answer will emerge.

He's cleared a space at the wall's base where he burns incense. There, he's placed several plump Buddhas—smiling, serene figures; and just above them he's tacked up pictures of Jesus and Mary. There are also Orthodox icons, and draped around the Buddhas are thin gold necklaces from which dangle Stars of David. When he prays, as he has taken to of late, he wears a yarmulke. Can't hurt to cover all the bases, he thinks. Ivan belongs to all religions; he is promiscuous in that way. (Misha, who professes to believe in nothing, says, "Oh, Ive, don't be a simpleton.") He believes Papa was a Jew and his mother of the Orthodox faith, but Papa's face has always been like stone when questioned.

Ivan loves life—the *all* of it: the sky, the sun, the moon, the stars, right down to the passengers who puke in the back seat (five times this has happened!) or steal his money (twice!). Until seven days ago, he loved his family most of all: his papa, Louie; his brother, Misha; and his mother, Sonya. In his dreams (when he was sleeping) he sees her brushing long blond hair in front of a mirror. Then, as happens in dreams, she is brushing Ivan's hair and whispering words (he can feel her breath!) that vanish when he wakes—words that gently implore, then grow urgent, desperate. The dreams (he's told no one of them) began when he left home, and have grown more intense in recent months. He accepts them as one would accept a jewel whose authenticity might confound the best of experts. Ivan finds the mystery of this puzzle an agreeable ache in his heart, which has become a more complex organ over the past week. Does Nicky's tiny heart hold more than a yearning for food, touch, and safety? Nicky stares back, inscrutable.

If he does not sleep there is more time for love, Ivan thinks, as he dresses for the night, for work: a crisp, clean white shirt; a red bandana around his forehead; a string tie he'd bought on a trip to Arizona. He is not like the other drivers, who dress like slobs. Old Charlie, who died last month, had taught him the ins and outs of the business. "Dress sharp," Charlie said. "Take pride." Ivan carries a picture of him in his wallet but his memory is still vivid: five feet tall, plump, bald, and with a face that in another century would have exiled him to a leper's colony.

Ivan's early, so he sits on his front stoop in the late afternoon sun. The sun is good for the immune system, he's read, and to love as grandly as Ivan loves, he needs to keep his health. He eats a bag of pumpkin seeds, his only meal of the day—he's lost all appetite these seven sleepless days—then sets off to the garage on Ninth Avenue. He heads south down Avenue A, then west on Houston. He is in the mood to take it slow. The air is sultry; it soothes like a warm compress. The sidewalk is crowded with people walking half the speed that fall and winter will compel. He limps, slightly, but the pain ebbs as he pushes on.

At First Avenue, he waits for the light to change. Ivan waits for lights. He does not dash between cars. Not like the others. I have Old World values, he thinks, eternal values. He wants badly to tell Misha about Taz but can't. Ivan and his brother are twins, fraternal. They do not keep secrets. (Taz—and Ivan's dreams of their mother—the rare exceptions.) They are close, like two fingers crossed for wishes, for luck.

In recent months, someone has split them apart. His name is Kevin, a man with whom Mish has fallen in love. He is an older man, easily thirty-five, whose hard, muscled body and booming voice speak of strength, the future, while his cratered cheeks betray illness.

Ivan has considered schemes to break Misha and Kevin apart, his imagination conjuring Misha's fate should he stick with Kevin. ("There's nothing wrong with Kevin. He's in great health, he just works too hard. You worry needlessly," Misha says.) None of his plans have worked, or he has judged them too cruel, and instead, after eighteen years where never a day had gone by without seeing and talking to each other (Ivan believes they spoke in their mother's womb!), they now speak *on occasion*. A clipped formality shapes their words. Last time they were together, "Damn him!" he'd said to Mish, in Russian. Misha was in Kevin's arms, stupid with love.

"It's my life! Mine," from Misha, also in Russian, his words slurred by drink. And Kevin, sleepy-eyed, bewildered, uneasy, looking from one brother to the other.

"To throw away?" Ivan asked, with a false smile to Kevin, and from Kevin came a look: is this about me?

Ivan poured Kevin more vodka, ignoring the hand placed over the glass. Then Ivan, who should not drink, drank straight out of the bottle until he gagged, as the room filled with Misha and Kevin's breathing, waiting. Against one wall was the desk Ivan had found in the street: it had been carelessly painted green and was peeling and chipped when Ivan spotted it on Avenue C. It was now restored, a brooding, majestic brown like fine Indian tea, a gift intended for Papa to remind him of home, of when he was a doctor. But instead, Misha laid claim to it, the gift to Papa lost in translation: "Kevin did all the work. It's ours, by right."

*Ours.*

And Papa, when told, dismissed the argument with the wave of a hand, "No squabbling, boys. I've no need anymore."

"Maybe you guys want to talk alone," said Kevin, rising.

"Stay," Misha ordered.

"It's your funeral," Ivan had said, the last words he'd spoken to Misha in weeks.

At Second Avenue, the light's against him. Ivan stops. He bounces in place, a prizefighter, warming up in his corner.

A tap on the shoulder. "Are you okay?" asks a woman, dark hair streaked with gray, braided, and tied with pink ribbon. She's pretty in a thin, nervous, nondescript way and wears a silver cross around her neck.

"I'm my own man," Ivan says, wishing at once he'd kept quiet.

"Of course you are," she says, stepping back.

"No, really, I'm okay," he says, switching to the language of the everyday, language he learned first from doctors, then Charlie and the other cabbies.

The light turns green. "Have a nice day," she says, before crossing the street.

"You too. Have a *great* day!"

He has made this his art, the everyday, in place of the words that race through his mind. He waits. He does not want to frighten her.

"Slavutich, Osokorki, Bortnichi," he says, softly. The names, when spoken, are calming.

On his skin, he feels, still, the bruises from leather restraints forced on him in hospitals. He does not like doctors. Or nurses. Or the tedium of life on drugs they insist he take, as do Misha and Papa. He does, though, feel for the attendants. They are only doing what they're told. There had been no need for hospitals in Kiev. He loved New York, but America brought him to hospitals. Was it the language? Something in the water? Ivan laughs. "Something in the water" is paranoid and Ivan is too in love with the world for paranoia.

He turns north by way of Hudson Street. Up ahead he notices a crowd gathered at the next corner. Drawing near, he sees they are murmuring, pointing toward the west, toward the river. Framed between buildings—hanging in the sky—is the setting sun. It is round and red and its light is soft; it's relinquished its power to blind, and Ivan and the gathered crowd can stare safely. A man with a briefcase, bulging stomach, suit jacket slung over his shoulder, tie loosened, says to Ivan, as if they were old friends, "It's like the flag of Japan. It's so cool!" He's as giddy as the teens he's likely to have fathered back home—in Tenafly, Morristown, or East Orange. (Ivan has a cabby's fine-tuned sense for the geography of faces, clothes, and voices, and has pegged the man for New Jersey.) "My father brought one back from the war," the man says. He looks at Ivan, eyes wide. "Really!" he says, as if trying to convince, while Ivan's thinking to ask, Which war? but fears betraying that it was America's war, not *his*—but *his* is now two countries, and Ivan forgets at times which is which, so he nods, keeps silent, lingers long enough for politeness, and walks away.

But on the next corner and the next and the next, again, people are murmuring, pointing at the same blood-red sun. Five blocks, five red suns. Ivan's now transfixed, impaled to the spot; he's swept back to the day Papa took him and Misha to Atlantic City. Papa had played the slots, letting his boys watch, saying, "You kids are too young" when they begged for quarters and later, "I've got a hot hand" at the blackjack table—words newly learned, which proved just true enough for him to get burned, another English lesson for the day.

A gust of wind, a truck's tuba-horn, the sun's disappearance beneath the toxic orange horizon conspire to move Ivan forward. The five red suns are a message in the sky: a winning streak, a payoff due, and he nears the garage and Taz burning with joy.

At the garage the talk is of baseball and girls, potholes and fares, good luck and bad. Ivan is quiet, a dreamy look on his face, which is judged beautiful by both men and women alike. A face gazed at often, directly, furtively, giving simple pleasure to some, the ache of longing to others. A narrow face: deep-set brown eyes; angular nose; skin smooth (he's tried to grow a beard but failed); hair straight, long, brushing his shoulders. He's aware of how eyes stroke him like fingers; he accepts the attention without much thought, understanding little of what it arouses in others, though in time he will learn.

The talk is background noise to his thoughts: his craving for sleep; plans to save Misha; Nicolai's soft fur; and Taz, who now glances at him as Ivan shyly looks away.

When he'd told Gabriella his fears about Kevin and Misha she'd put on a record, an old-fashioned LP. "Chopin," she said. The music made him sad. "Lose him?" she asked. He fought back tears. "Ivan, are you afraid you'll lose Misha? How could that be?" And he told her about Kevin's sculpted body and cratered cheeks.

"Oh, I see," she said, inhaling on a slender cigarette. "But he's in love, and that's rarer than you know. It's a blessing." Ivan balled his fists. "It's out of your hands, I fear." She'd reached out to stroke his hair, to comfort, but he'd turned away.

"Hey, how's my best little driver today?" Tony grabs at Ivan's crotch as if they were schoolboys in the playground and not in the garage, an immense underground cave, with countless poorly lit passageways that mystify outsiders. Here, amid the oil and exhaust fumes, Ivan is a star par excellence, which only makes Ivan hate this way Tony has of forcing from him a child's blush in front of the others: Lionel, from Jamaica, in dreadlocks, eating licorice, tapping out a Rasta beat on the hood of his cab, a song he's composed for his newborn child; Ali, a portly, good-humored family man from India, who lives in Jackson Heights; Jesus, who is new from El Salvador and lives with his aunt and eight cousins on East 118th, all ears, desperate to learn enough English, wary that Tony could fire him if he screws up as badly as he did last week when he took honeymooners to White Plains instead of the Waldorf.

And lanky, wispy-bearded, gum-chewing Taz.

Tony reaches for him again and Ivan grabs his hand and pushes it away.

"You've got a problem?" Ivan snaps, so unlike him that Tony jumps back a step and all eyes turn on Ivan.

From Taz to Tony, a confident, soft-spoken, "Leave him be," which can't be Taz, who's thin enough that a sneeze from Tony and he'd fall over, and who's spoken to them but a handful of yes's, no's, and maybe's in his week on the job. But it's Taz's voice that draws all eyes away from Ivan, who's surprised, touched, but undaunted; he's about to unleash "It's my fight" when Lionel steps between Ivan and Tony, offering Ivan a stick of licorice.

"Ivan, mahn. Good to see you."

Lionel's voice is balm even to Tony, who fiddles with the paper in his clipboard, muttering mildly, "So he talks," with a nod toward Taz.

Ivan accepts the licorice and bites off a piece. His mouth wakes to the tart flavor.

"Ivan, my friend, tonight's my night. I feel it in my bones. You will lose your crown and I will be the king of cabbies. Care to wager on the night? Twenty dollars, say?"

"You're on," says Ivan, forcing a smile. His back is to Taz, but in the past week he's learned to pick out the sound of Taz's breath and the steady champing of jaw and teeth, calmly working out his thoughts on a wad of gum.

"Hey, Lion," Taz says, "Me too?"

Tony, acid-voiced, looking up from the clipboard, says, "A real Shakespeare with words," flashing a smug grin, satisfied now that he's saved face. Ivan's on his toes, but keeps his silence.

"Sure enough, California boy," says Lionel. "Your money's good."

"Chop-chop," says Tony, clapping his hands, then slapping Ivan on the back. "Tea party's over, guys."

Lionel and Ali, with families to feed, take off. Taz lingers a moment. "Later," he says to Ivan, diffident, promising, an eyebrow raised, locking Ivan's gaze; then he's swallowed in the down ramp's shadows and Ivan's alone with Tony.

"My neck," he groans, but Ivan, turning, says, "Later," laughing so hard his tired body hurts.

She liked her coffee thick, dark, and sweet, in small cups she'd bought in Istanbul. Two spoons of sugar. She used a tiny gold one bought in Milan. "Stir five or six times, slowly," she'd instructed.

She moved gracefully about her room, crowded as it was with furniture, as if she'd memorized every inch of its terrain.

He'd met her on a cold rainy day in May. It was dark before sunset, the tops of buildings hiding in the clouds. She'd hailed him in Union Square, waving a cane of shiny metal. He pulled over and stepped out to give her a hand. It was not a walking stick, he took note, and then her dark glasses registered, and also the odd, wobbly turn of her head, as if she were one of those peasant dolls he'd loved as a child. She carried a Macy's bag and an umbrella in her other hand, which gave her a tilt, like a scarecrow, though she wasn't at all ugly or scary, just odd—a czar's unmarried daughter, perhaps: dusty, preserved, as if she'd only recently walked out of a museum.

He put a hand on the arm that held the cane but she pushed him away.

"No need, young man," she said, fumbling, managing with the door, bag, cane, and umbrella. "West End in the eighties, please, by way of Central Park," she demanded after she'd settled into the back seat. Ivan slid open the thick plastic partition; he didn't like barriers between him and his passengers. He liked to study them in the rearview mirror at red lights. Chatting with fares was his education in life. When closed, the partition left him deaf and nearly blind. Old Charlie had said, "If they don't shoot you from behind, once they're out, you roll down your window to get paid and there's a barrel in your face. Seeing as how they got the edge, you might as well get to know people. That's what makes the job."

A bullet busted his chest wide open, but to Ivan's way of thinking, Charlie'd had forty-eight years of college under his belt when life was done with him.

"West End and where?" Ivan asked.

"You just tell me when we're almost there, young man," she said, authority in her voice, German perhaps. Her voice did not sound kind but Ivan wasn't one for first impressions, eager as he was to give people a second, third, fourth, an infinity of chances at redemption.

How quickly she'd become a regular fare! A fixture in his life as necessary as food, as family.

"Your name?" she asked, an unexpected intimacy. He bristled. Ivan preferred to ask the questions. Besides, it was posted next to his picture, a mug shot: a young thief, a child conjured by Dickens, by Dostoevsky.

"Ivan," he said, begrudgingly, then slap to the forehead, forgetting, stupid me, she's blind as a bat, and his irritation softened into tenderness.

Driving through Central Park: "You should say E-vahn not I-vin. That's what is proper. You sell yourself short, otherwise."

"It was E-vahn in Russia. But I'm an American now." And silently, a thought: What business is it of hers?

"Yet another Russian. You people are simply colonizing this city. I loved St. Petersburg, but as for the rest . . ."

Ivan hit the brakes.

"I'm sorry, young man. My manners are poor when I'm tired."

"No problemo, lady."

"I'm Gabriella," she offered, as if they were at a bazaar, negotiating the price of a watch, a chicken, freshly cut roses. In Central Park, she said, "Take Eighty-sixth Street, and then turn right onto West End. It's the first building with an awning."

As he helped her out, she said, "E-vahn, I need a regular driver, twice a week. Are you my man?"

It began that way. She'd call the cab company, ask for him by name, and Margie's voice would crackle on the radio: "Ivan, it's your girlfriend."

*"Later"* is 2:00 A.M. Taz's face shines in the light cast by the Empire Diner at West 23rd and Tenth. It was happenstance, both of them dropping off fares at the same time and at the same place—London Terrace: a massive, ornate, square city block of apartments, the diner across the street.

"Do you ever sit still, dude?" Ivan's on his cab's hood, legs dangling. Taz is leaning alongside. Both are holding sandwiches.

And Ivan says, "Sure, all the time." He can't help it, this tap, tap, tapping—it's Lionel's song he's trying to remember, or maybe it's Morse code he's onto, a formula, higher mathematics to explain this feeling that's kept him awake all week.

"See," Ivan says. "Still, stillness, still-life," and he's frozen. "I can hold my breath, too."

"That's okay. You can breathe, bud. It's just like you were making me nervous."

Taz plays with his whiskers, gossamer blond, wispy, like Taz himself. Solid, yet not. An apparition that you can touch.

The second night Taz had been on the job—and Ivan's second without sleep—he'd said to Ivan, "Let's meet up for a break. I know this dive. It's this year's CGBG." Ivan had been impressed, envious that Taz had picked up the downtown lingua franca as if born to it. And they did meet, although in Ivan's rule book, a break is a quick bite, not an excuse to waste time. Rules keep Ivan on the straight and narrow. But for Taz, he's learning, he'll break rules.

They'd played pool. Taz drank beer. Ivan clutched a bottle and took pretend sips. Men's and women's voices mingled. There was laughter, the air was smoky. The crowd danced to punk, to grunge. Two hours had passed; it was no longer a mere break, but Ivan had not cared.

"Try eating," Taz now says, pointing to Ivan's sandwich, which is untouched; the sandwich an excuse to hang out with Taz, who's given up on standing to sit next to him on the hood of Ivan's cab.

Ivan loves everything Taz does, how he fingers his chin, the sloppy way he eats, the raising of his eyebrow, just the right.

The third night they'd met up on Eleventh in the west forties. A dark patch of street. "My neighborhood," Taz had said. "Hell's Kitchen," he announced as if it was China and he Marco Polo. Leaning against Ivan's cab, Taz lit a joint. They passed it back and forth, each time leaning in, hips grazing hips, fingers touching, Ivan on fire, looking up at a crescent moon and a scattering of stars in the city's night sky. Ivan doesn't do drugs. Another rule. (The second he's broken this week; it'll take three to know they fall like dominoes.) But this feeling for Taz, this sweetness— there's no way he could say no. And next, Taz took hold of Ivan's hand, pulling Ivan around so they were facing, Ivan leaning in. Lips, mouths were joined; there's no sweetness now, just fire. And Taz was no apparition, but flesh, bone, muscle; and next, Ivan's hands were up Taz's T-shirt. They both came so fast Ivan wasn't sure if anything had happened for real as opposed to all in his head, until he felt the wetness in his pants.

But Taz said, "Got to go," and he was gone in a shot, Ivan left with the crescent moon, the scattering of stars, and a feeling that he was falling, spinning.

He'd told himself it was just fooling around. Ivan doesn't do *in love*, just as he doesn't drink or do drugs. The numero uno rule. Papa and Mish and the doctors have warned. "Okay, sure," Tony's taunted, "Ivan's an equal opportunity offender. No one's safe from him, not the ladies *or* the boys." He can love Misha and Papa and every damn star in the universe, but *in* love—nope, nada. Yet there he was in his cab on Eleventh, in Taz's Hell's Kitchen, humming a folk song Papa'd taught him as a child, and next, looking up just to see . . . and no, the sky had not fallen.

But four days had gone by and they have not touched since that night on Eleventh Avenue.

Now, Ivan unwraps his sandwich. He's not hungry but fears he'll otherwise start tapping or bouncing. He glances nervously at Taz, but not wanting to stare he looks away, watching people pour into and out of the Empire Diner. Some are loud, some stagger; an epidemic of good spirits has spread. "I'm on fire," he says, mumbling, forgetting he's got to look cool to Taz, but Taz just says, "What's that you're saying?" and Ivan's safe. The words in my head, the words out of my mouth . . . got to watch it, he silently scolds.

Playing with fire, he thinks, rubbing wrists that hold memory.

The conversation stops. But this quiet between them feels good, until Ivan anxiously asserts: "I've been to Rome, you know. The Spanish Steps. The Sistine Chapel. In Paris, the Louvre; in Spain, I saw Goyas. And Venice. Really, I have." And he has, in his way. Papa's stories of each city, told in such detail—stories that Ivan made real by picture postcards he collected, illustrated books found in libraries, leafed through in bookstores, museums. "Papa promised," Mish complained. "He promised he'd take us," but Ivan understands that Papa would if he could, so the stories take life in Ivan's mind. And, for the millennium, if not sooner, they will see it all, Ivan's resolved.

But has Taz been to Rome or Paris or Madrid? Ivan commences tap, tap, tapping. But no bouncing. I'm bragging, he thinks, and feels the fool for it.

"But you're really from Russia?" Taz asks.

"Yeah, I'm really from Russia."

"That's so cool, but where's your accent? You should have an accent."

"I don't know," Ivan says. "I guess it got lost." He imagines it melting away like an early snow in the heat of New York City, America. It's an effort now to recall the taste, the smell of hot borscht on a cold Kiev night in their poorly heated apartment, or to feel the singeing revelation of a Russian summer. He's saving to go back before it's all forgotten. Not to stay; well, maybe not. But Mish won't go. He's a total American now. Not even to visit, as if the thought spooks him. And Papa, he just sighs, smiles, won't play his hand.

"Lost?" says Taz.

"Guess so."

"Say something in Russian." There's a challenge in Taz's voice.

"Ya tebia liubliu," he says, blurted out, not considered. "I love you."

"Cool," Taz says, smiling his smile.

Ivan studies Taz's eyes under the light of the street lamps, the diner's neon glow: is his glance merry or mocking, or maybe a show of respect?

"What's it mean?" Taz asks.

Ivan bites into his sandwich. There's food in my mouth he thinks, so I don't have to talk; then he says: "Can't talk, there's food in my mouth."

A playful punch to Ivan's shoulder. "Come on, Ive, what's it mean? Whad'ya say?"

Ivan doesn't want to lie, but if he says it in English he worries he'll spin so fast, he'll scorch anyone that comes near. Over and over he speaks his heart, but only in the mother tongue; and from Taz: "Oh, that's so cool, man, but what does it *mean?*" He pleads, "C'mon, Ive, tell, tell."

But Ivan won't. Not now. Not yet.

Gabriella lived in a residential hotel. He was invited up in June. "Please come at four," she'd said. He'd slept the day away, but restlessly, and took extra pains to dress. Her room was filled with the smell of coffee. ("It's Italian. The only kind one should drink. Don't you agree?") She had a double bed, with a canopy like you'd see in an old movie. A halogen lamp was at her bedside. ("They scare me. Do they scare you?") There was a rocking chair with a cushion; a worn, velvety green armchair; a desk columned with manila folders, showing its age in markings; and a green banker's lamp. There were photos on one wall, framed, and more propped on the desk. Ivan glanced over them, curious, but too polite to look closely. Stacks of old newspapers, magazines, shelves of books—"I can never throw away what I haven't read," she said, "and I cannot part with anything that's interested me."

"Oh," Ivan said.

"A conundrum," she replied, moving papers off the armchair, motioning him to sit.

He didn't know that word, but nodded anyway.

"Reading is more and more an effort. My vision was not always so poor. Large-print books, special glasses; Braille's the next step, but that would be admitting . . ." her voice trailed off.

"Are you a professor?" he asked.

"I'm an autodidact," she said, briskly, adding a smile.

"Huh?" he asked, sensitive to a wariness in her voice.

"I'm self-taught. The college of life."

He laughed. "Me too."

"I know," she said. "I sensed that about you right away."

There was a hot plate, a small refrigerator (cups and dishes stacked on top) and a sink, which was deep and wide, like you'd find in a basement.

It's tidier than he'd expected; surely someone came in to help?

He looked around some more and noted a bureau with a three-sided mirror and a short padded stool.

Gathering up courage, on a visit in July he asked, "Why do you need lamps?"

"For my guests, of course. Also, I see forms and movement 'as through a glass darkly,' one might say."

"Oh, yeah. *Comprende.*"

On that first visit, she told Ivan that she was a psychotherapist, that she listened and she healed, that her specialty was men damaged by war. She listened to her patients, her "boys," her wounded souls, for an hour, an afternoon, an entire day, depending. Ivan enjoyed the sound of her voice, barely taking in what she said. The armchair was comfortable and he felt at home. While she filled the room with words, he noticed the bed board. He could make out faded images of birds and branches. Someone's image of paradise, he thought. A window, which was so covered with soot that the outside world filtered through in gray, even on a sunny day. There was also a dusty TV and an old phonograph player, records in their jackets stacked against it.

She poured coffee for him; they ate scones.

"They're warm."

To the question in his voice, she replied, "The delivery boy arrived only moments ago."

He apologized for the crumbs that fell on the floor.

She waved him off: "If I can't see them, they're not there."

He tried to guess her age. Her hands were smooth and freckled, but there were fine lines around her mouth, which was lipsticked in red. Her hair was curly, full, blond, with a trace of orange; her forehead creased, weary. He was no good at ages. He just knew that she was younger than Papa; her full lips were too sensual for an old lady. He thought to ask if she'd been married, but held back.

He visited often, always on her invitation. He spoke of his childhood in Kiev, the mother he never knew, his papa, his brother. She would say, "Yes, Ivan. I see." He spoke of his failure in college, his longing to visit home with Papa, perhaps to stay— he was so confused—and, finally, staring at his feet, his hands, looking into her dark glasses, which soaked up the light and gave nothing back, of Bellevue.

Day seven, plus one, without sleep. His brain feels like a muscle that's bruised. He's walking down the ramp to his cab and sees Taz driving out. Taz slows, waves a hand; he says "Hey," not "Later," not "Let's meet," and then speeds away. Is what's between them something he made up? Is Taz weary of him? Sometimes, when he was very young, he'd grow angry at Misha, even bored with him, wishing for another brother. It shamed him, such disloyalty.

The evening sky is a scrim of thin gray clouds. The air is misty. It clings to people, cars, buildings. A garment of translucent silk, it obscures Ivan's vision as if these were shadow figures in a dream, or maybe this is how Gabriella sees the world?

He spots a fare on West 34th: a man wearing a dark suit too warm for a steamy night who stands in front of Penn Station, one hand up in a cautious gesture like he's scratching the air, the other holding a briefcase. Ivan smells his evening meal ticket. He makes a quick U to snag him, earning pissed-off honks from cars and cabbies. The fare says, "Staten Island, please, thank you, sir," and wriggles out of his black suit jacket. Can't be more than Ivan's age and, suit aside, looks too tender to be a stockbroker, a lawyer, or the usual white collar; more a lamb among wolves, Ivan quickly assesses, adjusting the rearview. He's easy on the eyes, so Ivan asks, "Where you from?" The lamb's head is covered with a fuzz that's so blond it's white. He's got the brave look of a boy his first time away from home.

"Utah," he says, as Ivan chooses the best route to the Verrazano.

Ivan's about to do the back-and-forth and say, "Where in?" and "What brings you here?" but the lamb starts babbling about religion. "I'm a missionary," he says, and goes on about people he calls latter-day saints. Ivan thinks he means saints born yesterday or thereabouts. Some other time he might have asked, but the boy has a nervous, honeyed voice, like he's reading a script, auditioning for his high school play. Ivan is touched, so he nods obligingly and says, "Really?" to be polite, but also because the lamb's babbling quiets Ivan's yearning for Taz.

Midway across the bridge, the boy pauses and looks over his shoulder. "Sir, can you stop, please?"

"Uh, I'm not supposed to."

"Please."

The traffic's light and there's a breakdown lane, so why not?

"I just want to look at the skyline. I've been here a week, but I've not seen it at night." Ivan eases to a stop. The lamb twists himself around and Ivan looks too. The city towers at sunset, brilliantly lit as if each one was alive, bazaar merchants in a competition to be noticed: Wall Street, the Trade Center towers, Chrysler, Empire State, Woolworth, Citicorp. Off to the side, there's Liberty's torch, and, down below, ferry lights moving in silence. Ivan forgets. It gives him a shiver.

"Wow," the lamb says. "They say it's a godless place, but unless it's the devil's work, this is, well, you know, it looks like heaven."

"Yeah, you've got a point."

"Thanks, sir," he says. Ivan's not used to such respect. It feels good.

He noses the cab back into traffic. The lamb's babbling slows to conversation. "So, like I was saying, I'm a Mormon. What are you?"

"I'm a U-man," Ivan says, by way of a joke.

"No, I'm serious," the lamb says.

Ivan's rule number six or seven is don't talk religion. Advice from Papa.

132

"I'm serious, too," he says.

A few red lights later, in the rearview, Ivan sees the lamb's opened his briefcase and holds pamphlets in his hands. "Do you believe in heaven?" he asks.

"Believe. Now that's a big subject. Don't know if I can cover it in the time we have. It's big, huge, enormous as the Grand Canyon."

"Utah's near the Grand Canyon. Well, near compared to New York. I've been there lots."

"Me too," Ivan says with authority.

Last year, Mish and Ivan took Papa there for his birthday. They rode a train to Denver, then rented a car. "See America!" Papa had said. One night, after Papa was asleep in the motel, they went back and lay at the canyon's edge. There was a full moon, so you could see outlines of the canyon but not the colors. Misha took some mushrooms, which was okay by Ivan, except for the way Mish said, "Vanushka, you know you can't." And then Mish started saying, "Choo-choo, choo-choo," like he was a train and Ivan choo-chooed along with him. They laughed, then were quiet, listening to the night. "Aren't the colors fucking amazing?" Misha said, breaking their silence.

"You've got that right, li'l bro," Ivan replied, not letting on that he saw colors in the dark, that he didn't need mushrooms.

They lay quiet, looking up at the sky. "Which do you think is bigger," Misha asked, "the Grand Canyon or the Milky Way?"

"Wrong question, Mishka. The point is not how big they are, it's how small *we* are."

"But together, you and me," Misha had said, "we're as big and grand as this canyon and all the stars put together."

Ivan says to the Mormon, "I believe in love." He's got this fear going now that it'll never be the same between him and Misha on account of Kevin.

The lamb has him pull up on a street of modest homes, with porches and tiny lawns fringed with shrubs just visible in the fading light. He looks lonely framed in the rearview. Ivan turns off the ignition, which a cabbie never does in a strange place. The house they've stopped in front of is dark. The lamb hands him a twenty and a ten but makes no move to leave. Ivan listens to the crickets. Night has taken command.

The lamb says, "Jesus is love. So you must believe in Jesus." His voice cracks. Then he takes to babbling again about those saints. Whatever floats your boat, Ivan thinks, not unkindly. He's imagining him and Taz on a train crossing the Canadian Rockies with their white-capped mountains, or maybe on the Siberian Express in winter, looking out on expanses of snow, endless, blinding. "Nothing like it in the U S of A," he'd say, proudly.

The lamb stops talking and, through the open partition, hands Ivan those pamphlets. "Read these and you'll learn about our ways."

Ivan takes them. Their fingers touch and he takes the boy's hand in his. It is warm, and unexpectedly large. "Sure, I'd like to learn more." The boy's lost his brave face, and Ivan's awash in tenderness, like he's the other brother Ivan once longed for. Ivan had tried so hard to look brave in school those first days, speaking his accented English learned from TV, clinging to Misha, who seemed braver, faster. He wants to comfort the lamb, give him something to assuage his fish-out-of-waterness. What Ivan can give best is Ivan. He'll peel off the lamb's sticky clothes, sponge him down in a cool bath, take him to bed, let him explore with those large, pale hands. "It's okay, it's okay," he'll say.

"I'm house-sitting. My aunt and uncle. They've gone to Salt Lake to visit my folks," the lamb says. "My name is John. What's yours?"

"Ivan."

"Come in for coffee, Ivan? I don't know a soul in New York, not really." He's still holding Ivan's hand. "I'm lonely."

In bed, John's intense and quick, edging onto rough; his hunger for touch, for sex, comes and goes like a storm in summer.

And after: "I've never done this before. Only dreamed."

"This?"

"What we did. I don't know what to make of it."

"Oh. It is what it is."

"Stay with me?" John asks.

"Sure." Maybe sleep will come in this most unexpected place.

John pulls the sheet to cover them and rests his head on Ivan's chest. "There's just one thing," he says, sitting up.

"Yeah?"

"Do you mind if I take my eye out?"

"Okay," Ivan says, thinking contacts. But the lamb lowers his head and cups his palm under an eye; then he lifts his head and holds out his hand, displaying an eyeball.

"It's glass. I take it out when I sleep. I lost my eye when I was two. From cancer."

"Oh. I'm sorry."

"Don't be. It's okay. Here, take it."

And Ivan's got this eye in his hand. It's round like a marble, two-sided: one side is a perfect eye, the pupil gray, speckled with blue; the other side is porcelain-white. Ivan rolls it in his fingers. The smoothness is delicious. He's reluctant to give it back. He wants it as a trophy, like proof he's been to the heart of the Amazon or climbed Everest.

"Can I look inside?"

The lamb looks confused.

"Inside, you know, where your eye was?"

"Sure thing," he says, laughing. "Most folks are too afraid to look. But everyone wants to." He stretches his eyelid open. Ivan's holding his breath, half afraid he'll discover that the boy's really a robot or an android from another planet; but really he fears, or hopes—the feelings are one—that he'll see the lamb's soul, some kind of pulsing white light. Smooth beige flesh, though, like the inside of a cheek, is what he finds.

"Disappointed?"

"No," Ivan lies.

"What you see is what you get," John says, a victory grin on a face that's now lopsided, with one eye closed, the other opened wide.

Soon, he's asleep. Ivan kisses him softly and slips out of bed, thinking he'll maybe pick up one more fare before turning in, maybe catch sight of Taz, whom he's forgiven, kind of, for blowing him off.

Day nine without sleep is about to begin, but tonight he's not counting.

He took an interest in her photographs in old-fashioned dark wood frames, covered in glass. One caught the light from a lamp, as if hanging in a museum. He pointed at a middle-aged couple and a young girl of maybe ten. It was set in a studio, staged, stripped of setting, clues. "You? Your parents?"

She stepped closer to look. "Yes," said Gabriella.

He wanted to ask more but her cautious *yes* warned him off. She kept a regal silence, but he sensed she could strike out, or worse, close her door to him. He'd told her about Mish and Kevin. Today he'd told her about Taz.

She understood.

He could not lose her.

He tried to guess her parents' ages, and from that, how old Gabriella was now, but the family seemed suspended in time, refusing to be pinned down by the style of clothes, the cut of her mother's hair, or her father's mustache. They were not American: that he could tell by their haughtiness, broken only by a sly smile on the young Gabriella's face—a ten-year-old's impishness. Their foreignness drew him closer to her. She was sighted then, a girl with lively eyes caught darting off to one side as if she'd spotted a cat, much to her delight.

There were other pictures of her family. All looked to have been taken the same year. No before, no after.

"I have pictures, too," he said.

"Bring them. I'd be honored."

Could she even see his pictures? Perhaps if she held them close?
He was afraid to ask. What else could he give her? A jewel? But
she'd not be able to see it glisten. Would its touch delight her? Or
he could give her the desk, *his desk*. Damn Kevin—and Misha,
too—rose in him, bitter, like the taste of anchovies, of bile.

He opened a window. The breeze was warm. He sat on the sill.
The view was west, of the Hudson, of New Jersey. Clouds from
the afternoon's storm were breaking. One, in the distance on the
horizon, the largest, was dark where it began and then, as it rose,
an intense white, purified of its baser elements. It floated across
the sky and caught a ray from the sun; it glowed with fragments
of golden light, an Orthodox dome, a blimp in a celestial circus.

"Thank you for opening the window."

"How did you know?"

"My ears work quite well, thank you very much, and the air
after a storm smells deliciously fragrant, even in New York. You
have good instincts, Ivan."

"I have to go to work," he said, leaning out the window.

Too far. She held her breath. "Come back in," she wanted to
say. But then he would realize. Did he know already? No, he was
too trusting for his own good. As a blind woman, she could stare
at him recklessly.

"Ivan, do come in," she said, calmly. He no longer spoke in
a pressured onslaught of words. She'd done him some good. He
stood in front of her and she ran her fingers over his face, brushed
back his hair, and sealed in his newfound peace.

At Grand Central he snags a monster fare to Amagansett. A
lucky end to his night. It's early morning and a yellowy gray light
is coaxing nighttime shadows from their resting places. It's the
hour before all hell breaks loose. The fare is a softspoken man in
his forties, fifty maybe. Straw hat not quite covering hair that's a
thinning brown; a Hawaiian shirt, three top buttons open; a tan
that ends below the neck. He has a quick smile: jaunty, you'd say,
until it fades. Then he sighs and slides down in the seat.

"Your summer home?" Ivan asks. He's got nothing against these rich guys and their homes in the country. But nothing *for* them either. He's curious, though. They're a species apart.

"No," he says, "I'm not in the same league, so to speak, as the people who summer. I just live there." He pulls out a handkerchief and spits into it. "With my . . ." he pauses, then stammers, "si- si-si-significant other. Or I did."

"Huh?" Ivan grunts. He's accustomed to people saying more than they intend. When they're not ignored, cabbies are like bartenders and priests.

"He's dead. Sometimes I forget that little detail." Straw hat speaks just above a whisper. A chuckle where Ivan would have expected sadness. His face is tanned but gaunt. His eyes are deep in their sockets in a way that has Ivan flashing to his bony, undressed skull. He's where Kevin is headed. In the rearview, now, a tepid smile. He's one of *those* people. They made their mistakes. Ivan doesn't mean it harshly, except where Kevin's concerned. Just an observation. Ivan's made his missteps, too, just not the ones these old guys made. Still, they should have known better, he can't help but think.

Straw hat is silent as the miles pass. He and Ivan are separate cocoons of thought. It's not that Kevin is evil. He's friendly to Ivan, shows respect, treats Misha well. But the belief that he should know better and stick to his own kind and not put Misha's life at risk is what drives away the sympathy Ivan feels for most people.

The sun's arced well above the horizon when they arrive. Straw hat's fallen asleep. Ivan watches him for a while. He looks serene and Ivan's loath to wake him up to what's real. A dog barks. Ivan reaches back—a light touch to the shoulder. It's part of the job. Straw hat leaves a large tip. "Live well, kid," he says. A squeeze to Ivan's hand that holds the money, and he disappears into a white cottage in need of paint and a garden run wild.

The next night, Ivan decides to call it quits early. Drops the cab off at 3:00 A.M. and heads home. It's going on day nine and his mind is all Taz, all the time. But without sleep, he'll scare him off—if he hasn't already—speaking all the thoughts in his head. This kind of love he's learned to circle around, but now he craves it more than he fears it. That he won't run from Taz has been decided, and damn Misha and Papa if they're proved to be right.

Again.

Once, in the tenth grade, after school, a girl, her skin ebony. A kiss. Another. Fumbling. Touch, sweet and terrifying. After: he could think of nothing else. "I'll take you to Abyssinia with me," she'd said. "I was born there. You'll like it." His thoughts raced. Words, too. Days, weeks later, "Fever speech," she said. "You frighten me." He spun like the whirling dervishes that had visited Kiev. Later, much later, when he'd told the doctor—weeks had passed and time rolled in on itself and he remembered only Papa and Mish saying to him: "Slower, slower," and then Papa had been angry and Mish cried and Ivan, recalling the dervishes and that he himself was one, grew desperate for someone to put out a hand, yet he swatted away any and all that reached for him. He was spinning, certain that speed would take him toward God and those who would stop him were devils and if only he could explain; but they came at him with needles that made time turn to sleep and when he awoke he was in a hospital, Bellevue it was called, but he could see no bells through the window and then he was telling the doctor about a kiss and what followed and the doctor nodded and said, "So you made out with the girl," as if that was all there was to it, and Ivan said no, and the doctor said, "Ah! You fell in love."

When Ivan returned home, Papa said, "The doctors advised me: consequences must be taken into account." Consequences! It was not like losing himself in the streets of Kiev. The word *remember* lay on the lips of Papa and Misha, only a finger need be raised, a brow furrowed to remind Ivan. And it was understood that Ivan could love the city, the planet, love the entire universe, love grandly, but no, he could not love any one person outside his family.

Voices echo from below: Tony's, and then it's Taz. Ivan heads down the garage's main ramp to find him. What's past is history. He will not let go of Taz. He is eighteen. He is strong.

"Hey," he says, meeting Taz, who's on the way up.

"Hey you," Taz says.

Tonight, they're in synch.

They climb from the depths of the garage—it's three ramps deep—out onto Hudson St., where bad city air smells clean by comparison.

Taz gives Ivan a friendly bump to the shoulder and Ivan bumps back and now they're walking up Hudson, bumping back and forth, Taz laughing, so Ivan knows he's safe. There's no need for words; between them is gravity's power. Ivan's dreaming: if he could, he'd build Taz a city as rich as Venice; he'd be his gondolier in this city of love. They reach the corner where Ivan goes east and Taz north. But they don't. They stop. Taz, hands in pockets, rocks back and forth on his heels. The air's hot, muggy, nasty as spit. Ivan is bracing for a *See you tomorrow*, but Taz looks him in the eye. "Uh . . . my place?"

Six flights up. It may be Hell's Kitchen, but Ivan's floating up to heaven. It's a one-room tenement that's seen better days. The air inside suffocates him with smells: the essence of Taz. There's a mattress, a snarl of sheets, several chairs, clothes strewn, a window with bars, a large table half-crowded with dirty dishes, half with notebooks and a computer. A bordello-red bulb dangles from the ceiling. The walls are white, green: a paint-job aborted. And books: books are everywhere—stacks of them on the floor (they have to navigate around them), and even more stuffed into bookshelves.

Ivan's never taken well to reading in English and what he can read in Russian is worthy of the eleven-year-old he was when he left.

Taz takes two beers from the fridge, tossing one to Ivan, who snares it as if this were everyday. Next, Taz opens the window and air, river-cool, smelling of fish, seaweed, and salt rushes in so a person can breathe, and Ivan does, deeply, reminded again that it's a port city he now calls home. Taz leans against the window and empties his bottle in a few gulps.

"You read a lot?" Ivan asks, shifting his weight from foot to foot. His mind is in a rare state: empty of thought.

"Yeah. A lot. I write, too, but it's mostly crap."

"That's cool," Ivan says, at a loss for words, wondering where to put himself, when Taz, finishing his beer, pulls Ivan down onto the bed, pushing aside the mess of sheets and clothes, his tongue exploring Ivan's mouth; and then Ivan's pulling Taz's T-shirt off— *The Dingo Got Me* it reads on the front; *Guess Who's Next?* on the back—and in turn, Taz is unbuttoning Ivan. "Aren't you hot always wearing long sleeves? I've been dying to ask you," Taz says in a moment when their mouths are unglued. But right away he's kissing Ivan again, not waiting for an answer. Then they're side by side, Ivan stilled by the gaze of Taz's pale blues and Taz whispers, "I've been waiting all week for this," and Ivan hopes this won't be a quick fuck, which it isn't because in the middle of kissing and stroking and sighing, Ivan lets go, falling into sleep, his head now cradled by Taz, who groans, "Ivan, dude, wake up." Ivan does, briefly, half in dream. "Taz," he says, the first time the name's escaped his lips. More words, murmured in Russian, follow.

From Taz: "What's that you're saying?"

In English: "I'll take you home with me. I will. You have my word on it."

Taz, reflective, sad, if Ivan's eyes were open to see, says: "You can't go home again, little buddy."

"No, I will," Ivan says, in Russian, in English.

"Not possible," Taz says, gritting his teeth and nestling Ivan's sleeping body into his.

Gabriella reclines in the bathtub. She inhales deeply on her cigarette. On the exhale, she says her name, *Gabriella*, extending the last syllable into a sigh, as if she'd felt a breeze on this hot summer day.

She'd started life an O'Connor, Mary-Ellen O'Connor. Her Irish grandparents had migrated past the rolling green hills to the arid heat of west Texas. They'd heard of oil. The nearest town of any size was Odessa. The oil had run dry, as did their money. So they settled in the dust. It was a hoot when the shoot-out at Waco gave it glamour again, of sorts. She had a sister who'd married and a brother who'd died in Vietnam. Although by then she was long gone. A baker's dozen names lay between then and now.

She rubs her head's knobby smoothness with a soapy washcloth. Her hair failed to grow back as promised after the chemo. "It happens," said the doctor. He was young, embarrassed, as if it was the first time his rule book had failed him. "The treatment might have uncovered a condition called *alopecia*. A preexisting tendency," he'd said. "Alopecia," Gabriella says now, trying it on for size as she might a new dress. Worthy of a Greek tragedy, she thinks. "Medea, meet Alopecia," she says, laughing, coughing. The diagnosis of alopecia was easier to take from the other doctor, whose bushy eyebrows turned up at the corners, his dark beard splotched white as if an angry patient had thrown milk at him. "What's a tendency?" she'd asked and he shrugged, putting down her chart, his lips beginning to mouth words that were swallowed before they emerged. She followed the movement of his Adam's apple, imagining the words thoroughly digested.

You're lucky to be alive, is what he intended to say.

She'd been a Susanna once. That was her favorite name. A Susanna Gibson, traveling the hill towns of Italy with an Englishman. What was his name? She squeezed the washcloth, wringing out dirty, soapy water and with it, the memory of his name: Guy. Guy Winfield, or Butterfield, or Copperfield; whichever, he'd come gift-wrapped with a girlish fantasy of a manor house and rolling green fields, borrowed from the novels she'd read by flashlight long after her father's stern "lights out."

She'd claimed to be Canadian when they'd met at a cafe in Pisa, her west Texas twang long gone. She could still feel the exhilaration now. Dear God, how she had been capable of losing herself in love.

He'd ditched her in Perugia. In a church of all places. She recalled the delicate pastels: the turquoise, faded blues and greens of the archway above the church doors. Inside was a painting of the Madonna and Child. Several. She let herself fancy the notion of having a child with him, but when he'd carried on about a wife and children, she'd thought: how pallid you are, your emotions, your skin. She gave herself to a day of despair and was over him. She was like that, Mary-Ellen O'Connor of west Texas.

She stands, pulls the plug on the bathtub drain, and wraps herself in a towel. On those July days in west Texas when the heat made the air visibly ripple, she'd lock her bedroom door, point a fan toward her bed, and lie on it naked, covered by a wet towel. When the winds kicked up, the air outdoors browned in a fury of dust, swirling, blinding.

She'd read somewhere they lived in the bed of an ancient sea.

In Umbria, she tried on Alessandra, then settled on Gabriella and on the arm of a Vietnam vet. Pete was younger but not young. He'd wake during the night screaming, pounding his pillow, the wall. She was frightened, excited. He seemed to speak in tongues though it was likely a smattering of Vietnamese. He'd told her of all the many times he'd cracked up. She listened to his tales of buddies blown apart—mines, grenades, children spraying bullets—and yes, it was worse than growing up with parents whose lives had left them rocks in place of hearts.

She followed him to New York. She learned the language of posttraumatic stress. Her listening helped, he said. She met his friends: the Joes, Jimmys, Phils, Andys who lived at war at night in their dreams. "She'll listen," he'd said to them. "She's got more wisdom in her big toe than those bozos with degrees."

It came to her: her life had been lived for pleasure, guided only by impulse, cloaked in, enraptured with freedom; but within her there was nothing of value. The west Texas dust had settled in her pores, not easily shaken. And oh had she tried.

"She heals," Pete said. And if they believed, she often did heal, and her new life was born. She alluded to camps—Hitler's, or Stalin's; these men seemed not to care or know very much about either. And the word *camps* had a sacramental quality that pleased her. To some, she claimed to have known Freud. ("I was such a young girl at the time.") Her accent shifted: a touch German, Polish, Czech; on occasion, she was Flemish, when she sensed her audience required a deeper note of obscurity.

The men were in pain and needed a woman's heart, open but mysterious. She said her sight was failing, suggesting she'd seen too much. She added the dark glasses one year, a cane the next. They saw in her lost vision a saintliness. Yes, it was a bold touch: blindness.

But cancer—the fear it brought, the dread. You can't sass the Grim Reaper, she learned.

Pete and his buddies stood by her.

And her lies gave her a voice that spoke truth, wisdom, compassion.

Now, after fifteen years, none knew her as sighted.

Gabriella drops the cigarette in the toilet. She puts on her wig, fiddling with it until it looks natural; strawberry blond suits her so much better than the muddy brown she was born with. Although they're hidden by her glasses, she draws in her eyebrows. Yes, vanity lingers.

Ivan is due at four. Poor, lovesick Ivan. He's not slept for days. It worries her. All for a silly boy from L.A., a city filled with silly boys and silly girls with their leather-skinned parents.

"Taz," she says aloud, holding onto the sink's edge, then laughing so hard she fears she'll break the surgical scars on her abdomen. Taz-mania and manic Ivan, a punch line to a joke she'd never tell, although "never say never" was her father's favorite saying. He'd say it with a wink to her at the dining room table, bypassing her mother's downcast eyes. He was a tease until he wasn't. And when he insisted on collecting his due, she'd taken all the money she could steal from his wallet and that cookie tin where her mother hid her own runaway savings, enough to put him and west Texas behind her and kill that thing that grew in her womb.

Ivan wakes. He stretches, yawns, his eyes open to daylight. Above, a molded tin roof. A thought: I'm not at home. He reaches over: emptiness. "Taz?" he asks. He's alone, but not lonely. Taz's pillow, his sheet, his clothes—they all hold his smell: salty sweat, deodorant, sex. And there's the memory of his touch. Ivan recalls waking earlier, hard, pulling Taz into him and Taz, quiet, grunting in rhythm with Ivan—or was it a dream?

And so many books. Beside the bed, one lies open, its pages roughened by use, notes in red ink scrawled in the margins, lines marked Day-Glo yellow. It's a thick book: *You Can't Go Home Again*. Who is this Thomas Wolfe? If he could read it, perhaps he'd know Taz better?

The sound of a key, the lock, tumblers, the groan of rusty hinges, and Taz says, "Hey you." He's holding a grocery bag to his chest.

"Where'd you go?"

"Food. Breakfast, little buddy."

Afternoon light floods the room through the single window. The bars lay down stripes.

Taz pulls out cereal, milk; then he slips out of his clothes and into bed. "You sure got sleeping down to an art." Taz leans on an elbow and studies Ivan with a playful smile. Ivan can see Taz's chest—delicate, concave—his heart's beat visible. Ivan's mind is calm.

"Are you really a writer?"

"Yeah. Not a great one. But I've dreams."

"Read me something."

Taz reaches for a book.

"No," Ivan says, "Something you've written."

"No. Can't. It's crap. I told you that." Taz looks away, back. His eyes stare past Ivan, who turns his head and looks at the ragged line where the half-painted wall goes from white to green.

"Please."

"No," he says so harshly that Ivan jumps, as if struck by lightning. My first mistake, Ivan frets. Please smile, he prays, looking into eyes that have turned guarded, distant.

"That's okay," and Ivan reaches out to hug him closer. Taz twists away, stands.

"Wait," says Taz. He picks out a book from a shelf. It's a thin paperback. He flips through its pages. Ivan watches intently. Taz's body is bony, white, sallow. Ivan's not fully taken him in before. His face is pink from the summer sun, as is his left forearm, which has poked out from his cab window. He's a boy-man, a creature that needs protection.

Taz finds what he wants and turns back to Ivan. "This is for you," he says.

"What is?"

"A poem."

"By you?" Ivan asks, then regrets.

"No. Not in a million years. A dead white guy. A genius."

The sun's tracked past the window, throwing the room into shadow. Taz turns on a lamp Ivan's not noticed. It casts a yellow light. He sits on the bed and clears his throat:

*"i like my body when it is with your body. It is so quite a new thing. Muscles better and nerves more. i like your body. i like what it does, i like its hows."*

He stops, stands, then looks down on Ivan. "I need a glass of water. You?"

"No thanks." Ivan's enthralled, drunk on Taz's voice. When Taz returns to the bed, Ivan says, "That was beautiful," thinking: does he mean it?

"Not done yet." Taz sips his water.

"Oh, sorry." Ivan lies on his back, hands behind his head.

*"i like to feel the spine of your body and its bones, and the trembling-firm-smooth ness and which i will again and again kiss,"*

He pauses, kisses Ivan on the stomach, lights a cigarette, coughs. Ivan stares at the tin ceiling with a fleeting curiosity as to who made it, who's lived under it.

Ivan would tell that Mormon boy there's more to love than Jesus.

*"i like kissing this and that of you, i like, slowly stroking the, shocking fuzz of your electric fur, and what-is-it comes over parting flesh. . . . And eyes big love-crumbs, and possibly i like the thrill of under me you quite so new"*

Taz stops. Is there more? Ivan's afraid to ask, or move, or even blink. To stop time is what he'd do if he knew how. To expand the silence. The poem was for *me*, he thinks. "You sure you didn't write that? You could have. I know you could."

From the street comes the grinding sound of a garbage truck; the air's grown hot, heavy. No river-cool this evening.

Taz says, "But I didn't." The silk is gone from his voice, replaced by an edge that's knife-sharp.

It's every day with them now. Ivan can't get enough of Taz: his smell, the taste of him, his touch. Each day begins with a poem. Sleep is brief, deep. Sex leaves them reshaped.

"Your skin is moist, dark, like an olive," Taz says, biting Ivan's arms and neck, then resting his head on Ivan's shoulder.

"Olives are sour."

"An acquired taste, buddy."

"And *your* skin is pale, like you're a ghost or you've seen one."

Taz pulls back, raises an eyebrow.

"What?" says Ivan. "Something wrong?" He's met no one like Taz.

"Nothing."

Taz has that faraway look in his eyes again. He lowers his head, hiding his face, sighs, and brings a hand up. To wipe away a tear? Ivan wonders.

"You sure?"

"Yeah," he says, but doesn't convince.

Ghosts disappear, Ivan knows. You can put your hand through them. He touches Taz to be sure. He presses. Feels his heart beat. His touch leaves Taz's skin a blushing, fading pink. Ivan's walking the high wire without a net. He's long since stopped his meds. He's defied the consequences. Ivan's in love. Anything is possible now.

In September, a storm: wind, rain, the city's left chilled, clean. The first leaves, yellow, fall and fill the sidewalks, clog the gutters.

Ivan and Taz have just eaten breakfast and now lie on their sides in bed, face to face; each has a hand on the other's hip.

"What are you writing?" Ivan asks, carefully. In sex, Taz is open, transparent. But the person who is Taz is volatile, easily frightened away. This business of learning another is seductive, fraught.

"The Great American Novel."

"What's it about?" Ivan once struggled with English. Now, speaking it, he's at ease. "But you don't get irony, sarcasm," Misha has often said, patiently, impatiently.

"Bad luck to tell."

"What's the title?"

"Can't say; doesn't have one." Taz turns away and curls himself up tightly.

Ivan massages the clenched, cobblestoned muscles of Taz's back. "That's cool," he says, untwisting Taz, who resists, but Ivan's strength catches Taz by surprise. He sits on Taz's chest, pinning his arms back. "Read me some," he dares.

"Not yet." Taz's face has emptied of expression. His eyes are dark, emptied of blue, all pupil, as if the color had leaked out; it's his faraway look, one that Ivan has grown accustomed to, but is still unsettled by. He recalls the masks Papa bought for him and Mish. "They're from Venice," Papa said, which Ivan believed, no matter how often Misha said, "Don't be stupid. He bought them on Canal Street." The masks were white, with black hair, red lips, and cheeks dabbed with rosy paint; there were small holes for the eyes and a slit for the mouth. They had frightened him. He'd thought they were what's left of people whose souls have been sucked out by a demon.

Ivan lets go. What can he do for Taz? He'd give him anything right now.

"I bet your parents are proud of you," he says. It has not occurred to him until this very moment that Taz had a family, a life, before he'd appeared that day in the garage.

"You think?" Taz asks, childlike, meek.

"Tell me about them, your mother, your father."

"One father. One mother." Taz gives Ivan a shove, which lands him on his back. Taz crouches and offers Ivan a hand, then they sit naked, cross-legged, knees touching.

"That's it? No brothers or sisters?"

"Just me. The apple of their eyes." Taz smiles, proud, scornful: behind the smile there's a joke Ivan's not in on.

"Do you love them?"

"What's love?"

"Be serious," Ivan says. Taz is playing with words. He feels the stirring of anger, which is not Ivan (Kevin the exception, but for good cause), certainly not part of the new world he now finds himself in.

"Poetry's serious. Writing's serious. Can't waste what little I've got."

"Of love?"

"Yeah."

"And me?" Ivan says, wishing he hadn't, holding his breath; now he can't look Taz in the eye.

Taz runs the fingers of both hands through Ivan's hair, making a part down the middle that had not existed before. He brushes his lips against Ivan's. "You're my muse."

"Is that love?"

"It's better."

Ivan's appeased, unsure, knowing just that Taz's touch says more than words.

"You're lucky."

"How?" Taz throws his head back. Laughs deep from his belly.

"My mother died."

Taz cups Ivan's face in his hands. "I'm sorry. You never said."

"But I've got a father and a brother and I love them and there's lots left over."

"You're one lucky dude, in that case."

Ivan, perplexed: "How can you not know if you love your mother and your father?"

"Didn't say I didn't. Said I can't waste it."

"That's cruel and I don't believe you."

"It's my life and welcome to it."

"Taz, Taz, Taz, Taz. I think there's no way you don't love your parents. No way."

How exhilarating it is to say Taz's name: the freedom he now has.

Taz gives Ivan another shove that's less playful. "Ive, give it a rest." He turns away, picks up a book, leafs through the pages, looking for something he can't find.

"Taz," Ivan says, again, insistent. He feels a pain in his chest that someday he'll know is the beginning of heartbreak.

"Let it go, Ive. Please just let it go."


"Hey, Lionel!" Ivan shouts.

"Hey, Russkie! What's happening?"

"Life is good."

A brisk fall wind has made its way down into the first level of the garage.

"Yes, that's for sure, except when it's not," Ali pipes in.

"Your friend pulled a no-show," Tony says, from the doorway of his office, clipboard in hand.

"Huh?"

"Yeah. Baby says he's sick." Tony walks over to them with a deliberate, lazy stride.

"Oh?" says Ivan.

"Didn't you know? Thought you two were *joined at the hip*."

"Leave him be," Lionel says.

"*Whatever*," says Tony. Then, lips brushing Ivan's ear, whispers, "See me in my office later if you're lonely." Ivan does not believe in hate. Tony is for sure the one who's lonely. He feels sorry for him. Ivan has Taz in his life, after all.

"Mouths to feed," says Ali, a signal to disperse.

A few fares into the evening Ivan calls Taz. The phone rings, once, twice, ten times. He calls again. Twenty rings. Not even Taz's message machine's: *Hi, this is Taz. Sing your song.*

Twilight is early now, the darkness quick to descend. Ivan pulls his cab over, sits quietly and observes: at a red light, cars and cabs gun their engines, buses and trucks spew fumes. People on the sidewalk are all in a hurry, even the old folks carrying groceries. The men and women in suits, briefcases in hand, are racing— where? Exceptions: teens, boys and girls, Dominican, Puerto Rican, most likely, saunter or the boys swirl around the girls.

The light changes. Cars take off, pedestrians edge into the crosswalk, risk being hit—*even dead, we'll sue you fuckers*, they glare. A cab cuts off a car, a horn's leaned on. The cabbie shouts "Asshole!" A man on the corner screams "Motherfucker!" at the cabbie, who seems to aim at the man, missing him by inches.

Times like these, Ivan wonders, what holds it together, this city that he's come to love? There's a street-level view only a cabbie has. He sees the mayhem, the fear, the hate, and you'd think it would all fly apart, some centrifugal force, flinging all the cars and the people out to the moon or Mars or Saturn. Maybe Saturn's rings are made of what's left of the Mayans and Incas, the Greeks and Romans? Papa won't talk about the past, but Ivan knows how Papa's life in Russia contained three wars, with purges and blood-lettings in between, as if Russia were a rotting walnut that God had taken a nutcracker to, again and again, chewing, then spitting out pieces in disgust.

But here, now, this world, this New York, America, did hold together. It was a mystery to Ivan, whose thoughts might begin to race, spin out of control, at any time. He's a whirling dervish who in some past frenzy had likely spun off pieces of himself that comprised those rings of Saturn's and who now craved the embrace of Taz, who never hurried, who read him poems, who quieted Ivan's mind and soul with the touch of his voice.

It was Taz with his blue eyes that took Ivan's measure, for whom Ivan could think of nothing he could give in return besides love, but uncertain that love was magic enough to free Taz's fingers to scrawl words on the page like his Thomas Wolfe.

The next day. Ivan's early. He and Tony are alone in the garage.

"Quit," says Tony.

"Where's he gone?"

"How should I know? Kids like him come and go. Say la fucking vee."

"Where?" Ivan says, just short of a scream, standing toe to toe, feeling he'd rip Tony's head off, despite the fifty pounds and several inches in Tony's favor.

"Ivan, you're a fucking pest." Tony rolls his brown eyes upward and flashes his cat-that-swallowed-the-canary smile. Strolls behind him. Puts his hands on Ivan's shoulders. His lips sloppy on Ivan's neck. It's no puzzle what he'll have to do to learn from him where Taz has gone. So it's quid pro quo in Tony's back office, blinds down, pants at his ankles. Rule number eight or nine: don't sell your self-respect, now broken. It hurts. Tony's not the gentler sort. Ivan, desperate, ashamed, tries to relegate this event to just another transaction: a monster cab fare with a loudmouth drunk, worth the price.

Afterwards: "Home to La-La Land," Tony says, the words now ugly. He swats at a gnat with his heavy arm, and then zips his fly. He drops the condom in the trashcan and rips a page from a notebook.

An address that means nothing.

*His name is Scott.*

Ivan's a rag doll, limp; by rights, he should crumble to the floor.

"He went home to Mom and Pop, sunny California, beaches. I'd go, too, if I were twenty years younger and didn't have a wife, three kids, and a fucking mortgage." Tony rests a finger on Ivan's shoulder and guides him out of the office. He spits, then spits again, as if ridding himself of self-pity, his envy of Taz, of rich college boys, of foreign boys who get to fuck them. And he succeeds; there's a version of sympathy in his eyes. He puts an arm around Ivan. If Ivan were alert to the world beyond his thoughts, beyond his skin, which feels inflamed, he'd see the sadness in Tony.

"Ivan, it's the way of the world. Time you learned. You can have the night off, if you want; so go get smashed and then catch yourself some sleep. Okay, kid?"

Ivan walks up the ramp and out onto Hudson. His blood is poison. Ivan fears it will spurt from his ears, his nose, his mouth, even the pores of his skin. Is this what Taz does alone, writing? Spilling his blood on the page? Is Taz okay? Did he run out of blood to spill? Ivan thinks: I'll go to L.A. Taz needs me. But Scott? He says the name; spoken, it has the flavor of something foreign, unnatural. Suddenly, he's doubled-over, retching his last meal on the street. People walking by glance in distaste and hurry their pace.

If he goes home, he will lock the door and not leave. He will not eat. He will not drink. He'll write on the wall. He'll explain to Nicky what's happened. He knows himself better than Mish or Papa realize. He is not a fool. He'll not be made a fool. His cab is his other home. He can drive in circles and not spin out of control.

He turns and heads back into the garage. This time, there'll be no leather restraints, no doctors, no needles, no drugs. He can't tell Mish and Papa, as much as he needs them. *Consequences,* they'll say. We warned you. But it was not a mistake, this being in love. And he will find him, his Taz, this Scott.

Later that night, Ivan cuts off another cab at West 54th and Seventh, heading with two suits in his backseat toward Lex and East 88th. Rain slickens the street. He turns on the wipers. They squeak. At 57th, he brakes hard at a red light, grips the wheel to pull out of a skid, almost hitting another cab. The other cabbie screams, "Fuck you!" They line up at the light. Ivan guns his engine. On green, he speeds north, through Central Park.

The suits in the back shift nervously. "Take it easy, pal," says one, knocking on the open partition. Ivan slams it shut. Ivan doesn't give a goddamn. He's picking up speed tonight. Placing bets on himself, adding pressure, counting fares, dollars, so as not to think about Taz: his voice, his touch, the whereabouts of him, which is known: California, L.A. But that's known to Ivan in images from TV, movies, magazines: palm trees, beaches, freeways, tans.

At East 88th, another fare jumps in as the two suits exit. He's wearing a trench coat.

"So what do you do?" the fare asks.

"Huh?"

"What do you do when you're not driving a cab?"

The rain's heavy now, wind-driven. While stopped at a light, under a street lamp, Ivan checks the rearview. The new fare's not young, not old, but headed that way; a face that's just begun to crumple, jowls under a fisherman's hat. Owlish glasses. Professorial.

"I'm a magician," he says, thinking: What's it to him? Besides, Ivan does the interviewing here. "College," Papa had said. "College," Misha had echoed. But two months in and he was out. No room to bounce, fidget, breathe. "Logorrhea," a professor had said, handing him back a long essay. "I don't understand a word of it. I do hope you're a genius, that I've missed the point."

The light turns green and they're off, moving slowly in traffic.

"I've never met one before," trench coat says, condescending, curious.

Ivan hits the brakes, pulls over. "Here's a trick," he says. "Ride's over. Disappear."

"What?"

"Outsky," Ivan says, adding nasty to his voice.

"You some kind of a nut?"

"Out and yes."

Trench coat exits, glances back, scurries off. Rain throws colors on the windshield. This is not Ivan. He spots a phone booth. Punches in numbers.

"Mish?"

"Vanushka. You okay?" Misha asks, hesitant, vulnerable.

"What are you up to?"

"Company tonight."

"Kevin?"

Misha, whispering: "Ive, give him a chance. He's a good person. He likes you. Can't you even try?"

Ivan so wants to tell Mish why it doesn't matter if Kevin's a good person, but now he's scared. Taz, he wants to say. *Taz*. But to say his name now risks an uncontrollable stream of words, among them—*I am in love*, and, *he's gone*.

Instead, Ivan says, "Give the devil his due, you mean," then regrets it.

Silence.

The sound of Misha's breath, familiar, loved, missed. "I'd do the same for you," says Misha.

Ivan taps against the glass. He writes "Taz" in the fog. Beads of moisture condense and drip down.

"There's a customer. Got to run."

He exits the park on the West Side. Pulls up on 77th off of Broadway. People scurry, umbrellas in hand. The air's cooled. He sits and watches Papa in his doorman's uniform: Ivan's gift, long to his ankles, military, with gold buttons. He could be a general on the western front, except for the cap, more suited to a cruise ship than a battlefield. Papa, he'd longed to say, you're a doctor. But he knew the answer without the asking: "I adapt, one adapts. For my sons, it's an easy trade. Besides, the holiday tips!"

The minutes collect to an hour. Ivan steps out.

"Hi, Papa."

"Vanushka, you rascal," he says, while helping a woman into the lobby who's pregnant and pushing a stroller. "You're all wet."

They hug. Ivan tighter. Tighter than the night Papa said they were moving to America. It shames him now, Papa's job, and that he did not stay in college. But it feels right to hold him. Papa's breath has the odor of the cigars Ivan bought him last year. There's the smell of his wool overcoat, damp, familiar, a doorway back to childhood.

"Are you okay?"

"Never better."

"What brings you uptown?"

"A fare. Around the corner."

"Good money?"

"Good enough."

"Sure you're okay?" Papa asks again, but he's distracted by a woman burdened with packages. He holds the door open for her, then he gives Ivan the look.

"Sure as can be," Ivan says. Papa's mustache is dripping from the rain. Ivan knows he's not fooled. Papa can read Ivan's face and he will worry. Still, seeing him settles Ivan. But in the looks they exchange there's that stain they share; it's what draws him closer to Papa than Misha can be, yet keeps him and Papa apart—the doctor who's a doorman smiling for holiday tips, his son who's sane by the thickness of a hair, driving a cab, not in college, drunk on the words in his head, not the words in books.

"Got to get back to work," Ivan says and he's off.

He'll track Taz down. You can't run from love, is what he's learned this eighteenth of his years.

Gabriella studies her image in the mirror. No longer a beauty—yes, she was once, and undeniable traces remain—she counts her assets: good posture, firm breasts, a long neck that's just smooth enough not to betray age (she stretches her neck upward to create this illusion), and cheekbones that will carry her through another decade or two, she concludes. There are swollen tender lymph nodes, she knows, and sharp pains in her back, but she's chosen to ignore them. There may not be another decade, she understands. But she will not put herself in the hands of doctors and their poisons again. She has just this moment decided. She feels light, young, girlish. A young colt, her father had called her. Regret and bitterness unsettle her mind: that she misses him astonishes her.

Through the window comes the smell of wet pavement. There is the sound of rain. The radiator knocks, or is it clearing its throat after a summer's absence?

"Sit," she says to Ivan. "Sit close." He'd come after dark, un-invited, unannounced. The buzz from the lobby was electric; his voice through the speaker was broken, in pieces. He'd tapped tentatively on the door. His hair is long, wet. His eyes are blood-shot, with dark shadows below. He's quiet, then come words, a flood, torrential. She picks out: Taz, L.A., gone, Mish, poison, a plan, and Scott. She is confused. Who is Scott? She gives him ten minutes, and then touches his knee. "Slow," she says.

And he does.

Ivan stares into the dark lenses that cover her eyes and wonders: might one of them be glass?

"You are a young man of many enthusiasms, bursting with them," she says, unsure what to say to fix this beautiful, shattered boy. He is ill. The illness has a name. It would help her to think of him in that way. She struggles, unwilling to reduce him to a few cold words.

"But there can be a dark side to such enthusiasms," continuing, where? She brushes his unshaven cheek with a finger and he looks at her, compliant, waiting. In the next apartment a piano plays; a woman sings scales.

Gabriella's voice is hoarse today. The sound absorbs Ivan. She is wearing a new perfume: pungent, not the lavender he's accustomed to. She is wise. He can talk to her. When he arrives, she is always prettier than he remembers. Had he once thought her old?

"Gone," Ivan says. The word emerges after a long silence.

"I know." The sum total of all her wisdom.

"It wasn't a mistake." He looks all of twelve.

"What?"

"Love."

"Yes," she says, puzzled, but then thinks, yes, of course it would be love.

"They're wrong."

Who are they, she wonders; then, does it matter? Love is dangerous for us all she thinks to say but quickly calibrates: he's too young, too fragile.

"I'm going to L.A. to find him," he says.

"And then?"

Her words have an unexpected power. He looks dazed, deflated. His *plan* so easily brought to earth. His heaviness of spirit is new, intolerable. The others she counseled were broken men. But Ivan was incandescent. No, believe in miracles, she wants to say. Go find your love, your Taz. Instead, she takes off her glasses and thinks to kiss him on the lips.

He's never seen her eyes. They're green, like moss. Lydia Delektorskaya's eyes. He stands.

She reaches out for him, strokes his hair, his face. Takes his chin in her hand, studies his eyes, and finds a yes, a desperate yes.

He takes her to bed. He is tender. He comes to life. Or has she misjudged?

He leaves her sleeping; I've given my Gabriella back her sight, he thinks.

"I'm sorry," Ivan says. He hasn't fed Nicolai in days. The cage is dirty. It reeks. Still, there's forgiveness in Nicky's pink eyes. Ivan's brought lettuce and carrots. But first, he takes off the watches he's collected, takes down the clocks off the walls. Then he cleans the cage, sits at his wall, cross-legged, silent, like the monks he's seen in Buddhist temples (he knows this from pictures). He rocks like the old Jews he's seen in synagogues. He crosses himself. God will forgive his mistakes.

Hours pass.

He calls Tony. "I'm sick."

"Take care of yourself, kid."

He calls Misha, only to hang up at Kevin's voice. He feels like a newborn infant, his umbilical cord threaded with fiery nerves.

He calls Papa. "How's my rascal?" Papa asks, or is it a voice in his head, or is he asleep, dreaming? Gabriella says, her voice husky from cigarettes and life, "My Ivan," insisting on the long *E*. "Come up. We must talk."

Later, he lurks by Taz's tenement, in the dark. He looks up at the sixth-floor window. The air is warm, sticky from an autumn heat wave. It holds the dank smell of an evening thunderstorm, gathering strength to wash the city clean of its odors: garbage, sweat, peed-in doorways, exhaust fumes, dread. A delivery boy is buzzed in and Ivan follows his shadow. Taz's name is still on the mailbox. At his door Ivan makes quick use of a pocketknife and credit card.

As he fears, the apartment is emptied of Taz. He pulls on the light cord but nothing happens. Checks the phone but it's lifeless, too. A streetlight illuminates the room. The computer is gone; the dishes, unwashed, remain; also, the mattress, clothes strewn about, and the books. The books! He runs a finger along the spine of one, then another. Picks up Thomas Wolfe and turns the pages. If there's a message in Taz's notes, he can't find it. He lies down on Taz's bed. He searches for Taz in the smell of his pillow, his blanket, the sheets; and in the pile of clothes he's left: his T-shirts, frayed jeans, the prized flannel shirt, green, checkered with black, which Taz had claimed to have been passed down from his great-grandfather, Montana-born. He takes off his clothes. Dresses himself in those Taz has left. He lies like this for hours, vaguely aware of the sound of the rain and the thunder. After the storm passes, it turns cold again and Ivan wraps himself more tightly in the blanket. He notes, just barely, the changing light of day and night, the sound of rain returning, the silence when it stops, and the atonal symphony of traffic that begins at dawn. As long as he's surrounded by Taz, his smell, his memory, he feels no hunger or thirst. He wakes to pee and, as he had as a child, discovers he's wet the bed. Long ago, Misha helped change and wash the sheets, and kept his secret from Papa. He wakes, trembling—a bad dream? No, he's cold, shivering. He tries to close the window, but it's old and the outside leaks in. He puts the flannel shirt back on; it extends down to his knees.

A dream: he's playing a flute and they all follow: Papa, Mish, his mother, Gabriella, the Mormon lamb, Kevin. There are others he doesn't recognize. He leads them to a canyon. Taz stands there, dressed as a doorman, waving them over the edge. "Hey," he says to Ivan. The others each say Ivan's name as they pass by; he's warmed, briefly, at the sound of his name. Then they are all gone and there is silence, then fear, and the rush of thoughts, words, feelings; he spins, faster and faster. He breaks into two parts that press him closer and closer, to God, to the Devil, to heaven, to hell.

Morning. Time returns. He wakes to the jukebox sounds of the city. He wiggles his fingers, his toes. He yawns. A cramp in his calf brings him to tears. He stretches to loosen the knot and when the pain is gone he's filled with a new smell, his own—

fetid, unwashed—not Taz's, whose presence has faded, retreating into his books, which stare silently back at Ivan, keeping their secrets. He scratches. His body is covered with red welts from bed bugs or fleas. He showers, eats a bowl of cereal and sour milk, moldy bread, black coffee.

He dresses, leaves, walks slowly down the stairs. Outside, the sunlight is blinding. He shades his eyes. The sky is a rich, gleaming blue as if it's been given a fresh coat of paint. It's warm in the sun, cool in the shadows. Between buildings he watches clouds appear near the horizon and race across the sky, leaving streaks of white and gray. A half-moon has lingered into day. The city throbs with purpose. It is alive.

He sits, as usual, in the green armchair. Gabriella's prepared coffee and offers freshly warmed scones. There is no longer a pretense of dark glasses.

"Here," he says. "I came to show you these."

He hands her a photo album. Its weight surprises her. Or is it her weakness? The cover is mahogany-brown; a gilt-edged border surrounds two words in Cyrillic. The pages are thick, yellowed, curled at the edges. She pats the space next to her on the bed. "Sit here and we'll look at your pictures." He hesitates, then does as he's told, like an obedient child. He avoids her glance, as if he has a secret. He's ready, anxious even, to move on; that's what it is. She wonders: will I ever see him again?

"Turn the pages, Ivan," she says, gently, forcefully. The world, she thinks, is made up of particles of loneliness and loss, not atoms and neutrons.

"This is me and my brother."

She sees two boys of about five. One is clearly Ivan, the other, a bit taller, with blond hair that falls forward, covering his eyes, must be Misha. They are in a park. The ground is snow-covered. They wear jackets and caps. Their clothes are threadbare, ill-fitting. Ivan smiles broadly; Misha looks serious beyond his years.

She thinks to ask whether he heard from Taz, but is silent.

He turns the pages. More pictures of the brothers, growing taller, older.

"Who's that?" she asks, pointing at a handsome, bearded man leaning against a building, wearing an old-fashioned hat that's angled forward, striking a rakish pose.

"Papa," he says.

A picture of a young woman. Her face is oval, her hair blond like the brother's. "Your mother?"

He nods.

"I dream of her," he says. "She brushes my hair and says, 'Hush, my Vanushka,' when I cry." He's never told anyone of these dreams until now.

"They are only dreams," she says.

"No, I hear her voice. I feel her touch. They are real."

"How can that be?"

He shrugs. "I don't know."

Another photo: the boys, age maybe twelve, flanked by their father. The backdrop is Central Park. She recognizes the angel, the fountain.

Ivan risks a look at her eyes. Their green has paled, flecked with light brown, like grass that needs rain. He strokes her hand.

"Have you talked to Misha? Have you boys made up?"

He shrugs again, then looks away, toward the window.

"Here, have another scone. More coffee."

He eats hungrily.

She thinks: Yes, this is his last visit. He is done with me, as I've been done with others. He's taken what he needs. A not unfamiliar business. What is true, in this moment: he is safe, and Gabriella feels kind, forgiving, and a sense of innocence she'd thought lost, discarded long ago. She will live forever, she will not. It is of no great concern anymore.

Taz's mother stands in the hospital's lobby. The walls are white. They gleam. Doctors and nurses, blurs of blue and white. Her name is Sara. Where is my son? she wants to scream. Outside, the

Santa Anas were fierce. They'd dried her eyes. She'd scratched the skin on her arms raw. She'd wanted to drive into a wall. Jerry should have come. He'd handled the hospital admission, he'd shielded her, but she'd felt it was time to see him on her own. Now she thinks: I can't do this alone.

She'd rehearsed explanations to her friends. They would say, "It's not your fault."

She takes the elevator to the fifth floor. There's a large, glassed-in room where patients sit, watching TV, playing cards and board games. No one is ranting or drooling.

She spots him at once, off by himself. He wears street clothes but his head is shaved, his face, too; he looks barely fifteen, not the scruffy twenty-one-year-old who'd fled to New York. *Dear parents*, he'd written. *I've fled to New York*. He signed it, *Taz*. "This is what they do at that age," she'd said to Jerry, searching his face for reassurance.

She grabs the arm of a passing doctor. "My son, Scott? I'm Mrs. Robbins."

"Come with me." He leads her to a small office. He has a placid face. Dimples. On the wall: diplomas. She counts six. Pictures: a wife, three children. A poster: snowcapped mountains. Shelves lined with textbooks. Fresh lilacs in a vase. This is not the snake pit. Not Bedlam.

Scott wanted to be a writer. She'd preferred a doctor, a lawyer. But she hadn't pushed. Jerry was "live and let live": "He'll come around, in time."

The trip to Australia had been long planned as a gift for graduating college. She'd been sad when she sensed that this might be their last vacation as a family.

He'd brought along a dozen or so books. "I'm reading my way through the great American novels. To learn from the masters."

She'd thought: Maybe he'll be a famous writer, and was surprised how much this pleased her. She'd imagined seeing one of his books in the window of her local bookstore.

When he was young, she'd worried: if he dies, I won't survive.

She'd prepared herself for a car crash, cancer, any number of catastrophes.

Not this.

She'd wished they'd had another child.

In Sydney: "I need time on my own. I'm going camping in Tasmania." Jerry agreed easily. She was inclined to hover. "Sara, this'll be good for him. A little time on his own in the outback— or whatever they call it—can't hurt."

He was gone a week. And Scott seemed happier when he returned. He'd grown a sad excuse for a beard. He smiled more. But after a day, she thought he smiled too much. She felt humored along by him, not his usual teenage sarcasm. He wasn't stoned. She'd spot that easily enough.

There was a moment, after dinner, outdoors, at a restaurant overlooking Sydney Harbor. Jerry had turned in early and she was alone with him. She could have asked questions. But which? Just go try to ask a boy his age questions. All the mothers she knew said it was hopeless. At a certain point, after the hormones struck, they'd agreed, you trust to fate, good genes, and a job well done. But Scott was different. He'd talked to her when her friends' kids had stopped. She touched his cheek. "The beard will grow in, Mom," he said. But she'd sensed there are times you don't ask. There are moments in life when the truth can upend all hope of peace. So she'd let this one slip by.

"He's heavily medicated," the doctor says. "But it will take time."

He talks on, but she's not listening. She stares at a purple blemish on his cheek.

If she's quiet, watchful, still, all this will pass.

"Are you ready?" he asks.

She nods.

She sits beside Scott. His eyes are slits. Who took away his eyes? she wants to cry out.

He holds himself rigidly, his face averted from hers. She puts a hand on his forearm. His skin is cold, unfamiliar.

"I love you," she says.

He licks parched lips.

"Would you like some water? Or a mint?"

"It's one endless wheel," he says.

She pours out the contents of her purse on a table, desperate for a mint, a stick of gum, to give him.

His voice clear, assured: "Time, space, the galaxy, all the stars. God's pinwheel. It just turns and turns, so we never die, never really die."

He looks alarmingly self-contained.

"But the truth is . . ." he says, pausing, turning toward her, eyes open, no longer slits, his pupils small dark points. She feels he's scanning her soul.

"You can't go home again."

Ivan arrives early. He takes possession of a booth—a bit of elbowing of others is necessary as three girls stand around it, dividing up their bill. He orders coffee. The Odessa is crowded, young, high-spirited. Friends wave to friends. He sees a tall boy with a blond beard enter. "Taz," he's about to shout. But it's not Taz, just a shadow. He's seen many such shadows for weeks. But less often, with time. Soon, he supposes, such sightings will dwindle to zero.

He spots Misha and Kevin. He stands and waves at them. "Over here!" he shouts.

Misha's cheeks are rosy. He brushes the hair from his eyes in that way he has when he's nervous. Kevin's grin looks forced.

Ivan, on his toes, engulfs Mish with his arms. "I love you, li'l bro."

"Me, too," says Misha.

Ivan hesitates, then hugs Kevin, who looks startled, touched, but accepts it awkwardly, gratefully. Ivan's decided to trust fate. Trust their love. If the worst happens he will care for, take care of his brother. But that is not for now.

They order breakfast. Kevin digs into his backpack and pulls out a package. It's wrapped like a present, complete with a red ribbon tied in a bow.

"What's this?" asks Misha.

"A present."

"For me?"

"For you both."

"What's the occasion?"

"This, today, us. We are the occasion."

The brothers look at each other. They debate who's to open it in glances until Ivan unravels the ribbon, tears the wrapping paper, and opens the box.

The brothers stare and offer up a baffled "Thanks Kevin," in unison.

"They're called cell phones," Kevin says. "It's the hot new thing. You can call each other anytime, from anywhere. I don't want you two not talking ever again. I can't take the pressure." He smiles shyly.

Ivan takes one in his hand. It's black, heavy. He puts it to his ear.

"I've set them up already," Kevin says. He hands each a piece of paper. "Your phone numbers."

Ivan starts in right away, punching the small numbered keys.

"Pull out the antenna first, guys," says Kevin.

Misha's phone rings. His eyes grow wide. He smiles. Ivan recognizes delight in his brother's eyes, his grin.

"Ive?" Misha asks into the phone. "Is that you?"

# WHO DID WHAT TO WHOM?

—𝔪—

Vinnie's flat on his back in Roosevelt Hospital. Transparent gases and tinted fluids, some dark and brooding, others pastel, pour through translucent tubes that join his body to a rogue collection of bags and machines. They curve, twist, and toy with the possibilities of beauty, filling the room like a new hybrid life form, equal parts plastic, metal, and human.

There is a window and the glimmer of evening light; it's more the memory of light than light itself. It's five o'clock, the sun has set, but nobody's thought to turn on the lights. I do, and scan the celery green walls and Vinnie's sweat-stained blue hospital garb. The room is in disarray. Vinnie's legs are entangled in bedding; he looks to be a child's castaway doll, recognizable, but barely. Stepping into a puddle of liquid, I hear the crunch of broken glass. I curse under my breath as I bump into the bed's metal frame and mutter, "Where the hell are the nurses?"

Vinnie stirs. He lifts his head. His eyes open slowly. They close again. He blinks several times and gulps hard, his large Adam's apple moving up and down a long, familiar neck.

I imagine he's thinking *Oh shit, Kev, am I still fucking alive?* and swallowing his disappointment.

*Vincent rips the tube out. Milky fluid mixes with blood, pours down his arm and hand, and forms pools of red, white, and pink on the* blanket and sheet. He watches as the colors ooze and flow around each other, merging into an organic cocktail that soaks into the mattress. The needle tears his skin and the skinny vein of his right arm, but he doesn't give a fuck; that's what he tells himself, *I don't give a flying fuck*.

Though he had been thin and wiry and his strength had taken people by surprise, little of it remains. But now he uses it to grab every object within reach. He flings them across the room: first the glass vase and its tired flowers; he watches as rose petals flutter, fall, and bless the floor and the shiny beige chair for guests. Then a radio, a writing pad, a picture of his cocker spaniel Gidget, an empty water glass, rosary beads, and an ashtray. *What the fuck is an ashtray doing in the room of a dying man?* he thinks, or maybe he says it out loud: there's no longer a difference for him. He heaves the ashtray as hard as he can at the window, but it bounces off the double-paned glass with a thud.

"I don't give a flying fuck," he says.

I walk round his room cleaning up the mess, pushing aside the broken glass with my foot and guiding it into a corner under a sink. Then I bend to wipe the floor with a wad of tissues, avoiding his eyes. The room looks to be the victim of a bad-tempered gust of wind. A white hospital curtain hides the room's other bed. Behind it someone snores fitfully.

"Hey, farm boy," he says, voice cracking, teasing a look and a smile from me. His eyes were once the palest blue of a sun-bleached sky, but now, drifting toward death, they are electric. I stare into them and think of E.T. on life support shortly before his trip home.

"Yeah. Hi, Vinnie," I say, eyeing a chair covered in vinyl and brown stains. "Long time, huh?"

Vinnie's eyebrows arch upward almost to a point, reshaping his face into a look of friendly puzzlement. Then come a tilt of his head and a shrug of shoulders, almost a twitch, as if to say, *No explanations necessary*. Or so I hope. But what he does say is, "Kevin, you won't believe what happened, you just won't," as if he'd last seen me only yesterday, as if being sick was beside the point when he had one of his stories to tell.

A plastic mouthpiece clings to his chin. It should be on his mouth and nose to give him life-sustaining oxygen, but the Vinnie I remember loved to talk, loved to tell stories and paint pictures with words, and paint me this picture he will, I can tell. Even if it kills him.

"Take a seat, pal," he says, "I don't want you falling down and getting hurt when I tell you what just happened."

*Vincent reaches under the bed for the magazines he'd hidden when first admitted. Where others stash painkillers and sleeping pills for their last-minute suicide, Vincent has long planned the last jerk-off. Last rites were in the air, days or weeks away. He could see by the looks on the faces of friends—taut faces drained of hope, muscles twitching—and in the firm touch of nurses dispatching their chores about his body. The last jerk-off would be his catholic-with-a-small-c exit, his soul-cleansing preparation for a triumphant entry into heaven.*

*But the magazines are gone and Vincent reaches into memories of feverish, manic nights in parks and bathhouses and dark, sacred spaces behind barrooms. For a moment, shadows take the shapes of Albert, Petey, Joe, and Kevin, which dissolve and re-form into strong, fleshy bodies that descend on him, and he sweats passion again in place of toxins.*

*Kevin was the best of them all, he thinks, making a snap decision that surprises him with its force, though Vincent was never one to hold a grudge against even the worst; Petey's theft of two hundred dollars when he moved out of the apartment on East Tenth, along with Vincent's midnight-blue Italian suit and his Lord of the Rings collection (in hardcover!) comes to mind. Then his thoughts drift back to Kevin: maybe the last always seems best. He wonders who he could talk to about this.*

*He rubs himself raw but the only thing hard about him is his bones. They stick up through sweat-soaked pajamas, through the stiff, dry parchment which has replaced skin that his lovers whispered was so smooth and unnaturally soft. Like a young boy, Albert had said, stroking his back in their apartment on East Second Street above the Ukrainian bakery with its smell of yeast.*

"It was like a movie," Vinnie says. "Kev, it's like I thought I was dreaming. I mean like I can't tell anymore most times if I'm dreaming, if I'm awake or dead, or what day it is or what time of day, and so's all of a sudden I open my eyes and my father's standing in front of me, cuffed and in shackles, two Feds on either side holding him by the arms." Vinnie's dropping his r's and g's like they never existed. It's talk that would guide any linguist to the precise block in Bensonhurst where he lived his first sixteen years in a red-brick, two-family house, one of thousands that line the farthest reaches of Brooklyn.

"So's I start to cry," he goes on, arms and hands flailing about as best they can under the circumstances, "which I never like to do in front of my dad, 'cause it's not very masculine and he notices that sort of thing, but I'm crying and tears, I mean, Kevin, they're pouring down my face like I'm a regular Niagara Falls and I'm saying 'Daddy, Daddy I love you' and I reach up to him and the IV comes out of my arm, spraying liquid crap all over the place."

Vinnie stops as his lungs clutch at phantom oxygen. He puts his respirator on, sucks greedily, and continues: "And I still don't know if it's a dream 'cause I had a scene last week with my Aunt Cecelia when I called her a cunt and she showed up the next day to give me rosary beads. She shoved them so hard into my hand that I got cut real bad; but I wanted to apologize for calling her a cunt, 'cause there was no excuse for that even if she is a bitch and all she wants to do is make sure I don't go to hell 'cause that's where she's going and she don't want me there for company. But I never did call her that, it turns out; it was, you know, like a hallucination. So I think this is one, too, but then my father, he looks at the two goons . . . Kev, you should have seen him, he is sooo handsome. His hair is only a little gray after two years in the pen and even though he's almost sixty you can tell there's not an ounce of fat on him and he's got a chest most guys would die for. My father, he's what you call a natural-born leader, so he looks at them—they're trying to hold him back—but now they do what he wants and they let him shuffle over to me, and he leans down and kisses me on each cheek and on the mouth like he's my lover, and I can't stop crying and I'm saying 'Daddy, Daddy I love you' and he's very serious about all this, 'cause he's a very serious guy, very, you know, dignified and all. Kev, I thought maybe he'd show up in prison stripes like in them old movies, but he's wearing a suit. It's one of those gray pinstripe ones, and I can tell it's real expensive, great tailoring—cuffs would you believe, he always liked cuffs—and double-breasted just when it's back in fashion, and he's got this white handkerchief in the pocket, which he pulls out to wipe my tears, and he says, 'Don't you worry, my sweet Vincent, everything will be all right. Don't you cry anymore; your father's here to take care of you.' I mean Kev . . .''

Vinnie pauses. His breath is slow, shallow. The man in the next bed, behind the white curtain, groans as he shifts his sleeping body.

"Are you okay?" I ask, my hand resting lightly on Vinnie's arm.

"Yeah," he says, puckishly. "It's just that for a moment I could see this gray cloud coming at me. It's dark in the middle like somebody threw a rock and it stuck there, and the rock, it's beating like a heart and it's sucking me in."

Vinnie takes a hit of air from his mask. His skin is so thin I imagine I can follow the air's passage into his lungs. He holds the high-octane oxygen in his chest for several seconds, the way he once savored the pleasure of a joint, and exhales slowly.

"So he's saying this crap to me," Vinnie continues, "and he's in shackles and he's going back to jail and I'm thinking what shit this is and what a fucking charmer he is and how handsome he is and why couldn't I ever find a guy as cute as my dad, and Kev, I'm hating and loving him at the same time. Now don't laugh at me, 'cause wasn't it you who said you could never figure how someone could grow up on the streets and be so fucking naive he'd buy an apple, if not the Brooklyn Bridge, off the devil himself?"

Vinnie's mouth stretches unbearably wide, an ear-to-ear smile.

"But, Kev, I'm believing this shit about his taking care of me like I always wanted when I was a kid and like I always believed those asshole lovers of mine would do. Then the nurse comes in, the nice one you know, the nice Chinese one who don't speak great English but sneaks me leftover Chink food instead of this hospital crap; not the high-and-mighty white bitch from Queens who had a hissy fit that time she caught me jerking off. So she says very nice and proper to the goons, 'Time's up,' and then I blink and they're all gone like they never were here."

From the hospital corridor, the soft clack of shoes drifts in. As if tagging along, the heavy smell of beef and potatoes follows.

"Kev, I guess this means 'cause they let me see my father that I'm dying, huh?"

I'm holding Vinnie's hand. It's cold, and the yellow cast of his skin has taken on a bluish tint. "Yeah, any day now," I say, and think: "*Any day now we shall be released.*" I can remember the melody but not who sang it. Once I would have sung it to him. Now, I put his respirator mask back on in silence. I ran into his ex-lover Joe in the lobby. He told me they gave Vinnie the last rites yesterday. That's why the Feds let his father out of prison for the day, although, Joe said, Vinnie had begged to see his father for three months. Maybe they thought Vinnie's impending death was another con job by old Sal. Maybe they thought they were looking at the larger picture and were just doing their job.

I'm doing mine now, stroking his cold, damp hand, waiting for him to die.

Just hours ago he'd called. "Hey farm boy," he said, his voice an octave lower than I remembered, frail and wheezy.

"Vinnie, that you?" I'd asked, knowing full well, holding the receiver tight to my ear with one hand, a sandwich in the other, listening to the crunch of iceberg lettuce in my mouth. He didn't answer right away and in the silence I could feel the lettuce dissolve. Had it been a year since I'd seen him, or, more likely, two? I scrambled to recall.

"Yeah, it's me. Bet you're surprised, huh?" Vinnie says, his voice stronger, more like I remember him.

At nearby desks people whisper on phones. From behind a fuzzy terra-cotta partition my boss's voice—"I'm sensational, baby, just sensational"—greets a new client.

"What's happening?" I ask, still chewing. The taste of turkey and rye (shamefully gratifying, I'd think later) spreads like a vapor through the roof of my mouth. My voice sounds as fake as my boss's as I think: I'm behind schedule, the day is planned, I've a deadline in the pit of my stomach—why is he calling after all this time?

I work in a large open office in a converted loft with high ceilings and tall windows that rise to meet them. Light from a small winter sun pours in hot, its power restored by the glass, belying the snowflakes outside adrift in the wind.

"Look," he says, "I need a favor. More than a favor, more like a sip from the milk of human kindness, you know, like some high-potency TLC, like I'm in trouble, like I'm swallowing my pride to call, like there's something I gotta do and I can't do it alone, so's get yourself up here, okay?"

"Where's there?" I ask, while thinking: I'm not who I was, surely he knows that. In the distance is an office building dating from a time when big city buildings were stocky, no-nonsense, and muscular. I'd never paid it much attention, but now it reminds me of an old photo of my father: broad-shouldered and thick-chested before muscle had turned to paunch, me on his shoulder, squinting in the light.

"1111 Amsterdam, at 114th, room 615," Vinnie says. I turn it into a small, square yellow note stuck to the wall. Later that afternoon, I will encircle it with blue and green notes, docile planets orbiting a sun.

"I'll be there tonight after work." For a moment doubting my intention, picturing an Upper West Side rooming house— wondering what trouble he's in, what story I'll hear, knowing for sure his dad will figure in it.

I don't know why I didn't think of the obvious—too frightened, I guess.

"Kev, I'm counting on it," he says, and I realize I haven't swallowed my turkey and rye. Swallowing frees the flavor of mustard, tangy with a kick to it. I recall a hot day more than two years ago in Riverside Park. Vinnie had pulled his shirt off. Sweat had poured down his smooth, lanky body, leaving streaked dirt on pink skin he'd wiped dry. There was the whiff of baby powder, the smell of grass, both kinds, and of the river. The sky was a hazy blue. I remember how much I wanted to touch him, but felt shy in public, in daylight. He sported an amiable grin that had me aching for him. We'd hiked from West 23rd to 110th and back down to 79th. I was new to the city and Vinnie was showing me places I hadn't been before. I could almost come on the smell of him. He'd slung a damp arm around my shoulder and said, "I love you, I just love you," but I'd feared it was just an enthusiasm, like for a beautiful day, a favorite movie, or his pooch Gidget.

I rock in my chair, phone cradled between ear and shoulder, and fiddle with a paper clip, pulling it apart so the bends became a straight line. I use my makeshift tool to herd pieces of turkey, crumbs, and lettuce shreds into a small mound of food.

"Kev, I just want you to know something. You see, I've changed. So don't go getting upset when you see me."

And that's when I figured out the obvious.

The sun had dipped behind the building across the street. Columns of small rectangular windows run up and down its squat length. In some windows, tiny sexless figures stand motionless. At this distance, the columns of rectangles with their miniature people look like strips of movie film.

Chilled, arms wrapped around my chest for warmth, I reach for the sweater I'd tossed onto a pile of reports stacked on the floor.

This triggers a small landslide as the documents slide over each other.

"I owed you a call," I say lamely.

"You don't owe me shit. The point being, all is forgiven."

Hours later, pinned by the crowd against a door on the uptown train, I will run through a list of the last people on earth I'd expected to hear from today. Vinnie would come after my father from his grave.

*Vincent sleeps: a deep, dreamless sleep. Eyelids float like lily pads on fragile, fluid membranes. He feels bathed by voices. His body tingles, scrubbed clean by passing sounds. He lies on a slab in space surrounded by black. Eyes pop open and he's staring into a madman's glittering eye: the TV has snapped on with a mind of its own, aiming white noise and static; it dangles in front of him from a bent steel arm. Then it's off again and Vincent's legs become ensnarled in blanket and sheets. The madman's eye is now a dull smoky green like an accountant's shade. He undoes the knotted bedding, extracting first one leg, then the other. He thinks: I was never good at knots. Only then does feeling rush back in.*

What remained of the evening light when I arrived is gone, replaced by a hotel's flickering neon sign whose light reaches from across the street and laps the walls of the room. Cars and buses rumble past. The Doppler effect of each is a rising and falling swoosh that beckons me away from this room. Vinnie's skin, pale in the best of times, is a yellowy white. I think of the blanched boiled vegetables of childhood and a feeling of shame squeezes the sincerity from my smile. Yet there's the sweet and tangy scent of mangos rising from his body and I wonder if someone has slipped Vinnie a bottle of cologne, or maybe I'm smelling some new antibiotic—or am I losing my mind?

In the two years since I'd last seen him there'd been no one special, but I'd had my fun. In later years, I had my share of lovers and boyfriends. I made my mistakes: new ones each time is what I told myself, salvaging pride, claiming wisdom; most were mistakes of not loving enough. But one came from loving too much, and it led me to tell a lie and it was unforgivable, although Misha would say, and did say the last time I saw him, "It's water under the bridge."

But that night with Vinnie it was still 1983 and those were the days before I'd gotten used to tubes and respirators, liver biopsies and blood gases, and strange foreign words: pneumocystis pneumonia, Kaposi's sarcoma, cytomegalovirus—words that stretched my vocabulary each year to the breaking point before mutating into linguistically treatable PCP, KS, and CMV. Those were the days and nights when wet dreams were replayed and reviewed, murky film noirs from the forties and fifties that always ended with the same question: *Who did what to whom? Who did what to whom?* And I awoke with no answers, only that refrain lingering like a Humphrey Bogart sneer. There were no blood tests, no positives and negatives, no HIV, no safe sex. It could be from kissing or quiche, poppers, or brunches. More than once I shuddered awake in that crack of time between middle of the night and dawn, thinking over and over, *But Haitians don't brunch*, as if I could make sense of things.

Those were the days when you died real fast and there was nothing, at least in bed, that Vinnie had done that I hadn't done, too.

*Vincent begins to cry and imagines his father standing there, and he says "Daddy, Daddy, I love you," and Sal leans over and wipes his tears and kisses him on each cheek, then on the mouth. Like a lover, Vincent thinks, though he knows better. Vincent understands, like he understands the peal of a church bell, that this is no ordinary kiss. Though his father often said he had no ties to the families ("I'm an independent operator," he'd say with pride), Vincent knows the Mafia kiss of death. He knows that in his father's eyes he's wronged and dishonored him, so he accepts the verdict, the kiss, the coarse feel of his father's dry lips on his.*

*Vincent feels Sal's warm, mint-laced breath on his face. Like the wind in Miami, he thinks, a place he's never been but often imagined he'd go with one of his lovers. Now, with his left hand (his right arm still hurts from the IV needle), Vincent presses Sal's face tightly to his. He feels Sal's surprise and, in turn, is surprised by his easy compliance. He feels his father's thick tongue and tastes his saliva, tobacco-stale, and, beneath it, the flavor of mint.*

"Hey, farm boy," Vinnie had said, the day we met, running his finger along the outer perimeter of my mouth, tracing an elliptical orbit. Intoxicated (beer all afternoon, but it was hardly the beer), I didn't protest, although his finger hurt my dry, cracked lips. Cold winds had blown all day, funneled south from my hometown of Buffalo, mercenary winds that ended Indian summer, dropping the temperature thirty degrees during the noon hour and creating a vacuum that sucked the air out of one's lungs and turned lunchtime smiles into frozen scowls. All of which, goose bumps included, had made me lonely and sick for home.

We sat across from each other in a crowded coffee shop on Second Avenue, the kind of place where people eat breakfast all day and the smell of toast, coffee, and grease ripples the senses. We'd laid claim to a booth next to a window and watched people on the street scan the interior tables for friends or quick hits of sex and romance.

He'd started calling me *farm boy* just hours earlier (he'd called in sick to work), after we'd made love in his apartment. He thought anyone raised north of Poughkeepsie woke up under fairy-tale blue skies to the rooster's crow, milked cows, and lost their virginity in a barn with those selfsame cows.

But then, I'd thought all Italian boys had dark hair, olive skin, and swagger.

Later, sprawled and spent on his bed, he had leaned up on an elbow and said, "No, I got it wrong about you and those cows. Now that I've gotten to know you, I think it must have been a warm and fuzzy-wuzzy sheep."

*Fuzzy-wuzzy* were his exact words.

After sex, we sat across from each other in his kitchen, the lines and angles of our interlocked legs shifting about—a Ouija board, I'd thought, trying to form the letter *W*: *warlock, witch, winsome, watch out, Uncle Wiggly* had come to mind. Later, he rested his head on my shoulder and I inspected his thick brown hair that grew almost to where spine meets neck. I lifted the back of his shirt and looked down his knobby backbone as if it were a staircase leading somewhere. I thought of the day I climbed up the stairs in the Sistine Chapel in Rome (a summer program abroad) and continued to sketch my impression of who he was and how he'd figure in my new life, my New York life, just begun.

"I'm from Buffalo," I said. "Steel mills, traffic, slums, universities, football teams, acres of gray wood-framed houses; no hay, no corn, no cows, and no farms."

He'd paid me no mind, and farm boy I was all afternoon and into the evening, when we agreed that sex works up an appetite. Walking to his favorite coffee shop he took my hand and I let him, like holding another guy's hand walking down a city street was something I'd been doing for years.

"This place we're going to is *so* great," he'd said, looking up at the murky black-and-violet sky lit by a slice of moon. He seemed to be searching the heavens for just the right word. "It's just so excellent, so special, so fucking superlative, so superb, so cool, so far out . . ." Pausing, he added, "Well maybe it's just okay, but you see I've been coming here for years. They know me, and that's important, you know, to know a person."

In the coffee shop, absorbed in Vinnie, I failed to notice our waitress approach. Two cups of coffee angled in from my blind side. They floated down with the unexpectedness and grace of flying saucers. The cups clinked softly as they landed and I was reminded of the barely perceptible sound traffic signals make as they change from green to yellow to red. Sometimes, back home in Buffalo, I'd sit in my car, stopped at a traffic light after a middle-of-the-night drive home from a concert in Toronto, vision clouded by beer and grass, my friends asleep in the back. I'd watch and listen, intently, as if each click of the traffic signal's mechanism carried a message about my future: click, yellow; click, red; click, green again; a glimpse into that future, but only a moment ahead, half a breath, not even. Eventually, a horn's blast would bring me back. I'd glance at a street sign, rust on its ivory surface, and, after dropping off my friends, head home where I lived with my mother, marking time until I could leave.

Vinnie continued to circle my lips with his finger, even as the waitress gaped at us, lips fidgeting, an impatient pencil in her hand. I liked this gesture of his, and the kisses on my hand, then my mouth, that followed (though his sense of geography still rankled). I stared at his thin, slightly crooked nose and spacious grin. I tried to reconcile my curly dark hair and short stocky body—but tight, like the bantam-weight wrestler I was in high school—with images of tall, brown-haired farm boys I'd seen on television and in dirty magazines. I tried to imagine what he saw in me that evoked the odor of hay and manure while all I could smell was the Old Spice aftershave my mother had bought at the JCPenney's in the Tonawanda Shopping Mall the summer after my father died, urging it on me gently, firmly, explaining that it's something girls appreciate.

Vinnie leaned back in his seat and took my hands in his. I looked about nervously. These touches and kisses had me yanking my head left and right, eyes scanning for the guys back home with baseball bats. The Formica tabletop, a greasy white flecked with black dots, separated us. With our fingers we played that game where you try to pin the other guy's thumb down. Each time Vinnie won, he'd twitch his nose like Samantha in *Bewitched*. That's how we'd met, on a subway train: Vinnie had sat across from me during the morning rush, eyes crinkled, nose twitching, wearing a green tie and brown corduroy jacket. He was a legal secretary, I discovered later, on his way to work. When the petite brown woman sitting to my left, with the bulging Bloomie's shopping bag and heavy gold earrings, got up, he slipped across the crowded aisle and squeezed in next to me. In the crunch our knees touched and he put a strong thin hand on my thigh.

"We're on the numero uno line," he said solemnly, with the air of a tour guide in the Vatican. "I know that," I replied, trying not to seem a hick and wondering how to be sure if this was a pickup. Back home no one was ever so direct.

"It's what I call the glamour line," he went on. Catching my glance at the cheerful orange-and-tan seats and bright lighting, he added, "No, not 'cause the trains don't look like they came straight from hell, like, you know, the C train. It's 'cause it connects the Upper West Side to the Village. It's a highway for the cutest guys in the city."

The next day he had off and he gave me the grand tour of his neighborhood, where he'd lived his whole adult life, he said, gravely. The city glowed red and orange in the October light. A bravado sun's generous, waning rays picked out ochre and silver tints in the imported rock of stately brownstones and the cheap brick and embedded glass of dingy tenement fronts alike. Yesterday's freeze gone and forgotten, I was high on New York and the sinsemilla we'd bought last night on the corner of First Avenue and East Ninth from the Rastafarian whose natty dreadlocks fingered their way down to his waist. Bouncing to the rhythm of the reggae beat from the boombox on the corner, I was buoyed by pungent, curry-laced air drifting out from storefronts. I silently mouthed *Bombay, Bombay, Punjab, Punjab, Punjab, Delhi, Delhi,* trying to make a song's lyric—I had come to the city to be a songwriter, after all—but the demanding aroma of Hunan and Szechwan provinces, the ecstatic smells of the sweet pastries and breads from Warsaw, Kiev, and Vienna, distracted me.

I was new to town, Vincent was my boyfriend—my first New York City boyfriend!—and Vinnie ("Only my father calls me Vincent," he said last night) was my guide.

Later, standing in line at his favorite Chinese restaurant, he said, "We get an extra hour in the sack tonight 'cause Daylight Savings Time ends at midnight," and he twirled himself around like some kind of punk ballerina. Stumbling out of his spin he lost his balance, grabbed hold of me, and added, "So don't go turning into no pumpkin on me, farm boy."

After dinner, he wove me and him up Avenue A, across Ninth, down First, over to Sixth, up Second. "This is where I lived with Albert," he said. "And here with Joe," his index finger jabbing into the wind. On each block a different lover. "And Petey and I lived over there on the third floor," he said, pointing to a row of burnished tenement windows reflecting the disappearing sun. "We had a view of the river and could see all the way to Brooklyn." Taken into his confidence, I felt honored and curious like I had that summer in Rome attending to our guide's every inflected word in St. Peter's.

As he walked, Vinnie's pale body and toothpick arms flopped about like the scarecrow from Oz. It was easy for me to imagine he had no bones, no joints, no muscles, just straw packed loosely into his baggy tan khakis and blue button-down shirt with its faded green Polo emblem. Light brown hair, straight as straw, fell over his eyes and ears. A smile stretched his face into the shape of a friendly Halloween pumpkin. When he stood still, which was not often, he leaned at almost a forty-five-degree angle to the pavement, so I called him my leaning tower of Pisa. He thought I said *pizza* and laughed. He laughed at all my jokes, even the ones he didn't understand.

We saw each other every day for six weeks. Made love in the afternoon on days he could call in sick to work. I never bothered to look for a job, thinking I could live forever on love and the small bounty my father had left me. Most nights he'd prepare dinner: a succession of red and green salads, pasta, his favorite cheap Beaujolais, candles surrounded by a growing mountain of purple wax on a black-topped table, and stories, always more stories: parents he didn't know; uncles and aunts who took him in only to begrudge and despise him; foster homes and beatings; brothers and sisters not seen since he was five and about whom he dreamed at night.

One day we sat on his front stoop, huddled close, the sun just warm enough to feel, sharing a beer and a joint. He sighed, long and poignant, and said how he was so comfortable with me, trusted me like no one else before, felt he could say anything. "You really understand me," he said.

"Sure, yeah, try me," I replied, leaning closer, body warm and blushing, eager to be trusted; and, as quickly, worries surfaced: he was seeing someone else; I had bad breath; he was dying of cancer. Back then, AIDS was still a verb, not a noun.

But what he'd said was: "My father, he's really alive. I didn't tell you the whole truth." That's all he said, despite my badgering.

Each night, he teased with a fresh detail. "My father," he said proudly, "he was on the cover of a magazine a few years ago."

That was it, no more, and when I asked for more he had a way of turning the subject into whose pants came off first. So I figured he was trying to impress; but me, I was still more impressed by wrestling with his torso, hands, and arms in ways I had only dreamed about in high school.

One night, he said, "He was in the mob, you know."

"The Mafia?"

"No, the mob, not the Mafia," he said, impatiently. "He was an independent guy, an independent operator, you could say. Nobody owned my dad," he added, fiercely fingering the buttons on his shirt.

And the next night, while he poured wine: "I robbed some banks, you know, just a few, not for much money."

I knocked the salad dressing over as I reached for my glass. "What were you trying to prove?" I asked, unsure if this was a put-on or not, recognizing the voice I had used with my father when he was four Scotches into complaining about his work.

"Just trying to prove I was a man to my father. Dumb, huh?"

"As long as you didn't get caught," I replied, still wondering if it was true.

My dad had been an angry lawyer and son of a lawyer, who'd died so constipated his gut bulged like he was pregnant with all the dreams he'd kept secreted away. I'd sat at his hospital bedside watching him in a coma, eyelids flickering so I knew he was still dreaming, thinking I knew more about what was inside him than he did, feeling some crazy glimmer of hope that it was not too late for him to give birth, to speak what was in his heart, knowing that soon I'd escape to New York where I'd be a songwriter—I'd wait tables for as long as it took! Knowing one thing for sure: I'd be anybody but him.

Vinnie had asked me about my father more than once, and each time I'd say he was not worth talking about. "Real disrespectful," he'd reply, shaking his head sorrowfully.

The next night Vinnie's story took a twist: "You know, last year I almost had a sex change operation." We lay in bed, Vinnie curled up behind me so I couldn't see his face. "It would have been the whole thing. I'd grown boobs and they were going to cut it off at nine o'clock the next morning."

"Why, Vinnie? Why?" First, I thought this is all made up; if I turn over and look into his face I'll know he's joking; then I wondered: was anything of what he'd told me the truth?

I began to wish he didn't trust me so much.

"It was because my father, he said *in front of the whole family,* 'Anything but a faggot son, anything.' Of course," Vinnie added, "I changed my mind at the last minute."

But by then I'd pretended I'd fallen asleep.

I didn't make a decision not to see him again, I just didn't answer the phone. For weeks it rang, sometimes all day and night, the rings making a hollow, insistent sound in my room as I'd stare out the window and watch people going in and out of the Korean fruit market across the street. Once I counted thirty rings before he hung up, quiet filling the room like silent prayers in a church.

Gradually, their frequency diminished: once every few hours, then once or twice a day. I knew they were him because I didn't know anyone else in town. I was twenty-two and looking for adventure, or at least that's what I told myself. Only not this much.

The Jamaican night nurse touches my shoulder and offers me a bed. I'm hot, my pants are sticking to the chair's vinyl, there's a cramp in my neck. "You're determined to stay," she says, "I can for sure see that." Half asleep, I wonder why she is singing to me.

"But I don't want to get comfortable," I say, making no sense, I'm sure, to her.

"Whatever . . ." she replies, pausing, pressing a metal chart to her chest. Her narrow face, which widens at the jaw, has an oblong, liquidy look. "And to think you're not even a relation. I will never understand you boys, making tragedies for yourself when they come to find you soon enough without your looking."

When I returned home from Rome three years ago, my mother greeted me with a swollen yet composed face, holding on to her tears as tightly as she clutched her purse in the crowded airport lobby. A telegram received after a hot day of altars, mineral water, and stained glass had summoned me home. YOUR FATHER'S HAD AN ACCIDENT. HE'S IN A COMA.

Leaning against the counter at the American Express office, I had tried to remember what he looked like, even as I'd remembered how relieved I was that summer to be away from the weight of his unhappy life.

*Vincent lies in bed. He's had diarrhea but knows it's between shifts and not a time to call the nurses. The last jerk-off; he can imagine making love to his father if he wants. (If I damn well please, he thinks.) He tries to undo the knot on the cord of his pajamas. Feeling his way with his teeth, he searches for a weak spot in the cloth.*

The light from the sign across the street blinks on and off. I listen for Vinnie's breath. It's staccato and labored. A reedy, contented snore from behind the white curtain reminds me that we're not alone. I don't know how long I've been awake. I know I fell asleep again because a piece of a dream sticks to me: I'm in a time machine with my father. Red and amber lights flicker. We fight for the controls. He says, "This is the only way to escape." I tell him I want us to stay where we are. I shout at him, but he can't hear me. I scream, and then I'm on a beach, alone, watching a swimmer far in the distance. The sound of waves crashing is deafening.

For the first time since he died, maybe since I was a child, I miss him.

*Vincent reaches for the apple-filled Danish Sal had brought that morning. He pulls it out of the greasy white bag, bites deliberately, and feels its sweetness in his mouth. He chews slowly. He thinks of Sal's cool, dry lips and warm breath, of Kevin's watchful eyes and furry chest. Ignoring a cramp in his gut, he determines to summon courage and call Kevin, not knowing what he'll say, just something to do with good-bye.*

Middle-of-the-night quiet has replaced the drone of cars from the street. I hear muffled voices from the hall, giggles, then a loud "hush up."

The Chinese nurse (from Singapore really, she'd explained), had said, "Count the seconds between breaths. One-one thousand, two-one thousand. When you get to twenty-five one thousand, he's gone." At last count he averaged ten-one thousand. Once I got up to twenty-one thousand before he began to breathe again.

Vinnie hasn't asked me to stay to the end, but I've been determined to, not knowing why. Now I understand that it's to see the moment of death, to witness the event. After my father died I began to worry I hadn't paid attention to the exact moment of his leaving. I was afraid I had blinked and somehow missed the most important part, and all I'd have to go by was the before and after. I imagined people could see this about me, my negligence.

Vinnie's feet stick up from under the blanket. I rub them and wonder if he can feel my hands. "It's the arch I love," I'd said to him one night in his apartment, holding his foot near the bed lamp. It was golden in the light cast by the lamp's yellow shade.

"But my feet are flat," he'd said, trying to wrestle his leg from my grip.

"The way the skin oh so subtly curves upward like the roof of a cave," I continued, tweaking his big toe. Through the open window a breeze elbowed aside the curtain, bearing the moldy fragrance of fall leaves.

"When were you ever in a cave?" he said, burrowing his heel into my heart.

"And the furrows, the folds of skin along the cavern's roof, like so many plowed fields."

"You wouldn't know a plowed field if it fell on you." Wiggling his big toe, he'd added, "Remember, you told me you don't know nothing about farms."

"And the circles within circles of your calluses are like sacred mystery fields in ancient England. Monuments that make Stonehenge pale."

"They're plain ugly. And Stonehenge wasn't no field, I saw the documentary about it. My toes, maybe my toes are like Stonehenge," he'd said, breaking my grip, pinning me on my back to show that I didn't know all the wrestling moves.

I try to open the window in the hospital room, thinking I'll stay awake if there's fresh air. The window sticks to its casement. It takes several hard shoves to budge. I give it a lot of shoulder, then it slides up, opening wide, revealing a dark sky. At its eastern edge there's a line of light. Cool, moist air floods in. Then fear, panic—neither word does justice to the stabbing feeling in my gut. *I've forgotten to count.* How long has it been? I pick an arbitrary number to start with, twelve-one thousand, thirteen-one thousand, fourteen-one thousand.

Vinnie gurgles and breathes.

*With his tongue Vincent rolls the pieces of sweet pastry in his mouth, struggles to stop the sweetness, to hold it, play with it, remember it.*

I waited the whole time while he'd told me about his father. Sat through the entire story, wondering how a dying man could summon such breath, jealous that he could love his father so easily, thinking now is the time to tell him how I really feel, how I felt back then, why I didn't answer the phone when he called. I waited for just the right moment, hoping I'd figure it out for myself and my words would come, pour out as freely as his. The right moment never did come, or maybe it did and stupid me didn't notice.

After he'd finished his tale, we sat in silence until his eyes half closed in what I would later learn was the dyings' version of sleep.

I watch Vinnie breathe. An icy breeze washes over me. I remember sitting in the snow in front of our gray-shingled house in Buffalo watching the traffic signal flash yellow. I'm seven years old and I've got my father in tow. He's indulging me. He pulls on my hand, says it's time to go in. I've explained, carefully, like he's the child, how I can predict the future. Just listen for the click and the light will turn red or green. He holds my hand and we wait. There is no sound in the late evening but the blowing snow, and no click, just the flashing yellow light coating the white ground. I can see him so clearly, his thick, athletic body made even larger by his blue army parka; but his face has no features and his voice has no sound.

When did he stop being happy? And when did I stop remembering what he looked like?

*Vincent lies in fluids and wetness—his own and the ones that gushed from tubes—and thinks, it's okay, it's okay, it's okay.*

The blinking sign lights the top half of the double-paned window. Irregularities in the clouded glass take on colors, crystalline sparkles of red, blue, green, yellow, and white. One summer holiday I remember my father holding sparklers in one hand, me in the other. The sleeves of his white shirt were rolled above the elbows. His voice was deep and gravelly, but each word he spoke was carefully shaped as if he were blowing smoke rings with a cigar.

I fall asleep for a few minutes, time enough to dream Vinnie and I are orbiting the earth together, two new moons endlessly circling, orbits almost touching. Each time I try to say I love you, his orbit takes him to the earth's far side, out of sight.

I wake, angry at myself for sleeping. I get up and stand over him, listening for his breath. There's a reassuring snort, and then silence. I resume my count. He breathes at eighteen-one thousand, but he's already shading into blue. I'm counting the space between breaths, counting the emptiness as it grows larger and larger. It's Vinnie's breathing that creates it, marking the boundaries where nothingness begins and ends.

I will never hear the sound of Vinnie's voice again.

Months after my father's funeral I sat at his grave trying to remember the shape of his face, the color of his eyes, how thick his brow was, the sound of his voice, asking myself, were his lips thin, was his chin small and receding like in the old photos, or had it thickened, like his neck, with age?

He'd lost control of his car. Hit a tree—a white spruce, I discovered, when I went to see for myself. The car tumbled twenty feet into a ravine. A gash in the tree was already healing. The cops tallied it an accident. But there was doubt. "An accident waiting to happen," my mother said. "He was sadder than you knew."

He'd lived for another week. Drifted in and out of consciousness. I waited at his bedside. There was still time, I thought. Time to speak the truth about the accident, the truth about whatever he liked. So I'd know, so I'd remember the sound of his voice. But he was silent, and so was I.

Forty-two-one thousand.

I'd blinked again.

For a time I sit and listen to the silence, then to the sounds of a waking city and the clatter of breakfast trays from the corridor. A spot of sunlight brightens the far corner of the room by the sink. I watch it spread, waiting for it to reach me. When it does, I sink into the warmth.

# EPILOGUE

## New York City, January 2001

Ivan calls at noon. "Mish, we're running late," he says.

"Ive, who's *we?*"

Smith is sleeping in. I've been in and out of bed all morning. Out of bed, I pace; in bed, I dream: dreams that disturb but coyly refuse memory.

"*We* are Leo and a friend of his."

"Why the friend?"

"A friend of Papa's."

"I don't want strangers. I don't want surprises."

"Not to worry, li'l bro, there's room in the cab."

"That wasn't my point, Ive. And where are you exactly, if you don't mind my asking?"

"No problem, li'l bro. We'll be there before dark, I swear."

"*Before dark* is late and it's vague."

In the background I can hear someone toot-tooting on a musical instrument. Ivan makes me delirious with confusion. Not for the first time, I want to wring my brother's neck. Throwing the phone at Smith's sleeping form buried under blankets is a weak substitute.

"Ouch," he says. "That hurt."

The fuzzy brown top of his head pokes out, followed by a furrowed brow, his gray eyes, blinking at the daylight, then half a nose.

"Liar. No way that hurt."

"Is it time to go?"

"No. Ivan's late."

"Tell me something new."

"He's up to something."

"Again, tell me something new."

In the living room I open a window, then sit on the ledge. The chill air is like a slap in the face. It does me good. The street has that Sunday hush to it where even the cars seem to be whispering. Then a bird begins to chirp like a maniac. What kind of stupid bird stays north in the winter? I should look it up. There was a bird that stayed, thrived even, in Kiev, during the winter. I once knew what kind. Thinking about this is a nice distraction until I remember my last dream before waking: it was of Kevin. It was urgent: his body, his touch; I was hard with passion. I try to think of Smith. Can you betray someone in your dreams? Of course not, but I can't shake the feeling; it's like the vile taste of some medicine that stays in your mouth.

The sky is terraced with clouds, shades and layers of gray, like an old man's beard. Falling from it, through a mist: sleet, rain, snow. It's a potpourri of $H_2O$, as if God can't quite make up his mind how to behave on this solemn day: the scattering of Louie's ashes, God's mortal enemy for seven decades. For surely Papa, if his word was true, had declared war against Jehovah at the age of five.

I have trusted Ivan with too much: the urn with Louie's ashes, picking up Leo as well as myself and Smitty. Smitty says I indulge Ivan too much, more than ever since Louie died. He thinks grief has clouded my judgment. He is right, but also wrong. It is a borscht of grief, lumpy with guilt and shame, in which one of the ingredients has gone bad. But there is no one I can talk to about this. Not the least, Ivan.

"What's done is done, li'l bro. Look to the future," he says.

The cab slows, pauses, waits in line, and then rolls into the belly of the Staten Island ferry. This was Leo's idea, to scatter Louie's ashes in New York Harbor. "He'll rest just off of Brighton Beach. So, whenever I go to the beach, I'll be able to talk to him."

It was a compromise. Ivan and I had insisted on the cremation. Leo had argued, his voice, without a voice box, raspy as a concrete mixer: "But Jews are buried in the *ground*. It's wrong, what you boys want to do. And besides, how can I visit him if he's not in a cemetery?"

To which I'd said, "Leo, you know how Louie and religion didn't mix. In a cemetery, he'll lie very annoyed for eternity. Is that what you want?"

Ivan nodded in agreement.

I felt bad for Leo, although I was certain of Louie's opinions. I glanced at Smitty; give me a way out of my stubbornness was in my look.

"No one leaves this room until a decision is made," he said, sternly.

A fidgety silence had followed, until from Leo: "Okay. You are his boys. I'm just a friend. Ashes. But out over the ocean. He loved that damn ocean."

Ivan backs into a parking spot. It's a complicated maneuver as the cab is large and the space small. He always has to back in. Why can't he nose in headfirst like everyone else? The light is dim. The air smells of exhaust fumes. It reminds me of the garage where he keeps his cab. Leo sits up front. He holds the urn. Smitty and I are in the back. Between us is Leo's friend, Estelle. She is also Papa's friend. More than a friend. Leo had called today, an hour after Ivan's call:

"Misha, maybe Ivan hasn't told you this yet . . ." I'd pretended to be in the know. I have my pride.

She is a nice lady. Quiet. She wears one of those down coats that goes all the way to her ankles. It's pink edging into lavender and has a fur collar. There's a scarf that covers her hair, which is a cheerful shade of chestnut brown; the scarf is a somber burgundy and is tied under her chin. When Ivan arrived to pick up Smitty and me, she stepped out of the cab and gave us each a hug. She held me for a long time as if she knew me.

"You must be Misha," she said. "He spoke of you often."

She caressed my cheek.

"He was very proud of you, both you and your brother," she added. "More than you can know."

Louie had not spoken of her at all was what I'd thought. He'd kept her secret. After Leo's phone call, I was furious. How dare Papa! I didn't begrudge him happiness. It was not as if I thought he must stay true to our mother's memory. I knew better than that. But still, he'd been selfish. I knew he had Leo's friendship, but I'd worried about his loneliness and would have been reassured to have known about Estelle. I complained to Smitty.

"So you're pissed your father didn't let you vet his girlfriend?" he'd said, leaving me to waving my hands in the air, ending the discussion.

During the cab ride to the ferry terminal, Estelle takes my gloved hand into hers. Every so often she squeezes it. Smitty talks to her in a quiet voice. Asking her questions. Showing good manners. She answers in no's and yes's. Her voice is not strong; it's sweet and quivers like a fading note from a violin that concludes a sad sonata.

We walk up the stairs of the ferry in single file and out onto the deck. The wind is blustery. It's bitter cold. No one else is out. The engine churns. I can see blurry faces inside through the steamed windows. What do they make of us, out here? Is anyone curious? Does anyone care?

Ivan leads us to the rail. He's carrying the urn, which I hope is not a mistake.

Leo puts a large arm around Estelle. She is ghostlike and fragile.

*Epilogue*

I wonder what Louie saw in her. Smitty puts an arm around me
and I lean into him. He whispers, "It's okay." He seems less a boy,
more a man, and I am grateful.

"Here?" Ivan asks. He looks first at me, then at Leo.

"Not yet," says Leo. "Let's do it at halfway between Brooklyn
and Staten Island."

"How will we know halfway?" I ask.

"I'll know," says Leo. "Trust me."

Another person who wants me to trust him!

And from Ivan, "Leo knows about this kind of stuff."

"Maybe almost halfway would be just as good?" I suggest, but
Leo is looking stubborn. "It's really cold out here," I counter, and
nod my head toward Estelle. Leo turns his face from me and I
concede to him master of ceremonies.

The sky is clearing in the direction of Staten Island and out
toward the ocean; the towers of Manhattan, partly obscured by
clouds, radiate a pinkish glow. That first night in Central Park,
when Louie and Ivan and I were huddled together in the horse-
drawn carriage, the buildings looked like a welcoming party
thrown by our new best friends. Now, they still seem like friends,
but preoccupied friends, friends with their own problems to deal
with.

A wet snow is falling. A gust of wind blows the flakes into my
face. Everything becomes a blur, so I take my glasses off to wipe
them dry as best I can. In the distance, over the ocean, there are
a few stars, twinkling. I know there are millions and trillions of
them I can't see. Is the number of stars in the universe equal to the
number of minutes in a person's life? In Louie's? Or the number of
seconds? Or maybe it's the number of times Papa's eyes blinked?
The number is as important to me as Leo's halfway mark between
here and there. I want to capture Louie's life before he leaves me
forever. Is that selfish? Then I am selfish. I am filled with selfish.
He was my father, not Ivan's. He was mine alone! And *my* friend,
not Leo's, not Estelle's. More selfish. Maybe selfish is okay when
your father is dead. When it sinks in, finally.

195

"Will you men just shut up and do it!" It is Estelle. Her voice harsh, clear, commanding. "He's dead. There is no halfway. Dead is dead."

"Now!" cries Leo. "Now!" shouts Ivan, and Leo takes the top off the urn, placing it on the deck, and then four hands, mine, Leo's, Estelle's and Smitty's, reach in and throw handfuls in the sea toward the night. It takes several scoops to empty out the urn. On my last scoop, the wind picks up and blows ashes back into our faces. I am not surprised: this happened when I scattered Kevin's ashes two years ago, along with his friends. A secret I've kept from Ivan; a secret I kept from Papa. I have become an old hand at this business.

What does surprise me is the music. Ivan has pulled out one of those wooden recorders from the inside pocket of his coat. He toots on it a few times, then, very slowly, plays "Taps." I think: My brother is nuts. He is really nuts. We stand in a circle around him, as if warming ourselves in front of a fire. Yes, he is nuts, but the music is beautiful. It is perfect. He is perfect.

"Thank you," says Estelle, softly, her anger gone. "You are so much your father's son."

She removes a glove and holds out a hand. Ivan offers a short bow, takes her hand and lifts it to his lips.

# ACKNOWLEDGMENTS

Leonard Gill, who was indispensable—for all the red ink he spilled onto the pages I wrote and for being the kind of friend he promised he'd be a long time ago.

Sheila Bihary, Sue Cattoche, and David Salvage, for listening to and reading pretty much every word, sentence, and paragraph I wrote when it all began.

Andrew Chen, Pam Dickson, Susan Ito, Myriam "Bela" Sas, Naoko Selland, and Cathy Spensley, whose insights into many of these stories—quite literally, as they were written—made all the difference.

Laurie Fox, for her wit, wisdom, and friendship in the trenches in which we've both struggled and fought.

Jane Eklund and Honor Molloy, two of the best writing pals for whom I could ask.

Paula Maso Carnes, who read these stories more times than I had any right to ask, sharing all of her thoughts, and who prayed for me, regularly and often during the dark times. Every writer needs one person to pray for them.

## Acknowledgments

Geoff McNally, my audience and my friend.

Margo Perin, who taught me how to live the life of a writer.

Alice Mattison, for her heart, as big and smart and tough as her hometown of Brooklyn.

Also, the following, who either read many of these stories with insight and enthusiasm, fed me, paid a bill or two or three, said the right words at the right time, provided a place to stay, helped me with my Russian, managed to spring me from a French jail, or all the above:

Rekha Balu, Lois Barish, Nancy Buckles, Bruno Charenton (the best French translator ever!), Kos Chebetaov, Michael Cunningham, Audrey Ferber, Patty Grossman, Susan Guerney, George Hodgman, Dorothea Lack, Marie Lee, Margot Livesey, Ericka Lutz, Mark McClelland (restorative yoga rocks!), Tom Pallo, Jule Pecor, Kaveh Rad, Claire Robson, Michael Scott, Georgina Sculco, Caroline Smadja, Hal Smith, David Tuller, Genanne Walsh, Ann Williams, Victoria Zenoff, and Connie Zhu.

My thanks to:

The Colony at MacDowell for their generous Fellowship.

Anne Evans and her staff at the Napa Valley Summer Writers Conference, where several of these stories found an early audience.

Canada's *Descant*, which first published "Ivan & Misha"; Steve Berman, for including that story in *Best Gay Stories, 2008*, Lethe Press; Joe Taylor, for including it in *Tartts Four: Incisive Fiction from Emerging Writers*, Livingston Press; and the *James White Review* for publishing "Who Did What to Whom?"

*Acknowledgments*

Mike Levine and the great folks at Northwestern University Press, Marianne Jankowski, Anne Gendler, Xenia Lisanevich, Jenny Gavacs, and those whose names I don't know but for whose efforts I am deeply grateful.

Corrine Haverinen and Shook Chung for graciously creating a website.

The late Gordon Smyth, who convinced me on the basis of two hurriedly written pages that a silly story about telephone booths was worth pursuing; and the late Anthony Panico, who inspired the only character in this book based on a real person. They don't come any more real. I hope I did you justice.

My agent, Judith Ramsey Ehrlich, who stuck with a mere short-story writer and who coaxed this book into existence.